Mrs Dalloway

Manchester University Press

Vanessa Bell, *Mrs Dalloway's Party* (1920)

Mrs Dalloway

Biography of a novel

Mark Hussey

Manchester University Press

Copyright © Mark Hussey 2025

The right of Mark Hussey to be identified as the author of this work has been asserted in accordance with the Copyright, Designs and Patents Act 1988.

Published by Manchester University Press
Oxford Road, Manchester, M13 9PL
www.manchesteruniversitypress.co.uk

British Library Cataloguing-in-Publication Data
A catalogue record for this book is available from the British Library

ISBN 978 1 5261 7681 3 hardback

First published 2025

The publisher has no responsibility for the persistence or accuracy of URLs for any external or third-party internet websites referred to in this book, and does not guarantee that any content on such websites is, or will remain, accurate or appropriate.

EU authorised representative for GPSR:
Easy Access System Europe – Mustamäe tee 50, 10621 Tallinn, Estonia, gpsr.requests@easproject.com

Typeset
by Cheshire Typesetting Ltd, Cheshire
Printed in Great Britain
by CPI Group (UK) Ltd, Croydon CR0 4YY

Contents

Preface   vii

Part I: Drafting *Mrs Dalloway*   1
Beginnings   6
Character in fiction   14
Septimus Warren Smith   24
Design   34

Part II: *Mrs Dalloway*: content and influences   46
London   48
Politics   57
Clothes   65
Proust   69

Part III: Publishing *Mrs Dalloway*   72
Proofs   74
First readers   82
A modern novel   89
Bloomsbury's enemies   101

Part IV: *Mrs Dalloway* out in the world — 107
Ulysses — 109
In the classroom — 115
Crossing borders — 126
Feminist revaluations — 134
Trauma — 141

Part V: *Mrs Dalloway*'s legacies — 143
'Books continue each other' — 144
Adaptation — 150
Mrs Dalloway as muse — 169

Coda: Twenty-first-century *Mrs Dalloway* — 174
Dalloway Day — 175
Pandemic — 177

Abbreviations and a note on the text — 181
Notes — 182
Bibliography — 199
List of illustrations — 208
Legend of Morris Beja map — 211
Acknowledgements — 214
Index — 216

Preface

In the first copy of *Mrs Dalloway* I bought, I wrote the date—28 December 1972. It was the Penguin Modern Classics edition, with a detail on the cover from one of Vanessa Bell's portraits of her sister, Virginia Woolf. Woolf is depicted lying back in a deck chair, some work in her lap, her face featureless beneath a large hat. The author is identified as 'the daughter of Sir Leslie Stephen and the wife of Leonard Woolf'. Britain at the time was three years away from the passage of the Sex Discrimination Act, which began the gradual process of removing legal barriers to women's equality: in 1972, a woman could not open a bank account in her own name. I was three years away from beginning my BA, but already hooked on Woolf. My collection of editions of *Mrs Dalloway* has swollen past any reasonable number now, and I've long forgotten what I thought about the novel when I first read it, other than that Woolf had become—as she remains—my favourite writer. But this book is not my story. It is the story of *Mrs Dalloway*, a novel described by its publisher in 1972 as 'the first novel of Woolf's maturity'.

In her introduction to the Modern Library edition of *Mrs Dalloway*, Virginia Woolf wrote that 'books are the flowers or fruits stuck here and there on a tree which has its roots deep down in the earth of our earliest life'.[1] Where might we find the

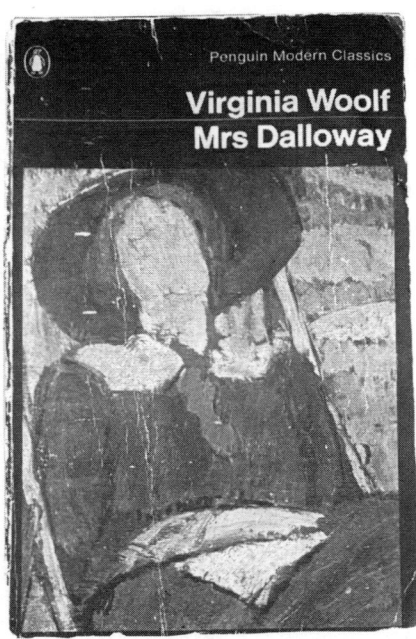

1 Author's copy of *Mrs Dalloway*, Penguin, 1972

seeds of Woolf's most celebrated novel? One suggestion for such a seed is the idea for a play that Woolf described to her friend Violet Dickinson twenty years before beginning *Mrs Dalloway*:

> Im going to have a man and a woman—show them growing up—never meeting—not knowing each other—but all the time you'll feel them come nearer and nearer. This will be the real exciting part (as you see)—but when they almost meet—only a door between—you see how they just miss—and go off at a tangent, and never come anywhere near again. There'll be oceans of talk and emotions without end.[2]

A similar-sounding idea recurs in a diary entry Woolf wrote two years after *Mrs Dalloway* was published, where she pondered 'a new kind of play', wherein a woman 'thinks', a man 'does', but 'They miss'.[3] Whatever subtle contribution it may have made to the genesis of *Mrs Dalloway*, this particular seed seems to have borne fruit in a later work—perhaps *The Waves*.

A more promising possibility for any speculation about the novel's origins is *The Party*, a 1920 painting by Vanessa Bell (frontispiece). It was included in a 1922 London Group exhibition at the Mansard Gallery but marked 'not for sale'. *The Party* was singled out in a *Vogue* review of the exhibition as 'a charmingly ironical vision of the social amenities that is also a very striking composition'.[4] The painting disappeared from view after 1922, resurfacing only in 1983 when it was sold to a private collector by the Anthony d'Offay Gallery.

Howard Ginsberg, a playwright and psychoanalyst, has told the story of how his late wife, Barbara, bought this painting when it was offered for sale after being discovered at Leonard and Virginia Woolf's Sussex home, Monk's House. Someone—either the gallerist or Quentin Bell—had renamed it *Mrs Dalloway's Party*. It seems never to have been hung at Monk's House, and after the 1922 exhibition there is no reference to it, not in Vanessa Bell's or Virginia Woolf's correspondence, or anywhere else. We know that an earlier work of Bell's, *A Conversation* (1913–16),[5] prompted her sister to 'wonder if I could write the Three Women in prose',[6] but there is no way of knowing what part the 1920 painting might have played in Woolf's thinking about *Mrs Dalloway*. Vanessa Bell made few narrative paintings, and Howard Ginsberg has often wondered what story the one his wife bought is telling: 'what is going on between the *embonpoint*, dominant female figure and the adoring, seated young woman? Why is the downcast man in black walking away?'[7] One scholar speculates, plausibly, that the seated figure might be Mary Hutchinson, the longtime lover of Vanessa Bell's husband, Clive.[8] Another has suggested that the painting 'may well have been one link in the complex evolution of *Mrs Dalloway* and a visual impetus for the party scene that closes the novel'.[9] We cannot know for certain. But there it is.

Mrs Dalloway began as it ends, with a party: 'all must converge upon the party at the end', Woolf wrote when she set down her earliest thoughts about beginning a new book.[10] That book is now one hundred years old. Among the many offspring of *Mrs Dalloway* are other novels, plays, operas, films, ballets, comics, memes, tattoos, walks and a steady stream of social media posts whenever the purchase of flowers is involved. Woolf's language lingers in the minds of countless readers and writers, who continue to incorporate it in their own creations in ways both large and small. In a recent dystopian fantasy, for example, a chef preparing dinner at a wealthy man's mountaintop colony, protected from a ravaged world, bizarrely finds herself assisting at the birth of a tiger cub. 'There was an anomaly, a breech. A cry from the beast. *Mrs. Dalloway said she would buy the flowers herself*, said Aida, plunging hands into the birth canal'.[11] An American writer walking back to her car after dinner with friends slips on the pavement, hurting herself badly. When she wakes the next morning, Clarissa Dalloway's words haunt her: '*She always had the feeling that it was very, very dangerous to live even one day*'.[12] There are times when *Mrs Dalloway* seems to be everywhere.

One of the many filaments connecting Clarissa and the tormented veteran Septimus Warren Smith is indeed a sense of nameless dread. Although they never meet, these characters are linked in a reader's mind by their awful fear of what might be about to happen, and by their mutual longing for release. 'Fear no more, says the heart', while Clarissa calmly mends the dress she will wear at her party that night. 'Fear no more, says the heart in the body', while Septimus lies peacefully on the sofa in the sitting-room, from the window of which he will soon plunge to his death. Perhaps it is Woolf's shimmering braiding of ecstatic joy in a lovely summer's day with the dark anguish of a mind broken by war, showing how such contraries pervade modern life, that gives *Mrs Dalloway* its continuing hold on our imaginations. This 'biography' of the novel tells its story with a focus more on the *how* than the *why* of its persistence. It assumes familiarity with *Mrs Dalloway*, but it is not a work of interpretation or analysis (though inevitably it stands upon the shoulders of the many insightful critics who have written about the novel since 1925). It will follow the novel's biography from conception to realisation; from publication to reception; and from dissemination around the globe to its reimagination in myriad forms and contexts.

Part I
Drafting *Mrs Dalloway*

Virginia Woolf was a messy writer. Her surviving drafts are often stained by cigarette ash or a dog's pawprints. The large wooden tables she preferred in her writing rooms were covered with manuscripts, bottles of ink, overflowing ashtrays and the notebooks she made for herself, ruling a margin on each page with a thick blue pencil. She did not write at the table, however, but sat each morning in a low armchair, a board to which she had glued an inkstand balanced across her knees to support the notebook in which she wrote her drafts.[1] She kept track of her progress, dating the day's work, sometimes totting up how many words she had written, and making a note of where she had been when she drafted a particular passage. In the afternoons she would type up what she had written, subsequently revising by hand, then retyping the pages until they were ready to be sent to a professional typist and on to the printer. She would continue to revise at the proof stage, too—a benefit of being her own publisher.

Leonard and Virginia Woolf's life had a rhythm defined by their work and their travels back and forth between their London homes and their country house. *Mrs Dalloway* was written in three places: Monk's House, in the village of Rodmell in Sussex; Hogarth House, on Paradise Road in Richmond; and 52 Tavistock Square in Bloomsbury. Years before either she or her sister had found the

2 Virginia Woolf at Monk's House, 1931

Sussex homes in which they would settle, Virginia imagined for Vanessa a countryside retreat with 'a little cottage in the trees at the bottom of the garden'. In that fantasy cottage, Virginia hoped she would have a room with a table, books, a looking glass and 'a curious cabinet, full of small drawers' in which her sister's children would hunt for secrets.[2] Woolf never did have a room at her sister's house, but in the summer of 1921 she was thrilled to report that she and Leonard were converting a toolshed at Monk's House into a garden room. It would have large windows through which she could look across the meadows of the South Downs to Mount Caburn.

In that garden room at Monk's House in August 1922 Woolf jotted down in her diary some plans for the work she wished to accomplish that summer before returning to Richmond in the autumn. She and Leonard went back to London by train from Lewes on 5 October. The next day she opened a fresh page in one of the notebooks in which she had drafted her third novel, *Jacob's Room*, to pin down some thoughts about 'a book to be called, perhaps, At Home: or The Party'. *Jacob's Room* was about to be published but Woolf's mind was full of ideas for her next novel. She intended it to be a short book that would end with a party. The first chapter would draw on a story she had just finished writing, 'Mrs Dalloway in Bond Street'. This, she thought, could be followed by another story she had been working on, titled 'The Prime Minister'. But if the modernist writers have taught us anything it is that our experience of time is rarely linear, that beneath the surface of every present moment the currents of memory run deep. Woolf herself wrote that life 'is not a series of gig lamps, symmetrically arranged', but more like 'a luminous halo ... surrounding us from the beginning of consciousness to the end'.[3] Therefore, although that outline in her notebook represents Woolf starting to plan her next novel, pulling together ideas that had been brewing for a while, it would not be accurate to see it as 'the' beginning of *Mrs Dalloway*.[4]

We can identify many sources for the world created by Woolf in her fourth novel, but no specific original inspiration. The characters who populate London on a June day in 1923, a day on which Clarissa Dalloway gives a party and Septimus Warren Smith ends his life, emerged from their author's imagination informed by her memories of growing up in Kensington, of living through the First World War, of her own mental breakdowns, even, as Clarissa says in the novel, of 'people she had never spoken to, some woman in the street, some man behind a counter—even trees, or barns'.

At the time *Mrs Dalloway* was beginning to take shape, Virginia Woolf had only recently begun to feel confident as a writer, despite having already been practising her craft for two decades. When Leonard read the typescript of *Jacob's Room* on a summer's day in 1922 he told her that it was 'a work of genius'. She wrote in her diary

3 Outline made 6 October 1922

that she had finally discovered 'how to begin (at 40) to say something in my own voice'.[5] After *Jacob's Room*, she felt that she could go on as a writer without needing praise. She had been excited by the challenge of developing the kind of short experimental fictions she had been writing since 1917 into the longer form of a novel. *Jacob's Room* had shown her how she could do so.

When she first conceived of *Jacob's Room* in 1920, Woolf was the author of two more or less conventional novels (although the apparent marriage plot of the first, *The Voyage Out*, is derailed by the premature death of its heroine), scores of essays and reviews, and was also the co-founder of the Hogarth Press. She and Leonard had launched their press with a pamphlet containing a story by each of them, Virginia's 'The Mark on the Wall' and Leonard's 'Three Jews'. As she began to think about the work that would become *Jacob's Room*, Woolf was also re-reading her first two novels, because an American publisher had just agreed to bring them out in the United States (both had been published in Britain by Duckworth, the firm founded by her half-brother Gerald). She asked friends to let her know before she sent the books off to America if they had noticed any typos. Lytton Strachey delighted her by saying that when he re-read *The Voyage Out* he thought it was '*extremely* good'. He particularly liked her 'satire of the Dalloways'.[6]

Clarissa Dalloway, Woolf's most famous character, makes a brief but significant appearance in *The Voyage Out*, a glamorous figure hitching a ride with her politician husband, Richard, on a merchant ship bound for South America. Woolf told Vanessa Bell that Clarissa was based on a friend from their youth, Kitty Maxse

4 Leonard Woolf at Monk's House

(née Lushington). She recalled in a memoir how the tea table at their parents' tall house at 22 Hyde Park Gate had been 'fertilized by a ravishing stream of female beauty' of whom the 'paragon for wit, grace, charm and distinction was undoubtedly the lovely Kitty Lushington'.[7] Kitty was one of those who disapproved of the young Stephen siblings' move to Bloomsbury in 1904 after the death of their father, the eminent late-Victorian man of letters Sir Leslie Stephen. Through the grapevine, Woolf heard that Kitty disliked her second novel, *Night and Day*—something Leonard wryly thought was quite a compliment.

Beginnings

Virginia Woolf was born Adeline Virginia Stephen in 1882, the seventh child of a blended family formed by Leslie Stephen and Julia Duckworth. Her father's first wife, Minny, daughter of the novelist William Makepeace Thackeray, had died in 1875, leaving one child, Laura, whose mental instability led to her being permanently cared for outside the home after 1893. Virginia's mother, Julia, had been widowed six weeks before the birth of her third child, Gerald Duckworth, in 1870. Following their marriage, Leslie moved into Julia's house at 22 Hyde Park Gate where she was living with Gerald and her other two children, George and Stella. Over the next five years the couple had four more children: Vanessa, Thoby, Virginia and Adrian.

Virginia Woolf's early life was a typical late-Victorian, upper-middle-class one in many respects, although both her mother and father counted many luminaries from the worlds of arts and science among their close friends. 'Outwardly an intellectual family', as Woolf described the setting of her childhood and adolescence, the Stephens also 'had floating fringes in the world of fashion'.[8] This was the world Woolf depicted in *Night and Day*, which opens with its heroine, Katharine Hilbery, pouring tea for her parents' guests 'in common with many other young ladies of her class'. Woolf has often been charged with snobbery, with having a narrow view of life seen from a privileged perch. But in fact this was an aspect of her character that she investigated rigorously, just as she explored her mental states, the effect on her of her earliest experiences of abuse and loss, and, always, the mysterious processes by which life is transmuted into art.

Julia's death when Virginia was thirteen upended the family's life. Her mother had been 'in the very centre of that great Cathedral space that was childhood',[9] indefatigable in charitable works, soothing the temper of her irascible husband and tutoring her daughters at the dining table. Julia was also a well-known matchmaker who had chaperoned her daughter Stella to balls where she might meet an eligible suitor. It was Julia who had introduced Kitty Lushington to Leopold Maxse, who proposed to her in the garden at the Stephens' rented summer house in St Ives, Cornwall. After her death, Stella stepped into her shoes, seeming to her younger half-sister to grow 'whiter and whiter in her unbroken black dress',[10] while continuing her mother's charitable visits and also suffering the unreasonable emotional demands of their twice-widowed father. Stella's engagement to Jack Hills, an Eton classmate of her brother George, gave the fifteen-year-old Virginia her 'first vision of love between a man and a woman'.[11] Three months after her marriage, Stella died, probably from peritonitis.

Had Julia and Stella not died prematurely, Virginia and Vanessa might have been brought out into late-Victorian society, groomed for marriage in the manner of other young ladies of their class. But, like the motherless sisters in Katherine Mansfield's story 'The Daughters of the Late Colonel', that pathway was blocked for the Stephen girls. George Duckworth took on the task of shepherding his half-sisters into polite society, with occasionally amusing but more often painful results. Fashionable Kitty Maxse, Woolf recalled, 'came nearest to his ideal' woman,[12] and George endeavoured to interest Vanessa and Virginia in the milieu that Kitty inhabited. Despite the misery evoked by her memories of being taken to dances and dinner parties by George, Woolf recognised that she always responded to what she would call, upon finishing *Mrs Dalloway*, 'party consciousness':[13] 'Any group of people if they are well dressed, and socially sparkling and unfamiliar will do the trick', she wrote in 'Am I a Snob?'.

Although the roots of *Mrs Dalloway* go down through the many layers of Woolf's past, the writing of the novel began with the figure of Clarissa Dalloway. While at work on the first draft, Woolf remarked in her diary that the 'social side is very genuine in me. Nor do I think it reprehensible. It is a piece of jewellery I inherit from my mother'.[14] In a 1903 journal, Woolf had outlined 'Thoughts upon Social Success', a reflection on the 'game' of society that she believed still had some redeeming qualities, even though it might appear superficial. As an example, Woolf invented a 'Mrs Thingemajig', who despite having lost her only son in the Boer War can still be amusing at a party.[15] The twenty-one-year-old writer found such fortitude admirable, anticipating Clarissa Dalloway's similar feelings about Lady Bexborough in the novel, who opens a bazaar 'with the telegram in her hand, John, her favourite, killed'.

Of three versions of Clarissa Dalloway that Woolf created, the one who appears in *The Voyage Out* is closest to her original model, Kitty. That Clarissa, however, is a quite different character from the woman who steps out of her Westminster home to buy flowers for her party. The satire that delighted Woolf's close friend Lytton Strachey is rather obvious—Clarissa is prone to saying such silly things as 'How much rather one would be a murderer than a bore!'[16] The Clarissa of the novel that bears her name is a more complex figure, still satirised (she is not sure whether it is the Armenians or Albanians for whom she is supposed to feel concern) but also shown to be a woman reflecting on the choices she has made that have brought her to 'this moment of June' at the age of fifty-one.

Clarissa Dalloway in *The Voyage Out* is relieved that Helen Ambrose, the sister-in-law of the ship's owner, 'though slightly eccentric in appearance ... was not untidy', and that her tone of voice is 'the sign of a lady'.[17] Like Woolf's own mother, who signed an appeal *against* women's suffrage, she upholds the Victorian doctrine of separate spheres for women and men. Her husband tells Helen's niece, Rachel Vinrace, whom he later sexually assaults, that his public life as a politician is made possible only by the domestic hearth tended by his wife, to which he returns at the end of each day.

Woolf worked on her first novel over several years during which her circumstances changed drastically. When their father died in 1904, the Stephen children moved from Hyde Park Gate—'that house of all the deaths' as Leslie's friend Henry James described it[18]—to 46 Gordon Square, in the then-unfashionable neighbourhood of Bloomsbury, where Thoby Stephen invited his Cambridge university friends to drop by on Thursday evenings. To the shock of their conventional friends and relations, Vanessa and Virginia would sit unchaperoned with young men till all hours of the night. Such was the origin of the Bloomsbury Group, a gathering of friends whose opinions, relationships and achievements continue to be argued over and parsed by friend and foe. 'The atmosphere of Hyde Park Gate had been full of love and marriage', Woolf wrote in 'Old Bloomsbury', contrasting it with Gordon Square, where 'love was never mentioned'[19]—at least not the kind that led to marriage.

This apparent idyll was once again shattered in 1906 when her beloved brother Thoby died from typhoid. He was twenty-six. On the day of his funeral, Vanessa agreed to marry Clive Bell, Thoby's best friend. After their wedding, the Bells would make their marital home at Gordon Square, while Virginia and her younger brother, Adrian, moved to lodgings in nearby Fitzroy Square. There they soon resumed Thoby's tradition of Thursday evenings 'At Home', one of several opportunities for a widening group of young friends to meet. Vanessa had begun a 'Friday Club' where painters and art critics could both exhibit their work and discuss aesthetics. There were regular meetings, too, of a play-reading society. All this activity attracted the notice of Lady Ottoline Morrell in Bedford Square, whose own weekly gatherings brought together many prominent writers, artists and intellectuals. Before long, members of the nascent Bloomsbury Group were also being invited to Ottoline's salons, where their circles widened further still. Ottoline and her husband, Philip, a Member of Parliament, were active campaigners for peace whose Oxfordshire home, Garsington Manor, would provide a refuge for many conscientious objectors, including Clive Bell, during the First World War.

A latecomer to this new Bloomsbury scene was Leonard Woolf, who had joined the Civil Service after graduating from Cambridge and been posted to Sri Lanka (called Ceylon at the time). There he received continual updates on his friends' lives and loves from Lytton Strachey, who cautioned him after Vanessa's engagement that he had better hurry if he wanted to court her sister. Lytton himself had proposed to Virginia in 1909, but both quickly realised that this was not a serious proposition. Returning to England on leave in 1911, Leonard did propose and, after making it plain that marriage was an institution she cared for very little, Virginia accepted him. They married in 1912. She had told Leonard that she wanted 'everything—love, children, adventure, intimacy, work' but felt no sexual attraction to him.[20]

When her siblings moved to Gordon Square in 1904, Woolf had been recovering from a breakdown at the home of her intimate friend Violet Dickinson, who had been close to Stella. Throughout her life, Woolf suffered from excruciating headaches that often left her bedridden and signalled the onset of more serious mental issues. In her biography of Woolf, Hermione Lee describes the writer as 'a sane woman who had an illness',[21] an appellation the critic Jacqueline Rose has suggested marginalises the 'madness' Woolf herself found a richly fascinating aspect of her own consciousness.[22] As she began to think about the book that would become *Mrs Dalloway*, Woolf wrote in her diary that at the age of forty she was 'beginning to learn the mechanism of my own brain'.[23] She would use what she had learned in creating the character of Septimus Warren Smith.

In 1913, Woolf suffered a severe breakdown and spent some time that summer in Twickenham at a private nursing home for women. That September, not long after returning to the lodging house where she and Leonard were living, she took an overdose of Veronal, a sleeping aid, and was only saved by the quick thinking of a fellow resident. Geoffrey Keynes, brother of economist John Maynard Keynes, was training to be a surgeon at nearby St Bartholomew's Hospital, from where he fetched a stomach pump. *The Voyage Out* had been accepted for publication by Woolf's half-brother Gerald in April, but the novel would now languish in proofs while she recovered, eventually being published in March 1915.

Leonard and Virginia moved in early 1915 to Hogarth House on Paradise Road in Richmond, where they would live until 1924. Recalling the early years of her marriage in 1930, Woolf described how her 'brains went up in a shower of fireworks. As an experience,' she continued, 'madness is terrific ... in its lava I still find most of the things I write about'.[24] As we will see, her experiences of breakdown at Hogarth House specifically informed her creation of Septimus Warren Smith in *Mrs Dalloway*, combined with what she learned about the trauma of combat from young men who had fought in the War. Among these were Siegfried Sassoon, a friend of Ottoline Morrell's; Ralph Partridge, who began working as an assistant at the Hogarth Press in 1920; and his close friend, with whom he had served in France, Gerald Brenan.

Woolf suffered another severe breakdown in March 1915, only recovering later that August. She and Leonard went to Asheham House in East Sussex, which Virginia had been renting for several years. Until 1919, when they bought Monk's House in the village of Rodmell after the lease on Asheham could not be renewed, the Woolfs would spend their time between Asheham and Hogarth House.

From the early days of the War, the threat of aerial attack hung over the residents of London, even though it would not be until 1917 that a German raid was carried out on the city itself. On 1 February 1915, Woolf described the effect of a 'terrific explosion' in St James Street:

> people came running out of Clubs; stopped still & gazed about them. But there was no Zeppelin or aeroplane—only, I suppose, a very large tyre burst. But it is really an instinct with me, & most people, I suppose, to turn any sudden noise, or dark object in the sky into an explosion, or a German aeroplane. And it always seems utterly impossible that one should be hurt.[25]

Even in the Sussex countryside, aeroplanes flying over Asheham House early on a September morning in 1917 caused Woolf to think a raid was imminent.

The 'preposterous masculine fiction', as Woolf described the War to Margaret Llewelyn Davies,[26] came close to home in 1917 when Leonard's brother Cecil was killed at the Battle of Cambrai, in France, and another brother, Philip, was wounded by the same shell. Visiting Philip in the hospital, Woolf surmised that her brother-in-law was 'puzzled why he doesn't feel more'. As she looked around the ward, she felt the 'uselessness of it all, breaking these people & mending them again'.[27] She had applauded Siegfried Sassoon's public 'Declaration against the War' that summer, telling Ottoline Morrell she thought that it 'was a splendid thing to do'.[28] Among books that Woolf reviewed during the War was Sassoon's *Counter-attack and Other Poems*, containing his 'Repression of War Experience':

And it's been proved that soldiers don't go mad
Unless they lose control of ugly thoughts
That drive them out to jabber among the trees.

In her July 1918 review for the *TLS*, Woolf wrote, 'We know no other writer who has shown us as effectually as Mr Sassoon the terrible pictures which lie behind the colourless phrases of the newspapers'.[29] Recognition that Woolf was a writer profoundly concerned with war and its effects was slow to emerge in the critical discourse, but she herself was in no doubt that her generation was 'daily scourged by the bloody war'.[30] She was revolted by the patriotic sentiment that led so many young men to glorify war, and resented the way that her childhood friend Rupert Brooke was canonised as a symbol of patriotism after his death in Greece in 1915. Septimus Warren Smith would embody many of Woolf's experiences and reflections from the period of the First World War and its aftermath. Preceded only by Rebecca West's Christopher Baldry in her 1918 novella *The Return of the Soldier*, Woolf's Septimus is one of the very earliest representations of a 'shell-shocked' veteran—someone enduring what is now termed PTSD.

At Hogarth House in 1916, recovered from her illness, Woolf settled into a busy routine of writing, publishing, organising meetings of the Women's Co-Operative Guild and assisting Leonard in his political work. Hardly a number of the *TLS* appeared during the War and subsequently without a review or essay by her (unsigned, as was the practice then) on works ranging across English literary history, as well as on translations from the Russian, poetry, memoirs and letters. Having inaugurated the Hogarth Press with their own *Two Stories*, the Woolfs followed that in 1918 with the publication of *Prelude* by Katherine Mansfield. By 1919, their output had increased to five titles, including *Poems* by T. S. Eliot.

5   T. S. Eliot at Monk's House

Character in fiction

In September 1920 Woolf was drafting a party scene in *Jacob's Room* when she was interrupted by a visit from Eliot. The appearance of *Prufrock and Other Observations* had led to an invitation from Leonard to send poems for consideration by the Hogarth Press, and this had developed into a burgeoning friendship. Seeing Eliot prompted Woolf to reflect that what she was attempting in her experiment with the form of the novel was probably being done better by James Joyce, whose writing Eliot praised highly. In 'Modern Novels', a manifesto she published in the *TLS* in April 1919, Woolf had included the Irish writer among representatives of a new generation challenging literary norms. Marking a divide between 'Edwardian' writers—H. G. Wells, Arnold Bennett and John Galsworthy—and her own 'Georgian' peers, Woolf argued that the former were 'materialists' whose fiction did not capture 'life or spirit, truth or reality' as it was experienced in the contemporary world. We are all continually bombarded, she wrote, by 'an incessant shower of innumerable atoms'.[31] It is the effort to convey this sensation in prose that characterised the work of several young writers, most notably Joyce.

Episodes of *Ulysses* were appearing in the *Little Review* while Woolf wrote 'Modern Novels', and *A Portrait of the Artist as a Young Man* had been serialised in the *Egoist* before the book was published in 1917. Asserting that writers should 'not take it for granted that life exists more in what is commonly thought big than what is commonly thought small', Woolf labelled Joyce 'spiritual; concerned at all costs to reveal the flickerings of that innermost flame which flashes its myriad messages through the brain'. For 'moderns', like her, interest lay in the 'dark region of psychology', not the materialists' focus on the external aspects of a person. She nevertheless found Joyce's focus on a single individual's consciousness limiting: the 'damned egotistical self', she soon wrote in her diary, ruined Joyce and also Dorothy Richardson, another contemporary who had, in advance of Joyce, attempted to render in prose fiction the experience of consciousness.[32]

With 'Modern Novels', Woolf was joining a debate about the nature of character in fiction that occupied many writers throughout the 1920s. She acknowledged that some in her generation had removed the 'handrails' on which readers depended for support. As is clear from her notes on the parts of *Ulysses* she read as they appeared in the *Little Review*, Joyce was a prime example in her argument. His novel was 'an attempt to get thinking into literature'.[33] To achieve this he was 'attempting to do away with the machinery'.[34] She returned to a similar idea just a few days before completing her first draft of *Mrs Dalloway* in 1924 when she wrote to a friend, the painter Jacques Raverat, that what she objected to in writers such as Wells, Bennett and Galsworthy was their adherence 'to a formal railway line of sentence, for its convenience, never reflecting that people don't and never did feel or think or dream for a second in that way'.[35] She noted Joyce's employment of cinematic techniques in his great experiment, something we can observe in her own use of jump-cuts, flashbacks and montage in *Mrs Dalloway* (she was certainly familiar with both avant-garde and popular cinema in the 1920s).

Woolf and Joyce have often been set up as antagonists, the surface similarities between *Ulysses* and *Mrs Dalloway*—both taking place on a single June day in a capital city—offered as evidence of Joyce's 'influence' or even of Woolf's plagiarism. Such views invariably rely on the casually nasty remarks Woolf made in her diary, that Joyce's book called to mind 'a queasy undergraduate scratching his pimples', or that it was evidently the production of a 'self-taught working man'.[36] But Woolf's discomfort at the 'indecency' in *Ulysses* was not the primness of a late-Victorian woman (who, after all, enjoyed Lytton Strachey's lewd poems very much). Her objection was based on the suspicion that it was a 'dodge' to convince readers that here was something unprecedented: 'Must get out of the way of thinking that indecency is more real than anything else' was another of her reading notes.[37]

When *Ulysses* was published as a book in February 1922, Woolf reaffirmed the generally negative opinion she had formed when it was serialised in the *Little Review*, although she also acknowledged that she had read it very quickly and might later revise her estimation of it (in fact she did so almost immediately when Leonard showed her a review by the American critic Gilbert Seldes that led her to admit the novel was 'very much more impressive than I judged'[38]). Although the opinion of 'Tom, great Tom', who thought Joyce's novel was 'on a par with War & Peace',[39] carried weight with Woolf, Eliot also told her that, despite its shattering of nineteenth-century norms, he did not think that *Ulysses* offered 'a new insight into human nature' in the way Tolstoy had.[40] It is more apt to think of those two groundbreaking works of modernist fiction, *Ulysses* and *Mrs Dalloway*, as in dialogue than as one echoing the other in pale imitation.

Woolf conceived of her experiment with *Jacob's Room* as a development from the short fictions she wrote during and right after the First World War. She included eight of these in *Monday or Tuesday* in 1921, which was illustrated with four woodcuts by Vanessa Bell and published by the Hogarth Press (the only collection of her short fiction to appear in Woolf's lifetime). Vanessa had provided two woodcuts for Woolf's *Kew Gardens*, published in 1919, and from then on designed the covers for all of her sister's novels, beginning with *Jacob's Room*. When Eliot read *Jacob's Room* he recognised that Woolf had achieved what she must have told him was her intention, writing to her that she had 'bridged a certain gap which existed between your other novels and the experimental prose of *Monday or Tuesday*'.[41] What the poet discerned was not widely appreciated at the time, however, and when *Monday or Tuesday* appeared Woolf felt despondent: readers 'dont see that I'm after something interesting'.[42] Yet a few months later she had shaken off her doubts, and acknowledged that she would probably never be a popular writer. Her appeal, she realised, lay in her 'queer individuality', the quality that attracted her in the writers she herself respected.[43]

By the time she finished *Jacob's Room*, Woolf was consciously positioning herself as a modernist writer with a particular relation to her readers. She had begun to think of writing a series of essays about how to read works of the past. Initially called 'Reading' in her notebooks, this series would take shape alongside her composition of *Mrs Dalloway* and be published as *The Common Reader* a month before the novel appeared. Woolf would maintain this pattern of moving back and forth between fiction and non-fiction for most of her life, 'so that I can vary the side of the pillow as fortune inclines'.[44] Indeed, her regular practice of flipping over the notebook in which she was drafting a novel and using the upside-down verso pages to draft critical essays provides a kind of concrete image of the way her fiction and non-fiction so often speak to one another.

While *Jacob's Room* was being typed for her American publisher, Woolf opened her diary in June 1922 to note that if her novel was received only as 'a clever experiment' she would 'produce Mrs Dalloway in Bond Street as the finished product'.[45] Throughout the first half of 1922, Woolf felt liberated, able to write as she wanted. She had made her case for a new form of fiction in 'Modern Novels' but was well aware of the headwinds she faced not only as a breaker of convention but also as a woman. Her friend Desmond MacCarthy's endorsement of Arnold Bennett's *Our Women* in 1920 had elicited a furious rejoinder from Woolf in the pages of the *Nation & Athenaeum*. Bennett believed that 'no woman novelist had yet produced a novel to equal the great novels of men' and that 'the average man has more intellectual power than the average woman'.[46] When MacCarthy, in his 'Affable Hawk' column in October 1920, agreed with Bennett, Woolf wrote 'The Intellectual Status of Women' as a rebuttal to both men (presaging the argument she would make in *A Room of One's Own* nine years later). All this occurred only a couple of weeks after the visit from T. S. Eliot that had stirred in her some self-doubt.

The challenge to convention in the work of those writers whom Woolf called 'Georgians' drew the attention of John Middleton Murry and Arnold Bennett in March 1923. Murry argued that D. H. Lawrence, Woolf and his own wife, Katherine Mansfield's, abandonment of plot was a dead-end for the novel. The 'problem of the novel' had not been solved by writers such as Proust, Joyce and Dorothy Richardson. In the face of what he described as an *'impasse'*, Murry argued that only in short fiction could such writers 'achieve creative perfection' because their longer works were 'fluid and fragmentary, brilliant and incoherent'.[47] Murry's point of view would have resonated with Woolf, who wrote on Christmas Day 1922 to Gerald Brenan that she believed writers of their generation could achieve nothing: 'Fragments—paragraphs—a page perhaps: but no more. Joyce to me seems strewn with disaster'.[48] Her sense of being embattled was exacerbated when Bennett, two weeks after Murry's article appeared, chose *Jacob's Room* to illustrate his argument in 'Is the Novel Decaying?' that the new generation of writers Woolf exemplified could not create characters that 'vitally survive in the mind'. For Bennett, Arthur Conan Doyle's Dr Watson 'has real life. His authenticity convinces everyone'.[49]

At first, Woolf seemed unconcerned, noting in her diary that Bennett's charges were 'only the old argument that character is dissipated into shreds now: the old post-Dostoevsky argument'.[50] She was thinking deeply about her new novel, not yet called *Mrs Dalloway*, for which she had 'almost too many ideas. I want to give life & death, sanity & insanity: I want to criticise the social system, & to show it at work, at its most intense'.[51] Woolf had taken out her diary to reflect on her own writing because she had just been looking at Murry's introduction to Katherine Mansfield's posthumously published *The Dove's Nest and Other Stories*, in which he quoted from her journals. The relationship between Mansfield and Woolf had been complex, ambivalent, but upon hearing of her death, Woolf admitted that hers was 'the only writing I have ever been jealous of'.[52] Mansfield may have been a rival but she was also the only woman writer with whom Woolf at the time felt 'a certain common understanding'.[53] In her journal Mansfield had expressed doubts about the honesty of her writing: 'All must be *deeply felt*', she wrote.[54] Her entry of 13 November 1921 would have caught Woolf's attention: 'I must try and write simply, fully, freely, from my heart. *Quietly*, caring nothing for success or failure, but just going on …'.⁵⁵ This was exactly Woolf's sentiment in 1923: 'One must write from deep feeling, said Dostoevsky. And do I? Or do I fabricate with words, loving them as I do?'⁵⁶ Even if Murry's and Bennett's criticisms irritated her, she was excited by her new novel, the structure of which was an absorbing challenge. Her working title for it now was 'The Hours'; she foresaw 'that this is going to be the devil of a struggle. The design is so queer & masterful'.⁵⁷

Woolf's response to Bennett appeared that autumn, first in the literary supplement of the *New York Evening Post*, and reprinted a month later in the *Nation & Athenaeum*. 'Mr Bennett and Mrs Brown' was the first version of an essay that Woolf revised and expanded over the next two years under two different titles.

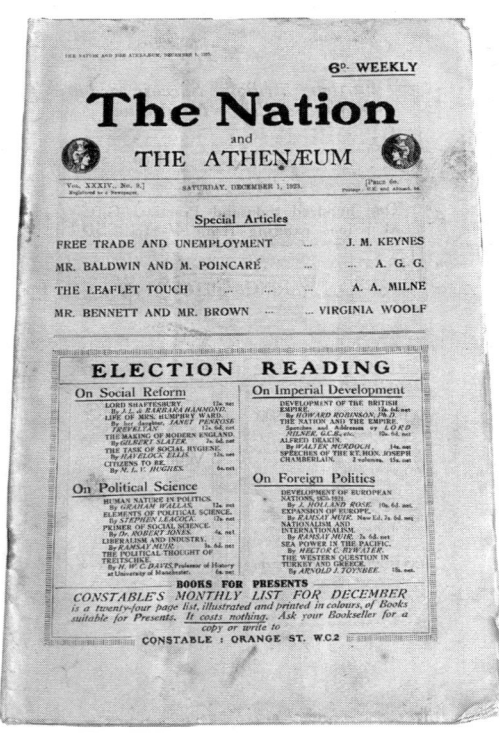

6 The typo in the title of Woolf's essay was not repeated inside

Its arguments in the version published in T. S. Eliot's *Criterion* in July 1924 under the title 'Character in Fiction' remain one of the clearest statements of her challenge to the writers she had labelled 'materialists' in 'Modern Novels'. In all its iterations, Woolf's essay agrees with Bennett that the essence of the novel is character-making. Their difference lay in what each considered 'real'. This was an existential issue as far as Woolf was concerned, for 'to disagree about character is to differ in the depths of the being'.[58] We might see this as foreshadowing the ferocious political battles of our own time over 'identity', which are arguments about different understandings of the human subject. In her essay, Woolf names that subject 'Mrs Brown'.

In May 1924 Woolf was invited to give a talk to the Heretics society at Cambridge University. 'Character in Fiction' survives in a heavily-edited typescript that shows how she reworked the arguments of 'Mr Bennett and Mrs Brown' for this talk, which was subsequently published in the *Criterion*.* The Cambridge talk has a couple of significant differences from the published version. In both, Woolf asserted that everyone needs to be a judge of character—because that is how we determine whom to trust, whom to marry—and that in the twentieth century people were thinking more than ever about character. In the typescript of the talk she wrote, 'If you read Freud you know in ten minutes some facts—or at least some possibilities—which our parents could not possibly have guessed for themselves',[59] but the line does not appear in print. As early as 1914, Leonard Woolf had reviewed Freud in translation, and in the year Woolf gave her talk, the Hogarth Press became the official publisher of the International Psychoanalytical Library, bringing out Lytton Strachey's brother James's English

---

* 'Character in Fiction' was then published with minor revisions under the original title—'Mr Bennett and Mrs Brown'—as the first of the Hogarth Essays series, which version was then published in two parts in the *New York Herald Tribune* in August 1924.

translations of Freud over the next few decades. Another difference between the talk and the published article is in Woolf's list of 'Georgian' writers. In the talk she named Joyce, Lawrence, Forster, Strachey, Eliot, Edith Sitwell and Dorothy Richardson, but in the *Criterion* version the two women are omitted. When she revised 'Modern Novels' as the better-known 'Modern Fiction' for her *Common Reader* collection, Joyce remained as the sole representative of the 'Georgian' writers whose challenge to convention Woolf defended while she was at work on *Mrs Dalloway*.

In letters to friends, and in her diary, Woolf made clear that she regarded *Jacob's Room* as a necessary experiment beyond which she intended to push in her next novel. Returning in 'Character in Fiction' to the figure of 'Mrs Brown', whom she had mentioned in passing in the first version of the essay, Woolf illustrates her argument about character-creation by telling a story about a journey from Richmond to Waterloo in which her entry into a train compartment interrupts a conversation between a Mr Smith and a Mrs Brown. Left alone with Mrs Brown when Mr Smith gets out at Clapham Junction, Woolf's narrator describes what she imagines to be the character of her travelling companion, because this is what novelists do. Acknowledging that no two writers would draw Mrs Brown in the same way (and also that she would be a different character in a French, or English, or Russian novel), Woolf argues that her trio of Edwardians would not notice Mrs Brown at all, being more interested in all kinds of things extraneous to her character. To Bennett, Dr Watson is real, but to Woolf he is 'a sack stuffed with straw, a dummy'.[60] And therein is the fundamental point that determines whether readers love the work of Virginia Woolf or cannot understand what her admirers see in it: what seems 'real' to us in the creation of a character such as Clarissa Dalloway?

'Mrs Brown is eternal, Mrs Brown is human nature':[61] to ask Arnold Bennett (or H. G. Wells or John Galsworthy) for help in creating a character for her is, Woolf says, like asking a bootmaker for help in making a watch. She quotes long passages from Bennett's novel *Hilda Lessways* to demonstrate what she means, concluding that '[o]ne line of insight would have done more than all those lines of description'.[62] Yet Woolf understood that hers was a minority point of view. The public is highly suggestible and will believe anything if it is repeated often enough, which makes the breaking of conventions very difficult. Writers such as Joyce—or Lytton Strachey in his biographies *Eminent Victorians* and *Queen Victoria*—are 'writing against the grain and current of the times'.[63] But 'on or about December 1910', Woolf writes in one of her most famous phrases, 'human character changed'.[64] There has been much speculation about what she might have had in mind. 1910 was the year in which Roger Fry's exhibition of post-impressionist painters at the Grafton Galleries in London caused an uproar, with guffaws and outrage from the public at works by Matisse, van Gogh, Picasso and others. Edward VII died in May 1910, and Woolf that February had participated in the infamous 'Dreadnought Hoax' on the British Navy.* Yet pinning a date on the great cultural, social and political transformations which occurred from the late nineteenth century into the early twentieth is probably futile. Woolf's thoughts on how the form of the novel could change to capture the 'astonishing disorder'[65] of modernity are an element in a fundamental shift in relations among what one of the characters in *To the Lighthouse* terms 'subject and object and the nature of reality'.

Woolf's detractors in the twenty-first century often echo the reaction that 'Character in Fiction' elicited at the time. The novelist Frank Swinnerton, who was a good friend of Arnold Bennett's,

---

* Danell Jones gives a thorough and insightful account of the circumstances of the hoax in *The Girl Prince: Virginia Woolf, Race and the Dreadnought Hoax*. Hurst, 2023.

opined in the *Bookman*, under the pseudonym 'Simon Pure', that readers never remembered the characters in Woolf's novels because her 'method is the vague and speculative method of an inactive dreamer'. The Edwardian writers she attacked create characters one remembers 'as one remembers real people'.[66] It is easy to see how futile arguing about such matters can quickly become: if one reader finds Conan Doyle's Dr Watson 'real' but another thinks he is a 'dummy' there is nothing empirical to appeal to in settling the difference of opinion. But 'Character in Fiction' is important as a manifesto explaining Woolf's aims as a novelist. *Mrs Dalloway* remains a significant presence on the cultural scene one hundred years after its first appearance, although some of the reasons why that is so will undoubtedly remain elusively idiosyncratic.

Septimus Warren Smith

Swinnerton's article was published in October 1924. On the ninth of that month, Woolf wrote the words that became the final sentence of *Mrs Dalloway*: 'For there she was'.[67] A week later, she recorded her feeling that she had 'exorcised the spell wh. Murry & others said I had laid myself under after Jacob's Room'.[68] Then she turned to a fresh page in a writing notebook—the second of three notebooks in which she drafted the novel—and on 20 October 1924 wrote the words 'Mrs Dalloway said she would buy the flowers herself'.[69]

The famous opening line of *Mrs Dalloway*, then, was in fact written two years after Woolf had first begun to plan the novel in 1922. It appears in the middle of a handwritten manuscript spread across three notebooks collectively known as 'The Hours', which now resides in the British Library.* 'The Hours' draft actually

---

* Leonard Woolf gave the three notebooks to Vita Sackville-West after Virginia Woolf's death in 1941.

begins with a scene of Peter Walsh walking in London. By the time she wrote that scene, Woolf had already written what she was considering as the first two chapters of her new novel: 'Mrs Dalloway in Bond Street' and a story she never published called 'The Prime Minister', which introduced Septimus Smith.

'Mrs Dalloway said she would buy the gloves herself' is how Woolf first reintroduced her character from *The Voyage Out*. Many elements that would reappear in *Mrs Dalloway* are already in place in the short story of 1922: Big Ben strikes the hours as Clarissa sets off on an errand one fresh summer morning, her thoughts returning to childhood memories as she walks through London. She thinks about her sister Sylvia's death, and how belief in God has faltered. The War remains present, in both Mrs Foxcroft's anguish at the embassy, because 'that nice boy was dead',[70] and in Clarissa's reflection that 'Thousands of young men had died that things might go on'.[71] The story ends with the sound of an explosion in the street outside the glove shop.

On the reverse side of the notebook page on which she put down her plan for a novel 'to be called, perhaps, At Home: or The Party' on 6 October 1922, Woolf wrote that same day the opening words of another story: 'The violent explosion which made the women who were serving gloves cower behind the counter'.[72] Two days later, she was startled to read in the newspaper that Kitty Maxse had died. She had not seen Kitty in many years, but all that day Woolf was haunted by images of her coming up from the past. After a week, Woolf noted that 'Mrs Dalloway has branched into a book; & I adumbrate here a study of insanity & suicide: the world seen by the sane & the insane side by side—something like that. Septimus Smith?—is that a good name?'[73] 'Mrs Dalloway in Bond Street' would be turned down for publication by T. S. Eliot, but accepted by the American magazine *The Dial*, where it appeared in June 1923. Woolf did not complete 'The Prime Minister' as a separate story, but its drafts served her as the second scene of

Mrs Dalloway, where the explosion of a car tyre is the device by which Woolf moves the narrative from the consciousness of Clarissa in the flower shop to that of Septimus in the street outside.

Clarissa Dalloway and Septimus Smith were always linked in Woolf's mind. She told Gerald Brenan that she intended them to 'be entirely dependent on each other'.[74] In 1932, Woolf responded to an American student's inquiry that as far as she could remember 'the character of Septimus in Mrs Dalloway was invented to complete the character of Mrs Dalloway; I could not otherwise convey my whole meaning about her'.[75] Woolf believed that Kitty Maxse, who fell over the bannisters in her home at the age of fifty-five, had committed suicide (although evidence for this is inconclusive). In her introduction to the 1928 Modern Library edition of *Mrs Dalloway* (discussed in Part III), Woolf wrote that 'Mrs. Dalloway was originally to kill herself, or perhaps merely to die at the end of the party',[76] but aside from this, there is nothing anywhere else that suggests Woolf intended Clarissa to die. (E. M. Forster, bizarrely, thought that Clarissa *did* kill herself the first time he read the novel.) Clarissa thinks a great deal about death but Woolf intended her party to affirm life. Hearing about the death of Kitty Maxse seems to have prompted Woolf to think more about the character of Septimus.

Septimus vows to kill himself in various drafts of 'The Prime Minister'. The surviving manuscript versions of the story all resemble the passage in *Mrs Dalloway* where Septimus Warren Smith is introduced among the crowd on Bond Street who have paused to speculate about the important personage who might be in the car that has stopped. In the story, Septimus is depicted in a restaurant at a weekly meeting of political activists, people who feel 'that this is the most depressing of all ages for people of Liberal principles'.[77] His sudden laugh for no apparent reason unsettles his fellow diners. Septimus imagines that his laugh has caused a hole to open in the wall: a liquid oozes through the opening and makes 'the outlines of things' quiver. He has a tremendous message to be 'communicated at once—at once!—there was no time to lose—to the Prime Minister'.[78] And when panic seizes him, Septimus thinks that it is 'necessary to kill himself' but 'not to bring discredit on one's wife'.[79] After writing ten pages of the story, Woolf made a note: 'Mrs D seeing the sane truth, S. S. seeing the insane truth'.[80] She showed Clarissa walking home with the gloves she has just purchased. Septimus, in a chilling foreshadowing of our own times, thinks of how he will assassinate the prime minister and then be immortalised in newspaper reports: 'He could do anything, for he was now beyond law'.[81] An undated typescript of 'The Prime Minister' ends with Clarissa following the gaze of the crowd up to where an aeroplane is writing letters in the sky.

Two streams flowing into Woolf's creation of Septimus Warren Smith stand out: what she read and heard about 'shell shock', and her own experiences of mental instability and the exposure to doctors that this entailed, particularly in the early years of her marriage. These streams at times converged. One of Woolf's doctors, Maurice Craig, was a member of the War Office Committee of Inquiry into shell shock that was established after the First World War, while another, Henry Head, gave testimony to that Committee. Yet another of the doctors Woolf was taken to see by Leonard shortly after their marriage, Theophilus Hyslop, had given (and published) a lecture about the paintings exhibited at Roger Fry's 1910 exhibition, *Manet and the Post-Impressionists*, in which, Woolf noted in her biography of Fry, he 'gave his opinion ... that the pictures were the work of madmen'.[82] As James Longenbach has written, 'the linked battles of modernism, sexism, and the Somme'[83] are examined in all of Woolf's postwar fiction. Her earlier experiences with the eminent neurologist Sir George Savage, who had recommended to her father that his 'delicate' daughter divert her mental energies into something more placid than writing, such as gardening, also informed her depiction of Sir William Bradshaw.

Early in 1921, Woolf observed signs of the peace that had followed the Armistice. Food prices had fallen, and there were 'very few wounded soldiers' about, although 'stiff legs, sticks shod with rubber, & empty sleeves are common enough. Also at Waterloo I sometimes see dreadful looking spiders propelling themselves along the platform—men all body—legs trimmed off close to the body'.[84] In Septimus Warren Smith, Woolf would represent those whose wounds were invisible. These were the men the populace would rather not notice. When Francis Hopwood, Lord Southborough spoke in the House of Lords in April 1920 in favour of the establishment of a Parliamentary Commission to investigate shell shock he acknowledged that many would prefer to forget all the 'insanity, suicide, and death' the phenomenon had caused during and immediately after the War; but this would not, he continued, be fair to those who were still suffering and who were 'still on our hands'.[85]

Woolf would have read Southborough's articles in *The Times* in September 1922, only weeks after she had begun to think about 'The Prime Minister' as the second chapter of her novel. Southborough explained that his Committee had wanted to move away from the term 'shell shock', with its connotations of injury solely due to artillery, but that it was too deeply lodged in public consciousness to do so. On the day Southborough published his first account of the work of the Committee (2 September 1922), a *Times* editorial regretted that it had 'failed to offer a clear definition of cowardice'. The notion that shell shock was a form of malingering persisted long after the War. During the conflict, 346 men had been executed for 'cowardice, desertion or other crimes',[86] and it is deeply resonant with this attitude that Dr Holmes cries 'The coward!' as he crashes into the room from which Septimus has just thrown himself to his death on the railings below. A week after Southborough's article, the explorer Francis Younghusband made the argument in a letter

7 Area railings in Tavistock Square

to *The Times* that the firmness of men's religious devotion—'the sentiment akin to love of country'—would ensure that 'the only fear they will have will be the fear of disgracing their regiment, their country, and themselves'.[87] Younghusband's conservative opinion exemplifies the attitude against which Rezia opposes her conviction that her husband is 'brave', even though she has been told that 'it was cowardly for a man to say he would kill himself'.

Under the subheading 'The Mental Cases', Southborough wrote that many of the soldiers conscripted to fight had already been suffering from mental conditions that would have emerged in the course of ordinary civilian life, but that the atrocious stresses of trench warfare exacerbated and sped up their manifestations. Some readers of his *Times* account might have been prompted by that subheading to recall a poem of Wilfred Owen's, published posthumously in 1920. In 'Mental Cases', Owen wrote of

> ... men whose minds the Dead have ravished.
> Memory fingers in their hair of murders,
> Multitudinous murders they once witnessed.

Such poems were key in exposing the vast discrepancy between the 'official' view of the War promoted by the government and the experience of soldiers in the trenches. Owen had been treated at Craiglockhart War Hospital in 1917, where he met Siegfried Sassoon. Sassoon had been sent to the hospital following his public declaration against the War, the government deciding that a court martial of the highly decorated officer would only give his cause more publicity.

Both men were under the care at Craiglockhart of Dr W. H. R. Rivers, whose open-minded approach to what were called 'war neuroses' contrasted with prevailing attitudes that tended to insist on physiological causes for the symptoms soldiers were experiencing, or saw them as efforts to avoid service.* The *Daily Sketch* of 10 August 1922, for example, entitled its news item on the release of the War Office Committee's report 'Shell-Shock or Funk: Difficult to Distinguish One from Other says Committee'. '"So you're in a funk"' says Dr Holmes to Septimus when the despairing Rezia calls on him to help her husband. Dr Maurice Craig, who had advised Woolf against having children and told Leonard that it was important for his wife to drink as much milk as possible, informs the doctors we meet in *Mrs Dalloway* (in 1922 Craig gave the Bradshaw lecture at the Royal College of Physicians, but his admonition to drink milk is also echoed in Dr Holmes's recommendation that Rezia give her husband more porridge to keep up his weight). A paper of Craig's on 'Mental Disorder' averred that 'there is one symptom which appears early and which stands out in strong relief, and that is hyper-sensitivity ... it is to me the symptom of all

---

* The relationship between Rivers and Sassoon at Craiglockhart is the subject of Pat Barker's novel *Regeneration*.

symptoms which gives rise to many others which in time may so disturb personality as to occasion definite unsoundness of mind'.[88] When Siegfried Sassoon visited Woolf in 1924, he struck her as 'a nice dear kind sensitive warm-hearted good fellow'.[89] Woolf named Sassoon and Owen as among those poets who made it possible to feel through literature the emotions aroused by the 'vast catastrophe of the European war'. Such emotions, she wrote in 'On Not Knowing Greek', 'had to be broken up for us, and put at an angle' to avoid sentimentality.[90]

W. H. R. Rivers gave a presentation at the end of 1917 to the psychiatry section of the Royal College of Medicine which he titled 'The Repression of War Experience'. Sassoon had written his poem with that title six months earlier. In the lecture, Rivers remarked that the men he saw at Craiglockhart had usually been told by doctors at other hospitals to try to 'banish all thoughts of war from their mind'.[91] Dr Holmes advises Septimus to throw himself 'into outside interests; take up some hobby'. A somewhat more enlightened doctor, whom Woolf consulted early in her marriage, was Henry Head. Head quoted Sassoon's 'Repression of War Experience' as an example of the 'evil advice' given by 'medical attendants' to soldiers suffering from war neurosis: 'Don't think of anything you saw in France, but play games and be with cheery fellows'.[92] In his testimony to the War Office Committee, Head stated his view that the origins of shell shock were mental rather than physiological.

In creating the character of Septimus Warren Smith, Woolf consciously drew on her own experiences as well as on what she learned about the traumas of combat from her reading and from personal connections. During the War, her cousin Herbert Fisher brought news 'from the very centre of the very centre' of Lloyd George's government, where he was a cabinet minister.[93] On one visit in 1918, Fisher told Woolf that the War would soon be over and that it only remained to work out the terms of Germany's surrender. Woolf's brother-in-law Clive Bell published a pamphlet against the War in 1915 that was quickly confiscated by the government. In *Peace at Once*, Bell directly addressed Gilbert Murray, the Regius Professor of History at Oxford, and one of Fisher's closest friends, because he believed him to have made the most convincing argument in favour of the War. Murray, Bell wrote, had at least

> tried to put into words his sense of the horror of war, and what he says is, as usual, worth attending to:
>
> 'Try for a moment,' an objector to our policy might say, 'to realise the extent of suffering involved in one small corner of a battlefield. You have seen a man here and there badly hurt in an accident; you have seen, perhaps, a horse with its back broken, and you can remember how dreadful it seemed to you. In that one corner how many men, how many horses will be lying, hurt far worse and just waiting to die? Indescribable wounds, extreme torment; and all, far further than any eye can see, multiplied and multiplied! And, for all your righteous indignation against Germany, what have those done?'[94]

Although Woolf was secluded while she recovered from a severe breakdown during the early part of 1915, she was certainly aware of *Peace at Once* when it was published in August (she told Margaret Llewelyn Davies that Bell's father had threatened to disinherit him 'if he writes more in the style of the pamphlet'[95]). When it was censored, Bell kept up a stream of letters to the *Nation* and to the *New Statesman* to make sure people knew what arguments the government would not allow to be heard. It is likely, therefore, that Woolf read *Peace at Once*, as we know that others close to her did. Bell objected profoundly to the promulgation by the government, and by apologists such as Gilbert Murray, of the idea that the War was being fought to defend 'national honour'. Such abstractions, he argued, obscured the fact that a nation was made up of individuals:

> A nation is nothing but a congeries of Mr. Smiths, Mrs. Smiths, and little Smiths. Bearing in mind this fact, that a nation is nothing but a collection of individuals, let us inquire what the individual stands to gain by war or lose by peace. We have agreed that to crush Germany the

Smiths who inhabit, and will during the next fifty years inhabit, Europe, must suffer great evils.[96]

It was Bell's opinion that the War was actually a contest between the ruling classes of various nations, using the 'Smiths' of their respective populaces to fight it for them at enormous cost. The War's supporters 'dare not face the realities of men, women, and children, so they glue their eyes resolutely on a trusty abstraction'. Although Smith is, of course, one of the most common English surnames, its use resonates in the anti-war texts of these two radical pacifists, Bell and Woolf.

Woolf conceived Septimus as someone who had 'been in the war' but might also be 'founded on me'.[97] She pondered, 'Why not have something of G. B. in him'[98]—Gerald Brenan, who had given up the military career his family expected him to pursue after the War to become a writer. Woolf also wrote that Septimus would be 'partly R.; partly me',[99] which has led to speculation that 'R' might refer to Rupert Brooke, with whom Woolf had once been close. Given that Brooke did not see combat, a more likely candidate is Ralph Partridge, who served on the Italian front in the War, as Septimus did. But in creating her extraordinary character, Woolf had to return to some of her most painful experiences. When the novel was about to be published, she wrote to her friend Gwen Raverat, 'You can't think what a raging furnace it is still to me— madness and doctors and being forced'.[100] When she was about to move from Richmond in 1924, she reflected on the years she had spent at Hogarth House, when 'aeroplanes were over London at night' and she and Leonard had started their press. 'I've had some very curious visions in this room too,' she added, in language that is closely echoed by Septimus as the section in which his death occurs begins, 'lying in bed, mad, & seeing the sunlight quivering like gold water, on the wall. I've heard the voices of the dead here. And felt, through it all, exquisitely happy'.[101]

8 Gerald Brenan

Design

In August 1923 Woolf said of Septimus that he 'must somehow see through human nature—see its hypocrisy, & insincerity, its power to recover from every wound, incapable of taking any final impression'.[102] A visit to Garsington earlier that summer, the refuge for so many conscientious objectors in Woolf's own circle during the War, had sparked a reflection on 'human nature'. On the day she sent 'Mrs Dalloway in Bond Street' to T. S. Eliot ('Mrs Dalloway doesn't seem to me to be complete as she is—but judge for yourself', she wrote[103]), she recorded her opinions about those she had encountered at Ottoline Morrell's estate.

She had met several young men there who were 'no bigger than asparagus' (Lord David Cecil, 'Puffin' Asquith and Edward Sackville-West), and wrote irritably that 'people scarcely care for each other. They have this insane instinct for life. But they never become attached to anything outside themselves'. But her ire was directed principally at her hostess: 'A loathing overcomes me of human beings—their insincerity, their vanity—A wearisome & rather defiling talk with Ott. last night is the foundation of this complaint—& then the blend in one's own mind of suavity & sweetness with contempt & bitterness. Her egotism is so great'. As so often with Woolf, the emotional pendulum swings back and forth: 'Yet on Saturday night I liked her'.[104] She chastised herself for hypocrisy, recognising that she had given Ottoline no inkling of her mood. (Although she never resorted to the cruelty of D. H. Lawrence or Aldous Huxley, who repaid Ottoline's hospitality with vicious depictions of her in their novels *Women in Love* and *Crome Yellow*, Woolf's private remarks about Ottoline were often very unkind, and their eventual close friendship had a long gestation.)

Woolf's thoughts then turned to her book, in which she was suddenly 'a great deal interested': 'I want to bring in the despicableness of people like Ott: I want to give the slipperiness of the soul'.[105] It was later this month that Woolf declared that she wanted 'to criticise the social system, & to show it at work, at its most intense'.[106] That 'system' in the novel is at once the political apparatus that wastes the lives of young men such as Septimus, and also the daily failings of personal relations. As she had written in *Jacob's Room* (a novel about a young man of promise who dies in the First World War), 'It's not catastrophes, murders, deaths, diseases, that age and kill us; it's the way people look and laugh, and run up the steps of omnibuses'.

Mrs Dalloway is a great war novel, an early instance of those works of the 1920s which made clear that the effects of war continue to reverberate throughout society long after the guns fall silent and the treaties are signed. This seems obvious now, when 'trauma' has become such a common term. But in showing how war's aftermath echoes through daily life, *Mrs Dalloway* was groundbreaking. Take, for one example, the skywriting aeroplane that draws Londoners' attention upwards. It first registers in the narrative when 'the strange high singing' of its engine mingles with the other city sounds enthralling Clarissa as she crosses Victoria Street on her way towards St James's Park. In Woolf's story 'Kew Gardens', the sound of an aeroplane embodied 'the voice of the summer sky',[107] but in *Mrs Dalloway*, when the crowd on Bond Street notices it, that same sound 'bored ominously' into their ears. A week after *The Times* reported on the shell-shock inquiry, the newspaper noted the new phenomenon of skywriting, pointing out its 'Wide Scope in War and Peace'. After the First World War, technologies ostensibly benign would invariably have violent uses as well. And as noted above, after 1915 the flight of an aeroplane across a country sky brought bombing to mind.

Life for her generation, Woolf felt, was 'tragic', 'like a little strip of pavement over an abyss'. Violence hung in the air, 'no newspaper placard without its shriek of agony'.[108] Septimus witnesses this: 'brutality blared out on placards; men were trapped in mines; women burnt alive'. Writing Septimus's 'mad scenes' taxed Woolf greatly while she continued to wrestle with finding ways to make the design of her novel work with her vision. A breakthrough occurred at the end of August 1923 when she envisioned 'beautiful caves' behind her characters that would connect. A few weeks later she described a 'tunnelling process, by which I tell the past by instalments, as I have need of it'.[109] Images of mining began to occur more frequently in her diary entries about the novel, metaphors which convey her sense of an archaeology of the self, the way in which memories are like veins of ore hidden deep within us until they are suddenly exposed, brought to the surface. Like many artists at the time, Woolf was conceiving of human subjectivity in new ways, trying to create fictional narratives that would communicate that conception. Writing *Mrs Dalloway* confirmed her sense that 'we're splinters & mosaics, not, as they used to hold, immaculate, monolithic, consistent wholes'.[110]

When T. S. Eliot asked Woolf if she would send him an extract from the novel she was working on (the *Criterion* was always on the lookout for fiction), she replied that it was 'too interwoven' for any part to stand on its own. Her insight is a clue as to why readers often find Woolf's novels challenging (indeed, by the time she came to write *To the Lighthouse*, she was not sure that 'novel' was the right word to describe what she was doing). In her many essays about reading and fiction Woolf explained that literary conventions set up expectations in readers; when these are not met, readers can feel disoriented, disgruntled, unsure how to deal with a text. We see this all the time, though perhaps it is more readily grasped in the field of visual art. Woolf was particularly close to the introduction to Britain of modernist painting and sculpture through her relationships with her sister; with Vanessa's husband, Clive Bell; and with Roger Fry. The response of many members of the public to Fry's exhibition *Manet and the Post-Impressionists* in 1910 was to reject the notion that a painting such as van Gogh's *Wheatfield with Crows*, for example, could legitimately be termed 'art'.

The 'nerve specialist' Theophilus Hyslop, echoing the majority of the British public's opinion, likened the post-impressionist painters' work to pictures created by inmates at the Bethlem asylum. As Hilary Spurling points out in her biography of Henri Matisse, it is very difficult for us now to understand how 'paintings of light and color, mediated through scenes of simple seaside domesticity', were viewed at the time as 'an assault that threatened civilisation as they knew it'.[111] After visiting Fry's exhibition at the Grafton Galleries, the poet Wilfred Scawen Blunt wrote in his diary for 15 November 1910:

> The drawing is on the level of an untaught child of seven or eight years old, the sense of colour that of a tea-tray painter, the method that of a schoolboy who wipes his fingers on a slate after spitting on them .... Apart from the frames, the whole collection should not be worth £5, and then only for the pleasure of making a bonfire of them .... These are not works of art at all, unless throwing a handful of mud against a wall may be called one. They are works of idleness and impotent stupidity, a pornographic show.[112]

His words could be those of a visitor to an art gallery exhibiting contemporary art one hundred years later, baffled or annoyed by experiments that challenge received ideas about what constitutes 'art' (or those of politicians today who have not even seen the work in person but dutifully perform their outrage).

For others, though, such as the young writer Katherine Mansfield, van Gogh's paintings taught 'a kind of freedom'.[113] Vanessa Bell echoed Mansfield's point in a memoir of Roger Fry, where she recalled what the 1910 exhibition had meant to her: 'it was as if at last one might say things one had always felt instead of trying to say things that other people told one to feel. Freedom was given one to be oneself'.[114] Clive Bell made his name in 1914 with a slim volume titled simply *Art* in which he brashly attacked the canons of visual art to make the argument that Matisse, Picasso, van Gogh and other 'revolutionaries' were in fact picking up an aesthetic tradition that had been diverted by an overemphasis on beauty and mimesis. He and Fry looked back to the fifth-century mosaicists of Byzantium for a connection to the modernist art they both championed.

Similarly, as we have seen, Woolf looked past her immediate forebears, the Edwardians, and rejected the 'fabulous fleshy monsters' created by them (as she put it in that Christmas Day letter to Gerald Brenan): 'The human soul, it seems to me, orientates itself afresh every now and then. It is doing so now. No one can see it whole, therefore'. This is why writers of her generation could only 'catch a glimpse of a nose, a shoulder, something turning away, always in movement'.[115] It is as if she is trying to capture in words the sensation of looking at a cubist work by Braque or Picasso. When the Bells in 1911 bought *Pots et Citron*, the first work by Picasso to enter an English collection, Vanessa told her sister 'It's "cubist" and very beautiful colour'.[116] Furthermore, as Julia Briggs has pointed out, Woolf's use of blank space in both *Jacob's Room* and *Mrs Dalloway* likely owes something to her having set by hand the type of Hope Mirrlees's avant-garde poem *Paris* for publication by the Hogarth Press in 1920. Mirrlees followed the practice of such French poets as Guillaume Apollinaire and Blaise Cendrars in her omission of punctuation, and of Pierre Reverdy 'who used blank spaces to create pauses in a text'.[117] The sense of flux, of some reality always just beyond one's reach, and the necessity of a reader's active engagement in creating the text characterises much of Woolf's fiction. This can either jar the reader who expects a more 'traditional', static notion of the self, or seem to another exactly how reality is experienced.

When Woolf told Eliot that her novel was too 'interwoven' to have any part broken off, she demonstrated her conscious choice to reject the comforts offered to readers by the conventionally structured novel in thirty-two chapters she had criticised in 'Modern Fiction' and 'Character in Fiction'. As she drafted her scenes—Clarissa walking to the flower shop, Septimus paralysed amidst the crowd on Bond Street, Peter Walsh suddenly reappearing in Clarissa's life—she maintained a running commentary in her notebooks, aware that what she was attempting was breaking the unwritten rules that guided readers' expectations. Unlike many of her modernist peers, however, Woolf was not only a writer of fiction but also a professional essayist and reviewer, to say nothing of being a publisher. She conceived of *Mrs Dalloway* and *The Common Reader* as 'two books running side by side',[118] and was also publishing other essays and reviews the whole time she worked on them.

Readers who encounter *Mrs Dalloway* expecting the kind of novel written by those Woolf dubbed 'Edwardians' often feel somewhat lost: what is happening, they may ask, and why? Who are these people? Although her initial idea was to have short chapters such as she had written in *Jacob's Room*, Woolf very soon moved away from this: 'No chapters. Possible choruses' she noted in November 1922. Woolf was greatly concerned with the *design* of her novel. Throughout her life she thought deeply about *form*, a key term in debates about aesthetics that run throughout the twentieth century. While at work on *Jacob's Room*, Woolf read Percy Lubbock's *The Craft of Fiction*. She did not engage very often with critics, but this book by Henry James's editor was one she returned to several times after first discussing it in 'On Re-Reading Novels' in the *TLS* in the summer of 1922.

Beginning with a further disparagement of the Edwardian writers, Woolf draws attention in her essay to the difficulty her generation has in reading older works of literature as 'wholes'. She explains that Lubbock believes that contemporary readers of novels are too distracted by their effort to identify with specific characters; or they focus on scenes they find particularly congenial; or compare the novel to the real world, and thus miss 'the book itself', a form that can be discerned only by reading according to the author's intentions. If we are reading correctly, according to Lubbock, we see 'the book itself, as the form of the statue is the statue itself'.[119] 'Form', Woolf points out, is a term drawn from the visual arts; she is not sure it is right to use it with regard to literary art (which is perhaps why she tended to use the term 'design' when referring to the challenges posed by *Mrs Dalloway*). Illustrated by her own reading of a short story by Flaubert, 'Un Coeur Simple', Woolf contends that 'the "book itself" is not form which you see, but emotion which you feel'. Lubbock's idea of 'form' is too concrete; it gets between her experience as a reader and what she is reading. When we finish a book, she continues, 'there is nothing to be seen; there is everything to be felt'.[120] Two years after publishing this essay, Woolf told Roger Fry that she had been writing again about Lubbock's book and 'trying to make out what I mean by form in fiction. I say it is emotion put into the right relations; and has nothing to do with form as used of painting'.[121] She would go on tinkering with 'On Re-Reading Novels' for several years.

What are the implications of her ideas about emotion and form for how we should read her books? A year after *Mrs Dalloway* appeared, Woolf gave a talk to a London girls' school titled 'How Should One Read a Book?' The book we read line by line is different from that book recalled after we have finished it, when we attempt to hold it in our minds as a whole. As we read, we build up connections, images, a sense of the world created by the narrative. Asked what *Mrs Dalloway* is 'about', someone might reply: not much. A politician's wife gives a fancy party, a young man traumatised by the First World War kills himself when his doctors fail to care for him. Or we might say, as Woolf did, it is about everything: 'I am stuffed with ideas for it. I feel I can use up everything I've ever thought'.[122] To read a book by this writer whose idea of 'form' is 'emotions put into the right relations' we need to understand that everything is related to everything else, that she is trying to achieve something that the necessarily sequential nature of reading works against. Woolf often uses repetition as a form of patterning, so that certain phrases will resonate with one another. For example, the last line of *Mrs Dalloway*—'For there she was'—echoes what has preceded it: Clarissa remembering 'there she was alone with Sally', who had suddenly kissed her; Peter remembering how she had always stood out to him: 'there she was, however; there she was'; and Richard, returning from Lady Bruton's to his wife: 'There she was, mending her dress'. Woolf's fiction puts great demands on our memory, and there is no helpful narrator pointing out what we should pay more or less attention to.

When Woolf wrote in her diary that she could 'use up everything I've ever thought', she was hard at work on the scene in Regent's Park when Septimus's ravings about his dead friend Evans walking towards him drive Rezia away from him in despair. This long diary entry of 15 October 1923 begins with an account of a terrifying night when Woolf set off from Monk's House to meet Leonard, who was coming back from a day spent in London at the offices of the *Nation & Athenaeum,* where he was literary editor. She could not find him. Walking in the dark and rain across a field, Woolf became rigid with terror. She took shelter under some trees at Iford, a nearby village, to wait for the bus coming from the train station at Lewes. When she knew that the 'last likely train' had come and there was still no sign of Leonard, she decided that she must go to London to look for him. She bicycled to the station through the cold wind and driving rain, bought a ticket, 'had 3 minutes to spare, & then, turning the corner of the station stairs, saw Leonard coming along ... He was rather cold & angry (as, perhaps was natural)'. Hiding her feelings as they walked home discussing a row at the magazine office, Woolf felt great relief, '& yet there was too something terrible behind it—the fact of this pain, I suppose; which continued for several days— ... & it became

9 Leonard Woolf at Monk's House, 1931

connected with the deaths of the miners, & with Aubrey Herbert's death the next day'.

In *Mrs Dalloway*, Woolf shows how difficult it is to separate emotions, one from another. Her fear of what might have happened to her husband was tangled up with and exacerbated by the memory of a newspaper story she had read three weeks earlier about the deaths of forty-one miners in a flooded pit at Falkirk, in Scotland. When she heard the day after her scare about Leonard that her sister-in-law Margaret Duckworth's half-brother had died, that news also attached itself to her feelings about what might possibly have happened to Leonard. The feelings she experienced on this night would be an 'old wound' still 'twingeing' a year later as she approached the end of her first draft of *Mrs Dalloway*.[123]

The same diary entry continues, turning again to her novel in progress, where she is writing the 'mad scene' in Regent's Park by 'clinging as tight to fact as I can'—presumably the facts of her own experience of mental breakdown.[124] She expresses doubts about Clarissa's character. Is she 'too stiff, too glittering & tinsely'? But she cheers herself by remembering her breakthrough that August: 'how I dig out beautiful caves behind my characters; I think that gives exactly what I want; humanity, humour, depth. The idea is that the caves shall connect, & each comes to daylight at the present moment'.[125] From the first, she had wanted her main characters to be seen by others, and to show, too, how they thought about and responded to others. Thus, we see Septimus through the eyes not only of his wife and his doctors but also of Maisie Johnson, (who in turn is viewed by Carrie Dempster) and of Peter Walsh, who mistakes what Rezia and Septimus are going through on a park bench for a lovers' quarrel. Similarly, Clarissa is glimpsed by Scrope Purvis, a neighbour in Westminster, affording us an external view of her. Both Septimus's and Clarissa's histories are filled in gradually as we come to know them in the course of the day. This was what Woolf called her 'tunnelling process, by which I tell the past by instalments, as I have need of it'. That she had taken so long to light upon this technique, she continued in her diary, 'proves, I think, how false Percy Lubbock's doctrine is—that you can do this sort of thing consciously. One feels about in a state of misery—indeed I made up my mind one night to abandon the book—& then one touches the hidden spring'.[126]

Woolf believed that readers were more interested in the inner life than external, objective 'facts'. Although in responding to 'Mr Bennett and Mrs Brown' in the *Nation & Athenaeum* the prolific novelist J. D. Beresford defended the Edwardian writers named by Woolf, he acknowledged that average English men and women were now 'more aware of their own diversity, more introspective, and hence more complicated'.[127] In her critique of Arnold Bennett, Woolf had remarked that describing a house in great detail did not necessarily convince a reader that anyone lived there. But without a narrator describing her characters, how would she convey a sense of them to a reader? One means was through other perspectives: 'Septimus ... must be seen by someone. His wife?';[128] 'Mrs D must be seen by other people';[129] 'Every scene should build up the idea of C's character'.[130] Woolf wanted to be sure that 'the inside of the mind' could be 'made luminous': 'that is to say the stuff of the book—lights on it coming from external sources'.[131] A month into writing the first draft, she wanted 'All inner feelings to be lit up'.[132] She wondered if there might be 'Possible choruses':[133] 'an observer in the street at each critical point who acts the part of chorus—some nameless person'.[134] These choruses might be 'links between chapters',[135] though she was not sure she even wanted to have 'chapters'.

In late 1922, she had begun reading for 'On Not Knowing Greek', an essay she wrote specifically for *The Common Reader*. The ancient Greek dramatists had invented the chorus as a way to communicate 'what was general and poetic, comment, not action ... without interrupting the movement of the whole'. Woolf wanted to find some modern equivalent to 'the old men or women who take no active part in the drama, the undifferentiated voices who sing like birds in the pauses of the wind'.[136] At times the 'choric' element of *Mrs Dalloway* is more evident than at others, such as when Peter drops off to sleep next to an 'elderly grey nurse' who is knitting on a bench in Regent's Park. There is a strong sense throughout the novel not only of communication without words but also of how no one is complete in themselves, that our 'selves' are in part created from the selves of others.

Woolf's essay on the ancient Greeks closes with a passage echoed in *Mrs Dalloway*. 'There is a sadness at the back of life' which the Greeks did 'not attempt to mitigate'. We turn to those ancient dramatists 'when we are sick of the vagueness, of the confusion, of the Christianity and its consolations of our own age'.[137] Thus, when Clarissa withdraws to her attic room thinking that there 'was an emptiness at the heart of life', Woolf is giving her character an 'Attic' (i.e. ancient Greek) reverie. Emptiness, absence, as so often in Woolf's fiction, was a key element of the design of *Mrs Dalloway*.

Part II

Mrs Dalloway: content and influences

The Woolfs enjoyed Hogarth House, where they had created the rhythm of their busy married life since 1915. The house boasted a very long garden, beautifully proportioned rooms and a view of Kew Gardens in the distance from the upper windows. But after several years there, Woolf longed to move closer to the heart of London. Leonard did not at first support her wish, worried about the effect on her health of the social stimulation she sought. 'Baffled & depressed' at the prospect of life 'mute & mitigated, in the suburbs', Woolf planned her escape. Despite the affection she felt for their house, and her pride in the Hogarth Press, she felt cut off in Richmond. If she were in the city proper she could 'go hear a tune, or have a look at a picture, or find out something at the British Museum, or go adventuring among human beings' without having to 'leave, guiltily, as the clock strikes 11' to catch the last train home.[1]

In January 1924 she signed the lease for 52 Tavistock Square in Bloomsbury: 'So I shall have a room of my own to sit down in, after almost 10 years, in London'.[2] The move would give her 'music, talk, friendship, city views, books, publishing, something central & inexplicable'.[3] Her delight called to mind a line from a fifteenth-century poem by William Dunbar, 'In Honour of the City of London': 'London thou art a jewel of jewels, & jasper of jocunditie'. Within a few months of settling into her new home she was walking back from the theatre 'through the entrails of London',[4] enchanted by 'a tawny coloured magic carpet' that effortlessly carried her 'into beauty'.[5]

It took Woolf a week to find the time to record in her diary the 'astounding fact' that she had written the last words of *Mrs Dalloway* at Tavistock Square on 9 October 1924, days after returning from their summer sojourn at Monk's House. She would now spend until the end of the year revising the drafts that were in her various notebooks. Determined to publish *The Common Reader* before her novel, she was unsure how much rewriting lay ahead. As she settled down to work on the manuscript in her large basement studio behind the rooms which housed the Hogarth Press, Woolf continued to reflect on several of the themes that had become part of the substance of the novel, thinking, as was her habit, backwards to her own past, and forwards to the next fiction she would write.

Having completed a novel that for once had not been interrupted by illness, she was feeling a little triumphant. She had broken through that '*impasse*' up to which John Middleton Murry had accused her of leading the novel form. Thinking about Murry inevitably brought Katherine Mansfield back to her mind, 'whom in my own way I suppose I loved', she wrote in a long diary entry on 17 October. By what name should such complicated emotions be called? Woolf was happy at the moment, overjoyed in her new abode and grateful for the deep friendship she shared with Lytton Strachey. He had just been to dinner, during which they had discussed their writing. Lytton said hers was 'of the school of Proust'. An old friend, Gwen Raverat, had written from France to say that she would like to see Woolf when she visited London. Adding to Woolf's contentment was the fact that Dorothy Todd, the editor of British *Vogue*, wanted to commission four articles from her at £10 each. Her reputation in America also seemed to be growing, leading Woolf to wonder if this time next year she might be one of

10 Virginia Woolf with Lytton Strachey

those people 'who know everyone worth knowing'. Was that even possible for a woman? She remarked that an election was coming up, 'the usual yearly schoolboys wrangle' (an echo of Septimus Smith's bitter mockery of the War as 'that little shindy of schoolboys with gunpowder').

London

To read *Mrs Dalloway* is to create a mental map of London as we accompany its characters walking (or riding on a bus) through the city. The novel has attracted cartographers ever since Morris Beja first treated readers of the *Virginia Woolf Miscellany* to 'The London of Mrs. Dalloway' in 1977. Beja's hand-drawn map was accompanied by a legend identifying where specific events took place, from Clarissa crossing Victoria Street in the morning to

Peter arriving at her party later that day. Soon enough, amendments were proposed, beginning with the Rev. Prof. Hamish F. G. Swanston's suggestion that, based on the textual evidence as well as his observation of houses in Westminster that had survived Nazi bombing, the Dalloways must have lived at 11 Lord North Street.[6]

Since the advent of GIS (geographic information systems) technology, creating maps of *Mrs Dalloway* has become an obligatory assignment for students who are reading the novel in their high school or university courses. Such endeavours range from the comparatively straightforward tracing of routes,[7] to more ambitious efforts like the '*Mrs. Dalloway* Mapping Project', which includes on its website a series of interactive maps of London that enable readers to follow particular characters.[8] Sometimes, students have literally followed in the footsteps of Peter, Richard, Clarissa and Septimus and filmed themselves doing so, posting their videos to YouTube in fulfilment of their assignment.[9] Maps are a common feature of editions of the novel published in the past few decades. The design of the novel was, we know, crucial to Woolf. A significant aspect of that design is her location of the characters in specifically identified parts of the city that she knew so intimately, and—like Clarissa Dalloway—adored.

By the time she moved to Tavistock Square, where she and Leonard would live until 1939, Woolf had already embodied her own love of London in Clarissa Dalloway. The completed novel opens with a great ode to London as Clarissa walks to the flower shop from her home in Westminster, across Victoria Street into Belgravia, through St James's Park, on through Green Park to the Ritz Gate on Piccadilly Lane, bordering Mayfair. She lingers by the window of Hatchards bookshop before turning onto Bond Street where she goes to buy her flowers at Mulberry's. With very few inventions (the flower shop, Mulberry's, is one) Woolf's characters walk through a London that would have been immediately recognisable to contemporary readers who knew the city or lived there, and that remains generally familiar today. Londoners in 1925 might have understood the reference to 'the Indian and his cross' as the Readymoney Fountain on the Broad Walk in Regent's Park, but more recent readers have had to depend upon annotations made by painstaking editors if they wish to identify some of the more obscure descriptions.

Clarissa's route connects on Bond Street with that taken by Septimus and Rezia, who continue on to Regent's Park before their appointment at noon in Harley Street with Sir William Bradshaw. In the Park, their journey intersects with Peter Walsh's meandering walk after surprising Clarissa at her house in the morning. Hugh Whitbread, whom Clarissa had encountered 'coming along with his back against the Government Buildings', continues part of the way with Richard Dalloway after their lunch with Lady Bruton, until the exasperated Richard leaves him 'at the corner of Conduit Street' to return home to Clarissa. The landscape of the city—its buildings, its parks, its monuments, its visitors and vagrants, its shops, its streets—is much more than a background. *Mrs Dalloway* uses the cityscape as an element of identity.

For example, as Clarissa walks towards Bond Street she contemplates her own death: 'did it matter that she must inevitably cease completely; all this must go on without her; did she resent it; or did it not become consoling to believe that death ended absolutely? But that somehow in the streets of London, on the ebb and flow of things, she survived'. Later, Peter Walsh remembers being with Clarissa on the top deck of a bus: 'she felt herself everywhere; not "here, here, here"; and she tapped the back of the seat; but everywhere. She waved her hand, going up Shaftesbury Avenue. She was all that. So that to know her, or any one, one must seek out the people who completed them; even the places'.

It is, of course, impossible to 'seek out the people who completed' anyone. Or the places. When Woolf felt that Clarissa was too 'tinsely', she reassured herself by thinking of all the other characters she could bring to buttress her. These characters, sometimes glimpsed in a mere sentence or two, are brought into the narrative by virtue of sharing the space of the city. The main characters are often unaware of connections that only the reader (or narrator) can make. For example, while Rezia and Septimus are in Regent's Park, a little girl named Elise Mitchell dumps a handful of pebbles onto her nursemaid's knee then runs straight into Rezia and falls down, making Peter Walsh laugh. Rezia stands her up, Elise runs back to her caretaker, and Rezia observes Peter letting the girl play with his watch 'to comfort her'. As she observes this scene, Rezia, in deep distress at her husband's condition, asks why *she* should be 'exposed', 'tortured. Why?' Subtly, therefore, a connection is made between Septimus and Clarissa—beyond the reach of the characters' minds—through the interaction of Peter and Rezia with the same little girl, a fleeting moment in a public park in London.*

Woolf often gives a glimpse of the inner life of her bit-part players, and can also convey a kind of mini-biography within very few sentences. Nineteen-year-old Maisie Johnson, just arrived in London from Edinburgh to take up a position in her uncle's business, is so disturbed by the 'queer' couple of whom she asks directions to the Tube station that she regrets her decision to leave home: 'Horror! Horror! She wanted to cry'. Fifty years later, the narrator tells us—that is, in 1973—she will remember this moment. Maisie, in turn, is observed by old Carrie Dempster, who predicts, thinking of her own hard life, that the young woman will be shocked to discover how her expectations will be thwarted: 'Get married, she thought, and then you'll know'. Rezia has no awareness of the effect she and Septimus have had on Maisie, just as Maisie is oblivious to Carrie's appraisal, but these crossed paths in

---

* This point is made by Irena Ksiezopolski, 'Props and Personages: The Significance of Secondary Characters in *Mrs. Dalloway*'. *Virginia Woolf Miscellany* 66 (Fall/Winter 2004), 23–25.

Regent's Park on a Wednesday in June add their substance to the world being built up by the act of reading.

Such small, intimate moments in the novel exist within a larger view of the city, one whose history is announced in the monuments, statues, palaces and great thoroughfares observed by the characters. The aeroplane that unites the gaze of disparate citizens carries the reader away with it as it soars 'over Greenwich and all the masts; over the little island of grey churches, St. Paul's and the rest till, on either side of London, fields spread out and dark brown woods'. Identity in *Mrs Dalloway* is composed through relations not only to other people but also to objects. The mysterious motor car with its famous, but unknown, occupant leaves behind it 'a slight ripple which flowed through glove shops and hat shops' and briefly unites the shoppers on Bond Street before they resume their business. But its presence and the questions it evokes have changed something: 'Something so trifling in single instances that no mathematical instrument … could register the vibration'. It has roused emotions in people who do not know anything about each other, and yet share the memory of what Clarissa has thought of moments earlier as 'this late age of the world's experience'. In the shops 'strangers looked at each other and thought of the dead … For the surface agitation of the passing car as it sunk grazed something very profound'. Communal memory contributes to individual identity.

The strangers who silently acknowledge 'the dead' would in 1923 have been thinking not only of the losses of the First World War but also of the harrowing deaths brought about by the influenza pandemic of 1918–20. *Mrs Dalloway* is haunted by that pandemic, not least because Clarissa has clearly survived it, though with a weakened heart. The choric element of Woolf's novel is imbued with the spirit of Sophocles' great ode in *Antigone* that speaks of the many achievements of humankind but cautions that there is no refuge from death.[10] London, its streets thronged by ghosts, is itself a kind of memorial. Woolf brings her own feelings about the city into the heart of the novel. Once she saw an old woman begging on Kingsway, holding her dog in her arms as she sang: 'There was a recklessness about her; much in the spirit of London', Woolf wrote. 'Nowadays I'm often overcome by London; even think of the dead who have walked in the city'.[11] Peter, Septimus and Rezia pass by this same woman, a 'rusty pump' envisioned in the narrative as an eternal voice bubbling up into a song of love and death.*

After a temporary Cenotaph (from the Greek for 'empty tomb') attracted nearly a million visitors to Whitehall in 1919, a permanent memorial to the War dead was unveiled in November 1920 by King George V. People again queued for miles to lay their wreaths. Woolf recalled the scene as if it were something out of Dante: 'such a lurid scene, like one in Hell. A soundless street; no traffic; but people marching. Clear, cold, & windless. A bright light in the Strand; women crying Remember the Glorious Dead, & holding out chrysanthemums. Always the sound of feet on the pavement. ... A ghastly procession of people in their sleep'.[12] The boys who overtake Peter Walsh as they march to lay a wreath at the Cenotaph seem faintly ridiculous to him, though 'one had to respect it, he thought'. The choric narrative hovering around Peter's consciousness makes the more sinister observation that 'life, with its varieties, its irreticences, had been laid under a pavement of monuments and wreaths and drugged into a stiff yet staring corpse by discipline'.

As several critics have pointed out, nearly everyone in *Mrs Dalloway* is shopping or, at least, looking at things to buy. Clarissa dawdles on her way to order flowers. She resists the urge to

---

* J. Hillis Miller deduced that the old woman's song is Richard Strauss's 'Allerseelen' (All Souls' Day), which tells of the 'one day in the year' on which the 'bereaved lover can hope that the beloved will return from the grave'. Miller 190.

11 Unveiling of the Cenotaph, November 1920

buy a brooch for her daughter, Elizabeth, displayed in a jeweller's window 'to tempt Americans (but one must economise…)'. She lingers at Hatchards' window, pondering what she might buy for Evelyn Whitbread, who has come to London, she just learned, to see a doctor. In the bookshop window an edition of Shakespeare's *Cymbeline* lies open where Clarissa reads, 'Fear no more the heat o' the sun/Nor the furious winter's rages'. 'Fear no more' recurs to Clarissa throughout the day, forming one of the more overt links between her and Septimus, who also repeats those words in the last hour of his life. On Bond Street, Clarissa recalls her father who had bought his suits there 'for fifty years', her father whose carelessness cutting down a tree caused the death of her sister, Sylvia. Passing a glove shop prompts the memory of an uncle who 'used to say a lady is known by her shoes and her gloves', things for which her own daughter seems to care little, her daughter who is in thrall to the badly dressed Miss Kilman (with whom she will go to the Army & Navy Stores on a shopping expedition).

Window-shopping and buying commodities unite the main characters of the novel. On his way to Brook Street for lunch with Lady Bruton, Hugh Whitbread pauses on Oxford Street by a clock provided by Rigby and Lowndes, each letter of whose name stands for an hour of the day. Hugh reflects that in exchange for this service, one is expected to purchase the socks or shoes displayed in their window. After lunch with Lady Bruton, Richard reluctantly accompanies Hugh into a shop where Hugh has spied a necklace he considers buying for his wife. But Hugh's pompous indignation when the man from whom he usually buys jewellery is out sends Richard back into the streets on his own vague quest to buy 'something; a present for Clarissa'. His modest purchase, a 'vast bunch' of red and white roses, stands in for the words he cannot utter to his wife, 'to say he loved her; not in so many words'.

Septimus's Italian wife, Lucrezia, whom Woolf modelled on the ballerina Lydia Lopokova, had been excited to move to London because she had heard from an aunt who lived there 'how wonderful the shops were'. And although Septimus takes her to the usual tourist sights—the Tower, Parliament, the Victoria & Albert Museum—it is 'the shops—hat shops, dress shops, shops with leather bags in the window' that move Rezia. As speculation runs up and down Bond Street about who might be in the mysterious car, Rezia wonders if it is the Queen, 'the Queen going shopping'.

The map on which it is possible to plot accurately the movements of Septimus and Lucrezia, Clarissa, Hugh, Richard and Peter covers a small area of London bounded by Victoria Street in Westminster to the south, Regent's Park to the north and Peter's hotel in Bloomsbury to the east. Only Elizabeth Dalloway strikes out farther than any of the others when, having at last escaped

Miss Kilman's clutches, she hops onto a bus, a 'pirate',* with no particular destination in mind but escaping the boundaries of the neighbourhood that defines a young woman of her class. Elizabeth's journey up the Strand ends at Chancery Lane, the centre of the legal establishment. It is 'quite different here from Westminster', prompting Elizabeth to think that 'she would like to have a profession', as if her impetuous journey emblematises possibilities hitherto unconsidered.

As in cities everywhere, London's neighbourhoods are stratified by class and privilege. Had there been no War, Septimus might have measured success by obtaining a house at Purley, a suburb expanding in the 1920s. Sarah Bletchley, who murmurs '"Kreemo" ... like a sleepwalker' as she watches the skywriting aeroplane, is one of the 'mothers of Pimlico', an area to the south of Westminster inhabited at the time by the struggling middle class. Clarissa's Westminster, Lady Bruton's Mayfair, Bond Street and Harley Street all signify status and wealth. Both Clarissa and Peter approve of the London 'season'. Its events are marked for Clarissa by cricket at Lords, horse-racing at Ascot and polo at Hurlingham in Ranelagh Gardens. Woolf was thoroughly familiar with all of these: 'Today is Cup day at Ascot', she wrote in 1920, 'which I think marks the highest tide of the finest societies greatest season—all superlatives that mean little to me—save as I catch the hum of wheels in Piccadilly on a fine afternoon, & passing carriages look in & see powdered faces like jewels in glass cases'.[13] Peter Walsh, too, as he approaches Regent's Park, notes approvingly what he sees

---

* Eleanor McNees explains that in 1925 a 'pirate' would have been understood to be one of the many unlicensed buses that cruised the streets of London with no set routes, looking for passengers. Eleanor McNees, 'Public Transport in Woolf's City Novels: The London Omnibus'. In Elizabeth F. Evans and Sarah E. Cornish, eds. *Virginia Woolf and the City: Selected Papers from the Nineteenth Annual Conference on Virginia Woolf.* Clemson University Digital Press, 2010: 31–39, 34.

through open doorways: 'Admirable butlers, tawny chow dogs, halls laid in black and white lozenges with white blinds blowing. ... A splendid achievement in its own way, after all, London; the season; civilisation'.

Politics

It is Peter who names the years since the end of the War a very important period of change in England. Having just returned from India, he finds that people look different from how he remembers them. What can be written about in newspapers is different, too, and he notices that women now apply makeup in public. His recollection of young men and women 'carrying on quite openly ... just having a good time' on board the ship he took home might recall the scene in Eliot's *Waste Land*, in which the 'roving hands' of a 'young man carbuncular' meet no resistance from a bored typist. Woolf had set the type by hand, letter by letter, for Eliot's poem of postwar desolation when the Hogarth Press published it in 1923, while she was writing *Mrs Dalloway*.

Peter's observations about Richard Dalloway's 'public-spirited, British Empire, tariff-reform, governing-class spirit' are the most overt approaches to what is typically understood as 'politics' in this novel in which Woolf wanted to 'criticise the social system'. A period of wide political change followed the War as the British empire declined in power, independence movements in Ireland and India increasingly made their presence felt and the Labour Party gained influence. The 'moment of leisure' that Richard envisages when he will take the time to write a history of Lady Bruton's family was, as contemporary readers of *Mrs Dalloway* would certainly have understood, about to arrive. The first Labour prime minister, Ramsay MacDonald, was elected in January 1924, six months after the novel takes place. That government was short-lived, but British politics was fundamentally changed thereafter.

The narrowest understanding of politics is represented by Richard's being a Conservative Member of Parliament at whose wife's party the prime minister will be a guest. In June 1923, Stanley Baldwin had only been in the position for a month when he arrives at the Dalloways' house (he is not named, adding to the impression of his insignificance):

> One couldn't laugh at him. He looked so ordinary. You might have stood him behind a counter and bought biscuits—poor chap, all rigged up in gold lace. And to be fair, as he went his rounds, first with Clarissa then with Richard escorting him, he did it very well. He tried to look somebody. It was amusing to watch.

The mocking tone of the narrative is contrasted by the behaviour of Clarissa's guests, who 'felt to the marrow of their bones, this majesty passing; this symbol of what they all stood for, English society'. The eminent people of Clarissa's milieu are little different from the 'ordinary people' in Bond Street earlier that day who had been transfixed by the thought that they 'might now, for the first and last time, be within speaking distance of the majesty of England'. Peter Walsh derides the 'snobbery of the English' when he observes the reaction to this pathetic prime minister.*

The political power satirised in *Mrs Dalloway* can allow no room for empathy. In 'Mrs Dalloway in Bond Street', Clarissa at least makes a vague gesture towards understanding that 'things'— the life she enjoys—are able to go on because thousands of young men have been killed. In the novel, Richard thinks of the 'thousands of poor chaps' who were 'shovelled together, already half-forgotten'. This amnesia is emphasised by one of those minor figures who appear so fleetingly, Mr Bowley (on Bond Street

---

* An article about the 2023 Conservative party conference quoted Woolf's description of Clarissa's prime minister to illustrate what a 'piteous figure' Rishi Sunak presented, an example of the novel's continuing resonance. Will Lloyd, 'Fools, Frauds, and Firebrands'. *New Statesman* 6 October 2023.

looking up at the aeroplane in the morning, and as a guest at Clarissa's party that evening): 'orphans, widows, the War', he thinks; 'tut tut'.

Such attitudes would have been anathema to Woolf and her Bloomsbury Group friends. Septimus enlists 'to save an England which consisted almost entirely of Shakespeare's plays and Miss Isabel Pole in a green dress walking in a square'. Clive Bell spent much of the War arguing against military conscription and seeking to improve conditions for conscientious objectors (such as himself, Duncan Grant, and Lytton Strachey). But Septimus was 'one of the first to volunteer', not a conscript. He 'won crosses' for bravery and went 'through the whole show'. We might think of him as one of the young men imagined by Philip Larkin in 'MCMXIV', queuing up outside a recruiting office in August 1914, 'Grinning as if it were all/An August Bank Holiday lark': 'Never such innocence again'.

As *Mrs Dalloway* begins, Clarissa shakes off reminders of the War's costs and losses: 'but it was over; thank Heaven—over. It was June. The King and Queen were at the Palace'. The novel as a whole examines memory and forgetting on this lovely day in June. Clarissa's story is shadowed—haunted—by that of Septimus, a reminder of things most wish to turn away from except via the officially sanctioned modes of two-minute silences or memorials appealing to those abstractions pilloried by Clive Bell. Woolf's close friend John Maynard Keynes left the postwar treaty negotiations in Paris in disgust, returning from Versailles to Vanessa Bell's home, Charleston, to write *The Economic Consequences of the Peace* in 1919. The warning he sounded in that famous book's introduction reverberates in *Mrs Dalloway*:

> In England the outward aspect of life does not yet teach us to feel or realize in the least that an age is over. We are busy picking up the threads of our life where we dropped them, with this difference only, that many of us seem a good deal richer than we were before.

This was how it seemed in England, and perhaps in the United States, but, Keynes continued,

> In continental Europe the earth heaves and no one is but aware of the rumblings. There it is not just a matter of extravagance or "labor troubles"; but of life and death, of starvation and existence, and of the fearful convulsions of a dying civilization.[14]

Woolf's awareness of political and economic issues was astute and well-informed. She had done extensive research during the War to assist Leonard in writing the book he published in 1920, *Empire and Commerce in Africa*. Leonard, who in 1924 became Secretary to the Labour Party's Advisory Committee on Colonial Questions, made the case there and in subsequent books that economics drove imperialism in Africa and India. Virginia Woolf's family itself had deep roots in India, where her mother was born. Her paternal grandfather was Permanent Under-Secretary for the Colonies, and an uncle had codified British law for India. Peter Walsh, who would have been in India at the time of the notorious Amritsar massacre in 1919, intends to ask Richard at the party what the 'conservative duffers' are 'doing in India'. In June 1923, Gandhi was in prison, charged with sedition. Lady Bruton's exclamation, 'Ah, the news from India!' at the end of the lunch to which she invites Richard and Hugh, indicates the fact that the newspapers at the time would have been full of reports about the turbulent situation.

Millicent Bruton, who 'had the thought of Empire always at hand', invites the men to assist in her scheme to encourage the emigration to Canada of well-bred English youth. As David Bradshaw has shown, such a plan was being promulgated in 1923 in the columns of *The Times*, another example of how topical *Mrs Dalloway* was when it was published.[15] The eugenicist concern with 'superfluous youth' finds its most chilling expression in Sir William Bradshaw's disdainful attitude to Septimus Warren Smith:

Sir William had a friend in Surrey where they taught, what Sir William frankly admitted was a difficult art—a sense of proportion. There were, moreover, family affection; honour; courage; and a brilliant career. All of these had in Sir William a resolute champion. If they failed him, he had to support him police and the good of society, which, he remarked very quietly, would take care, down in Surrey, that these unsocial impulses, bred more than anything by the lack of good blood, were held in control. And then stole out from her hiding-place and mounted her throne that Goddess whose lust is to override opposition, to stamp indelibly in the sanctuaries of others the image of herself. Naked, defenceless, the exhausted, the friendless received the impress of Sir William's will. He swooped; he devoured. He shut people up.

That Bradshaw would 'penalise despair' shows the 'social system ... at work, at its most intense'. The lack of empathy, the will to dominate, is manifest throughout *Mrs Dalloway* in a variety of forms. At her party, Clarissa senses with a shudder that Bradshaw is capable of 'forcing your soul', reviving her earlier premonition 'that something awful was about to happen'.

Nothing awful happens to Clarissa, though, at least not on this day. She would appear to be one of the targets of Woolf's criticism of the social system, cosseted and protected by it as she is. Such criticism can at times operate quite subtly. Richard returns from Lady Bruton's lunch with his bunch of roses and settles his wife down for her afternoon rest before he goes back to work. Where is he going, Clarissa asks? '"Armenians," he said; or perhaps it was "Albanians"'. He leaves; Clarissa lies back: 'no, she could feel nothing for the Albanians, or was it the Armenians? but she loved her roses (didn't that help the Armenians?)'. Trudi Tate has deduced that Richard must, therefore, be sitting on the government committee that was negotiating the Treaty of Lausanne. This 'final act of betrayal' of the Armenians, whose genocide by the Ottoman Turks during the First World War had been widely reported, was signed on 24 July 1923.[16]

Woolf's depiction of Clarissa's ignorance would seem to clinch the case against her as a 'perfect hostess' who has no understanding of how the world actually works, and whose apparent beneficence to her servants is superficial at best. In Mayfair, at Lady Bruton's house, the illusion is sustained that tables for luncheon lay themselves, that the food and the wine are not paid for but just appear. Clarissa might have a better idea of what is involved in giving a party, but it is the chorus, the narrative voice, not Clarissa, that whips away the cloak of invisibility that hides all labour when we are afforded a glimpse of the Dalloways' kitchen at the height of the party:

> Did it matter, did it matter in the least, one Prime Minister more or less? It made no difference at this hour of the night to Mrs. Walker among the plates, saucepans, cullenders, frying-pans, chicken in aspic, ice-cream freezers, pared crusts of bread, lemons, soup tureens, and pudding basins which, however hard they washed up in the scullery seemed to be all on top of her, on the kitchen table, on chairs, while the fire blared and roared, the electric lights glared, and still supper had to be laid. All she felt was, one Prime Minister more or less made not a scrap of difference to Mrs. Walker.

It would be understandable to agree with Doris Kilman that Clarissa 'came from the most worthless of all classes—the rich with a smattering of culture'. In awkward silence on the landing, Kilman rails against Clarissa in her mind: 'Fool! Simpleton! You who have known neither sorrow nor pleasure; who have trifled your life away!' But so easy an answer to the question of how we are supposed to judge Clarissa would belie the complexity of Woolf's novel and the strange, almost mystical, alliance between her and Septimus.

On Bond Street in the morning, Clarissa thinks of how her daughter cares nothing for clothes, cares only about her dog, and cares for Miss Kilman, 'who had been badly treated of course'. Various models have been identified for Miss Kilman, such as Louise Matthaei, who worked as Leonard's assistant on the *International Review* after losing her job at Newnham College, Cambridge during the War owing to her German origins. Described by Woolf as a 'lanky gawky unattractive woman, about 35, with a complexion that blotches red & shiny suddenly',[17] Matthaei is an obvious source for Kilman. Similar models for various characters abound in Woolf's diary and letters—a Stephen cousin who opens and closes a large knife during a visit; Walter Lamb 'full of palace gossip', just like Hugh Whitbread—but Woolf is a magpie, taking elements from anywhere that serves her purpose. Clarissa acknowledges Kilman's tireless self-sacrifice on behalf of Russians and Austrians, both in dire economic circumstances in the 1920s, but thinks to herself that the green mackintosh Kilman wears in all weathers is 'positive torture'. Throughout *Mrs Dalloway*, if we read attentively, the question of where we are supposed to position ourselves morally recurs, and the narrative gives us little to no help, insisting that we take responsibility for our own judgements.

One thing in particular that bothers Clarissa about her daughter's mentor is her religious belief. Kilman has channelled into religious devotion her rage against a world that has treated her so badly, but she cannot entirely disguise from Clarissa how she feels. Looking at Clarissa with 'steady and sinister serenity', the force of Kilman's resentment shocks her. But Kilman's supposition that Clarissa has never known loss has to be weighed against what we know of Clarissa's inner life, as well as the fact that she grieves for her dead sister. When Kilman and Elizabeth leave for the Army & Navy Stores, Clarissa reflects that love and religion are 'the cruelest things in the world' because they seek so often to impress their will on another, to possess and convert. 'Had she ever tried to convert anyone herself?' Love and religion destroy 'the privacy of the soul', she thinks, foreshadowing the obscure 'evil' she senses in Bradshaw's 'forcing your soul' when she learns of Septimus's death. The 'spirit of religion' with 'her eyes bandaged shut and her lips gaping wide' was abroad in the crowd on Bond Street that morning, and Clarissa opposes to its dogmas her 'atheist's religion of doing good for the sake of goodness'.

Woolf evokes sympathy for Kilman, as well as condemnation. On Victoria Street, Kilman tries to curb her feelings. She is self-conscious ('do her hair as she might, her forehead remained like an egg, bald, white') and sure she will never find a mate, putting her in the company of many women of the time when the balance of the sexes had been destroyed by the War. She shares Woolf's anxiety about clothes never suiting her ('how I hate Bond Street & spending money on clothes'[18]), as well as her antipathy to shopping. There is an element of this in Clarissa's moment of self-consciousness about her hat that morning when she runs into Hugh, although Sir John Buckhurst a little later on appreciates her as 'a well-dressed woman'.

Try as she might to mortify her fleshly desires, Kilman appals Elizabeth by greedily eating cakes whilst enviously eyeing more on another table in the tea rooms at the Army & Navy Stores. Elizabeth 'had never thought about the poor', but her youthful potential to fulfil the professional ambitions thwarted for Kilman allows her to evade the ire Kilman directs at her mother. Just as Kilman's unspoken judgement irritates Clarissa by diminishing the pleasure she has taken in her fine home since recovering from her illness, so Elizabeth feels 'so small' in her presence. Elizabeth's beauty and 'well cut clothes' are sharply contrasted with the sweaty, unkempt Kilman, but if our sympathies are leaning towards her, they are tempered, perhaps, by Kilman's desire to 'grasp' and 'clasp' Elizabeth, to 'make her hers absolutely and forever'. In a novel in which the imposition of one's will upon another is associated with characters to whom a clearly negative attitude is indicated, such as Holmes and Bradshaw, Clarissa's refusal to say of anyone that 'they were this or were that' sends our feelings in another direction. In a kinder moment, too, Clarissa thinks that her daughter's 'odd friendship' with Miss Kilman at least 'proves she has a heart'.

At a loss for words under the pressure of Kilman's self-pity, Elizabeth escapes and boards her 'pirate'. Distraught, Kilman lurches 'through all the commodities of the world' in the Stores, out into the street and finds her way to Westminster Abbey where people shuffle past the Tomb of the Unknown Warrior. The reader's image of Kilman's presence is augmented by a momentary view of her afforded by a Mr Fletcher, who is impressed by 'her largeness, robustness, and power' as Clarissa and Elizabeth had been. We should not forget that to impress means not only to evoke admiration but also to mark, to leave an impression on softer material. Neither Clarissa nor Kilman is a 'type': Woolf argued that character was the heart of fiction, and that character was endlessly complicated. She would not say of anyone that they were this or were that, for that would be to impose her own view on the reader, to whom she gave the materials with which to make up their own minds. At the party, suddenly reminded of her encounter that afternoon with Elizabeth's tutor, Clarissa thinks 'Kilman her enemy': 'She hated her; she loved her'. *Odi et amo.*

Clothes

In November 1924, a month into revising her completed draft of *Mrs Dalloway*, Woolf was distracted from her task by high society. She had been to a party given by Mary and St John Hutchinson to say goodbye to their house overlooking the Thames at Hammersmith because they were moving to one in Regent's Park. As with Katherine Mansfield, Virginia's relations with Mary, Clive Bell's lover, were complicated. When she had once told Leonard that Mary was one of the few people she disliked, he had corrected her: 'No ... one of the many you dislike & like alternately'.[19] Having tea with Mary at River House a couple of weeks before the party had led Woolf to think once again about the nature of friendship between women. When Clarissa Dalloway puts away her coat upon returning from her morning errand, she considers 'this question of love ... this falling in love with women.

Take Sally Seton; her relation in the old days with Sally Seton. Had not that, after all, been love?' Woolf believed the 'relationship so secret & private'[20] between women to be very different to that between women and men.

Elegant, fashionable, photographed for *Vogue*, confidante of T. S. Eliot and longtime paramour of her brother-in-law Clive, Mary fascinated and irritated Woolf by turns. They flirted, quarrelled and gossiped about one another. Woolf lied to her about the party, saying she had enjoyed it but writing in her diary that it was impossible to get to know other people when 'poised on the edge of a chair ... trying to laugh'.[21] 'Party consciousness ... frock consciousness'[22] was a seam in the novel she was revising, but she was not done with the topic, continuing to explore it in a number of short stories even after *Mrs Dalloway* was published. She noted that Clive Bell easily transformed himself on social occasions 'into an upper class man very loud familiar, & dashing all at once'.[23] He and Vita Sackville-West once ganged up on Woolf at a party to tease her about her hat (chosen for her by Dorothy Todd): 'they pulled me down between them, like a hare; I never felt more humiliated'.[24]

Choosing what to wear was nearly always painful for Woolf: 'going into rooms properly dressed is alarming', she wrote when at an early stage in the composition of *Mrs Dalloway*.[25] The feeling surfaces in the mind of Ellie Henderson, a guest whom Clarissa had not wished to invite. The invitation makes Ellie feel 'timid, and more and more disqualified year by year to meet well-dressed people who did this sort of thing every night of the season, merely telling their maids "I'll wear so and so," whereas Ellie Henderson ran out nervously and bought cheap pink flowers, half a dozen, and then threw a shawl over her old black dress'. Anxiety about clothes had deep roots for Woolf, who recalled in her memoir 'A Sketch of the Past' how when she was eighteen she had bought furniture fabric to make herself a dress:

> Down I came one winter's evening about 1900 in my green dress; apprehensive, yet, for a new dress excites even the unskilled, elated. All the lights were turned up in the drawing room; and by the blazing fire George [Duckworth] sat ... As I stood there I was conscious of fear; of shame; of something like anguish—a feeling, like so many, out of all proportion to its surface cause. He said at last: 'Go and tear it up.' ... the voice of the enraged male ...

Clarissa is certainly one of those women who merely tell their maids what they will wear, knowing how to present themselves. Elizabeth, who cares nothing for shoes or gloves, nevertheless goes out with Kilman in 'well cut' clothes, and 'looks lovely' at the party.

Despite her anxiety about clothes, Woolf always took note of them, understanding how they communicated. It was, too, a topic deeply entwined with her thinking about relationships between women. She was ambivalent about fashion, profoundly interested by her 'love of clothes ... only it is not love; & what it is I must discover'.[26] She embodies this love in Septimus's wife, Rezia: 'Every hat that passed, she would examine; and the cloak and the dress and the way the woman held herself'. Rezia's aesthetic sensibility is offended by 'Ill-dressing, over-dressing' just as it is delighted by the 'shopgirl who had turned out her little bit of stuff gallantly' or a 'French lady descending from her carriage, in chinchilla, robes, pearls'.

Apart from a passing doubt about her hat when face to face with pompous Hugh Whitbread, Clarissa Dalloway is generally confident about her clothing, relying on a favourite dressmaker who 'thought of little out-of-the-way things; yet her dresses were never queer. You could wear them at Hatfield; at Buckingham Palace. She had worn them at Hatfield; at Buckingham Palace'. Woolf, on the other hand, would never achieve the unselfconsciousness of her sister. Vanessa had come to Mary Hutchinson's party 'in her old red brown dress which I think she made herself'.[27] Clive Bell, Woolf told Jacques Raverat, had said to her that, 'just because Mary dresses well, and you and Nessa badly, you think her dull'.[28]

Woolf admired Ottoline Morrell's 'sealing wax green' dress at an evening party in 1920, noticing how she 'did control the room on account of it'.[29] Women like Ottoline wore their hats with confidence. At the premiere of Edith Sitwell's *Façade*, 'the London season of course in full swing', Woolf spied another society hostess, 'Lady Colefax in her hat with the green ribbons'.[30] Women in *Mrs Dalloway* seem to wear only green: Elizabeth is 'sheathed in glossy green'; Miss Isabel Pole wears a green dress in Septimus's charged memory; Miss Kilman never relinquishes her green mackintosh; at the party, Nancy Blow seems to have spontaneously 'put forth ... a green frill'; and, of course, Clarissa is mending her 'silver-green mermaid's dress' when she is surprised by Peter Walsh. Elaine Showalter has speculated that this proliferation of green clothing reinforces a connection in the novel between female sexual and natural cycles, the green 'a kind of leafing or natural exfoliation of the female body'.[31]

Her old friendship with Violet Dickinson was also often on Woolf's mind as she wrote *Mrs Dalloway*. Violet had been a friend of Stella Duckworth's and became the first among several intense relationships Woolf had with older women. Before she had even conceived of *Mrs Dalloway*, Woolf had mused after a visit from Violet, 'is love the word for these strange deep ancient affections, which began in youth, & have got mixed up with so many important things'.[32] Violet was intimately mixed up with Woolf's memories of her brother Thoby because she had been with them on the fateful trip to Greece in 1906 where he contracted the typhoid that killed him. Telling Violet that she was copying out the last chapter of a novel she had just finished, Woolf asked what she thought her and Vanessa's lives might have been like had they 'taken our opportunity and gone to Devonshire House'. If the Stephen sisters had, like Clarissa and Sally Seton, danced the night away at

Devonshire House in their fashionable clothes, might they have 'married better' instead of 'sitting so shabby as we do, without a set of furs between us and the family jewels up the spout'.[33] Woolf was laughing as she wrote to Violet. By this time Devonshire House, past which Clarissa walks in June 1923, had been demolished to make way for an office building.

Woolf had intended from the very start that *Mrs Dalloway* would culminate in a party. It has been the focus of an enormous amount of commentary, bringing together as it does the entire cast of characters from Clarissa's past at Bourton whom she has been thinking about all day, as well as the menacing Dr Bradshaw, the pathetic prime minister, Lady Bruton and various other minor figures. The party is haunted, too, by Septimus's ghost (David Bradshaw suggests that the curtain blowing out three times at the party 'signals the arrival of Septimus's soul'[34]). A party offered the novelist's eye an opportunity, as Woolf explained in her diary after Mary's gathering. She liked the way that at a party 'individuals compose differently from what they do in private. One sees groups; gets wholes; general impressions: from the many things being combined. No doubt Proust could say what I mean'. But she could not read Proust while she was revising her own manuscript, 'so persuasive is he'.[35]

Proust

That 'great modern chronicler of party-going and party-giving', as Proust has been called,[36] accompanied Woolf throughout her writing of *Mrs Dalloway*. She had asked Roger Fry about him in 1919, and read him first in French and then in English when *Swann's Way*, C. K. Scott Moncrieff's translation of the first volume of *À la recherche du temps perdu*, came out in September 1922. Proust had an immediate and profound effect on Woolf, 'an astonishing vibration and saturation and intensification', she reported to Fry: 'theres something sexual in it—that I feel I *can* write like that, and seize my pen and then I *can't* write like that'.[37] A few days before she set down her plan for a book to be called 'At Home: or The Party', she wrote again to Fry: reading *Swann's Way* had her 'in a state of amazement; as if a miracle were being done before my eyes'.[38] In 'Modern Novels', as we saw, she had complained that the Edwardian novelists always seemed to miss 'the essential thing'; 'life escapes' from their novels. But Proust, she told Fry, had somehow 'solidified what has always escaped'. She knew that Proust might influence her own fiction, though she believed that his writing in French about French culture would protect her against that: 'yet his command of every resource is so extravagant that one can hardly fail to profit, & must not flinch, through cowardice'.[39] Her response to Joyce, whom she read around the same time, could hardly have been more different, but clearly it was not motivated by anything like jealousy.

Woolf could not have failed to notice the congruence between Proust's and her own ideas about subjectivity. An often-quoted passage early in *Swann's Way* even echoes what she had termed in 'Modern Novels' the 'transparent envelope' of consciousness, composed of an 'incessant shower of innumerable atoms'. Woolf would have read in Moncrieff's translation that 'none of us can be said to constitute a material whole, which is identical for everyone'. Proust's narrator continues that 'our social personality is created by the thoughts of other people', and that, in turn, we hold so many ideas about other people that their own features come to seem to us 'to be no more than a transparent envelope, so that each time we see the face or hear the voice it is our own ideas of him which we recognise and to which we listen'.[40] Any influence of Proust on *Mrs Dalloway*, however, is not to be found in such direct echoes, but rather in the texture of its poetic language.

Lytton Strachey's telling Woolf that she was of the school of Proust would have delighted her. In *A Room of One's Own* she described the French writer as 'wholly androgynous',[41] but it is in 'Phases of Fiction', a three-part essay of 1929, that Woolf is clearest about why he was so important to her. *Mrs Dalloway* is, among many other things, a meditation on the difficulty of knowing another person, something Peter Walsh remembers discussing with Clarissa—'not knowing people; not being known'. For Proust, Woolf wrote, 'relations are not only with another person but with the weather, food, clothes, smells, with art and religion and science and history and a thousand other influences'.[42] His mastery in rendering the complexity of emotions struck her as unmatched, and her description of how Proust offers no guidance to the reader on where to lay the emphasis on a scene aligns very closely with many readers' experience of reading Woolf's own work. The 'common stuff' of Proust's novel was made 'of this deep reservoir of perception', Woolf wrote in 'Phases of Fiction' in words that could just as well apply to *Mrs Dalloway*. 'It is from these depths that his characters rise, like waves forming, then break and sink again into the moving sea of thought and comment and analysis which gave them birth'.[43] We might hear in this an echo of Clarissa's feeling of being 'laid out like a mist between the people she knew best, who lifted her on their branches as she had seen the trees lift the mist, but it spread ever so far, her life, herself'. *Mrs Dalloway* is by far a more Proustian than Joycean novel.

Part III
Publishing *Mrs Dalloway*

When Woolf told Violet Dickinson she had 'finished' *Mrs Dalloway* she meant that she was about to embark on a furious task of revising the entire book. As 1924 drew to a close in a frenzy of social engagements and the rapid turnover of a number of assistants at the Hogarth Press, Woolf worked as quickly as she could to have a typescript of the novel ready for Leonard to take with him to read when they went to Monk's House for Christmas. Woolf discussed cover designs for *The Common Reader* with Vanessa, and decided she would dedicate that book to Lytton Strachey. She spent her afternoons in the Press offices, just behind her studio. Woolf found her work at the Press a relief after the pressure of a morning spent writing and revising. Getting ready to leave for the country, she looked back on what had been an eventful year, the first in her new home. A tree that she was used to seeing through the skylight of her basement writing room had just been cut down, but she reflected that changing houses had not really changed her: 'I am absorbed in "my writing"'.[1]

At Rodmell, where the River Ouse overflowed its banks and the roads flooded, preventing the Woolfs from visiting Charleston at New Year, Woolf continued to revise her typescript. When Leonard told her that *Mrs Dalloway* was her best book yet, she wondered if he felt obliged to say so.[2] On the other hand, relying on him as her first reader, as she always did, she knew that he would not dissemble to protect her feelings.[3] Back in London in January, as she waited for the proofs to come from the printer, Leonard agreed with her that connecting *Mrs Dalloway*'s twin narratives would be challenging for readers. Woolf intended to show 'the sane & the insane side by side' but she wanted those two views of the world to be more than simply adjacent. The risk of her 'queer' design was that readers would not be able to understand that these different strands were supposed to be woven together, culminating in the complex emotional reaction Clarissa has at her party to hearing about Septimus's suicide.

Mrs Dalloway was published by the Hogarth Press on 14 May 1925 in an edition of about two thousand copies; a second impression was printed that September. The book sold 2,236 copies in the first twelve months. The Harcourt Brace edition was published on the same day in New York, the first time a novel of Woolf's was published simultaneously in America and Britain. Sales were so brisk that Harcourt reprinted 1,500 more copies in May and August. Both editions had the cream dustjacket printed in yellow and black with Vanessa Bell's distinctive design, which has usually

12 A sketch by Vanessa Bell for the cover of *Mrs Dalloway*

been understood to show the arches of a bridge reflected in water, seen through a window framed by curtains. A bunch of flowers and a fan at the bottom of the cover can be seen more clearly in one of Vanessa's earlier sketches (which version also has lit candles framing the central image). Booksellers in Britain had 'almost universally condemned' Vanessa's simple cover image for *Jacob's Room*,[4] but Donald Brace hoped that Leonard was planning to employ Vanessa again. 'I feel that Mrs. Woolf is now at a point', he wrote to Leonard on 16 December 1924, 'where her work may go far beyond the rather small circle which has admired it here in the past'.[5] He noted with pleasure Clive Bell's long appraisal of Woolf in the December 1924 issue of *The Dial*. At the time, Brace had not even read *Mrs Dalloway*, the publisher's travelling sales staff fanning out across the country with only the title to sell. By April he was able to tell Woolf he thought her new novel was 'wonderful'. She dared to hope it might be a success.

Proofs

Gwen Raverat seemed 'very tragic' when she came to see Woolf in October 1924.[6] It had been eleven years since they had last met, although Gwen's husband, Jacques, had written to praise *Monday or Tuesday* when it came out in 1921, picking up a lapsed correspondence. Gwen met her old friend in the basement at 52 Tavistock Square where the Hogarth Press hummed along, producing *Mr Bennett and Mrs Brown*—number one in the new Hogarth Essays series. Jacques Raverat had been diagnosed with multiple sclerosis in 1914, but now was only months from death, Gwen told Woolf. She had brought with her Jacques's only copy of Paul Valéry's *Eupalinos, or the Architect*, a dialogue he wanted Woolf to read because it 'contains a good many of the things I believe on life & death & art & the body'.[7] After Gwen left England, summoned back early to Jacques's bedside when he took a turn for the worse, Woolf worried about entrusting his precious *Nouvelle Revue Française* to the postal service because it had lost her copy of a French tribute to Proust the year before. She had signed the 'Hommage d'un groupe d'écrivains anglais' upon Proust's death.

Gwen, a granddaughter of Charles Darwin, and Jacques had been part of a Cambridge circle dubbed the 'neo-pagans' by the Bloomsbury Group, at whose centre was the charismatic Rupert Brooke. In 1911, Woolf befriended Katherine (Ka) Cox, a Newnham graduate and member of Vanessa Bell's Friday Club, who confided in Woolf about her love affair with Brooke. Jacques was in love with Ka, but she rebuffed his marriage proposals, suggesting he turn his attention to her friend Gwen, a student at the Slade school of art. Gwen and Jacques married in 1911. Woolf had strong opinions at the time about these various amours, telling her sister, 'Obviously (in my view) J. is very much in love with K: and not much, if at all, with Gwen'.[8] Hermione Lee speculates that there may have been an 'eruption of irritation'[9] on Woolf's part, of which she reminded Gwen shortly after Jacques's death. Gwen was sure to remember 'all those years ago when you used to come to Fitzroy Square, I was so angry and you were so furious, and Jacques wrote me a sensible manly letter'.[10] She told Jacques that his engagement to Gwen had taken on a 'symbolical character' for her at the time.[11] The Raverats were to have a curious part to play in the biography of *Mrs Dalloway* because Woolf took the unprecedented step of sending a proof to them while she was correcting it.

Jacques had flowers delivered from Vence for Woolf's forty-third birthday in January 1925. When she wrote to thank him, Woolf offered to send him a proof of her new novel. She mentioned that she had seen Ka recently, describing her in a way that almost suggested that Jacques had had a lucky escape: 'She has no feeling whatever for the arts'.[12] Seeing Ka and receiving Jacques's flowers had set her thinking about their shared past, 'when I so much wanted you to admire me'.[13] Woolf's sending Jacques her proof is another instance of what makes *Mrs Dalloway* unique in her oeuvre; it is also the only novel of hers for which she wrote an introduction. Although she had shared the earliest drafts of her first novel with Clive Bell, Woolf had not since shown anyone but Leonard her manuscripts, and even then only when they were more or less finished. Perhaps it was simply that she was terribly moved by the Raverats' awful situation, his death only weeks away, or that something about the tangled emotions of 1911 made them particularly apt readers for a novel in which the main character has always wondered if she made the right choices in love. Whatever the reason, Woolf's sending her own copy of the proof to Jacques was highly unusual.

Woolf typically ordered multiple sets of proofs. She would send one to her American publisher, Harcourt Brace, and one was used for the Hogarth Press. But she would revise the English and American proofs differently, which means that nearly all of her novels exist in different versions in those two countries. The situation is often much more complicated than even this suggests, however, as is the case with *Mrs Dalloway*. She had told Jacques she would send him a proof (a third set she had ordered for herself) on the condition that he not bother to write to her about it, 'or even read it'; she added, '*don't mention* it to anyone'.[14] She would certainly have been surprised had Jacques *not* read it. In some ways he was an ideal reader, not only because they shared a friendship that had begun in an atmosphere of anguished young love similar to that recalled in the novel by Clarissa and Peter ('when it came to that scene in the little garden by the fountain, she had to break with him or they would have been destroyed') but also because Jacques would have been likely to understand well Woolf's efforts to represent the inner life of her characters. Replying in September 1924 to one of Woolf's letters, he had said: 'When you write a word like *Neo Paganism* for instance, it's as if you threw a pebble into a pond. There are splashes in the outer air in every direction, & under the surface waves that follow one another into dark & forgotten corners of my past. You are not only a writer, but a printer & you'll see how difficult it would be to represent this odd phenomenon'.[15] This was a significant insight, because Woolf did indeed usually bear in mind how a revision at the proof stage of a book might affect the layout of pages that had already been set.

Although Woolf had intended to send a copy of the proofs to Jacques at the end of January, a bout of influenza delayed her until February when she and Leonard went back to Monk's House. She sewed together the pages and made a cover for the proof, which she inscribed 'Jacques with love from Virginia'.[16] On thirty-one pages of the Raverat proof—which is now in the UCLA library archives—Woolf made more than fifty corrections. She also typed a revision of the scene in which Septimus commits suicide and glued it onto the proof pages. In the American proof (now at the Lilly Library of Indiana University) there is a carbon copy of yet another typed revision of the same scene. The English proof has not survived (nor has Woolf's final typescript of the novel), but it has been possible for various editors to infer from the Hogarth Press edition of *Mrs Dalloway* what changes Woolf made on it that differ from those on the other two.[17]

When she sent the proof off to Jacques in France, she asked him, not seriously, to 'do a little rewriting on my behalf'. He was too ill to hold a pen but on 9 February let Woolf know that he and Gwen had 'already read the first 40 pages of *Mrs Dalloway*'.[18] His dictated letter was enclosed with one from Gwen dated 8 March that let Woolf know Jacques had died the night before. It was left to his widow to tell Woolf what it had been like to read the novel to Jacques. From what Woolf wrote to Gwen on 11 March it seems likely that one letter from Jacques about *Mrs Dalloway* has not survived. Woolf had been 'on pins and needles' sending it to him and was now 'exquisitely relieved': 'these efforts of mine to communicate with people', she told Gwen, 'are partly childlessness, and the horror that sometimes overcomes me'.[19]

Later, Gwen told Woolf that some of the mad scenes in the novel had been so painful that she could not bring herself to read them to Jacques, skipping over them: 'I think it may have been that in our state of mind just then we couldn't stand any more horrors'.[20] Yet she admired Woolf's honesty about Septimus's mental anguish, understanding that it was linked to the writer's own. Most people, Gwen thought, could not really face pain, or even talk about it: 'That is to say most people have to pretend it isn't so—but people who've been through it don't & can't—(like you, who've been mad) only one has to be awfully careful about how one writes or talks about it'.[21] A month later Gwen read the proof again. The novel seemed to her 'like a ballet ... All the movements in different directions both in time and in space, going on at the same time'.[22] It was the same point Jacques had made about the difficulty of creating in words a form for such experiences. Woolf must have felt confirmed in her sense that Jacques and Gwen would understand what she had been trying to achieve with her design that was 'so queer & so masterful'.[23]

Near the end of 1924 Woolf had begun to retype the whole manuscript, a process she likened to going over a canvas with a wet brush so that 'parts separately composed & gone dry'[24] would be joined together. She had worried then that the 'mad parts' did not connect with the Clarissa parts, but this was more in anticipation of what reviewers would say than doubts of her own. 'What you say about Mrs Dalloway', she told Gwen two weeks before *Mrs Dalloway* was published, 'is exactly what I was after. I had a sort of terror that I had inflicted something on you, sending you that book at that moment. I will look at the scenes you mention. It was a subject that I have kept cooling in my mind until I felt I could touch it without bursting into flame all over. You can't think what a raging furnace it is still to me—madness and doctors and being forced'.[25] The parts that gave Woolf such concern were evidently very powerful for her first readers.

It is clear from the revisions Woolf inserted into both the American and Raverat proofs that the scene of Septimus's suicide had continued to dissatisfy her. She added in both proofs an account of the thoughts Septimus has as he considers what means his room presents for ending his life—his landlady's bread knife? ('mustn't spoil that'); the gas line to the fire? (but there is no time because Holmes is coming up the stairs); a razor? (but Rezia has already packed his shaving kit). This was a moment in the novel that Woolf had already revised several times, shortening at the proof stage what had been a longer passage in 'The Hours' notebook, and then expanding it again before publication.

Another significant change Woolf made in the proofs occurs near the end when Clarissa withdraws into a small room by herself after hearing the Bradshaws 'talk of death' at her party. Something about this young man's suicide affects her profoundly: 'He made her feel the beauty; the fun'. That was how the line appeared in the proofs, but on the American set Woolf revised it, in her characteristic purple ink, to read 'He made her feel the beauty; made her feel the fun'. She must have deleted the line on the English proof because it did not appear in the Hogarth Press edition. On the English set of proofs, she indicated that a space should be inserted after Clarissa 'came in from the little room'. Thus the crucial passage was published in two different versions:

<u>English</u>
She felt glad that he had done it; thrown it away **while they went on living**. The clock was striking. The leaden circles dissolved in the air. But she must go back. She must assemble. She must find Sally and Peter. And she came in from the little room.

<u>American</u>
She felt glad that he had done it; thrown it away. The clock was striking. The leaden circles dissolved in the air. **He made her feel the beauty; made her feel the fun.** But she must go back. She must assemble. She must find Sally and Peter. And she came in from the little room.

This change resulted in the English version of *Mrs Dalloway* having twelve sections. A book of hours, perhaps. *Mrs Dalloway* is a novel whose day is divided by clocks that shred and slice time; dominated by the 'leaden circles' boomed over London by Big Ben; whose characters experience the strange elongations or contractions of time effected by memory. It would seem almost unremarkable that it should be divided into twelve sections, and yet that 'neglected and deeply significant aspect of this modernist novel's form', as one of its most recent textual editors has explained,[26] existed for decades only in the first edition published by Woolf's own Hogarth Press in London.

Although the twelve sections of the English first edition do not correspond to the hours during which the novel's action takes place, the number inevitably summons the idea of the sun's passage through the sky. Sundials and water clocks dating from around 1500 BCE in Egypt were marked in twelve increments for the day, the origin of the division that has persisted ever since. The first six sections of *Mrs Dalloway* in the Hogarth Press first edition take place between 11 and 11:30 as several actions occur simultaneously: Clarissa on her way to Bond Street and back home; Peter walking to and from her house; Rezia in Regent's Park with Septimus. In the seventh section it is a quarter to twelve, and in section nine it is noon as Clarissa lays her green dress on the bed while Rezia and Septimus are walking along Harley Street to their appointment with Dr Bradshaw. In the same section, it is half-past one when Hugh and Richard are at lunch with Lady Bruton; then it is 'Three already!', then half-past three, and finally the clock is 'striking, four, five, six'. In the next section, the tenth, Peter thinks how Clarissa must have written the note saying it was 'heavenly' to see him as soon as he had left her to get it to his hotel 'by six o'clock'. In the penultimate section, the prime minister's presence makes no difference to Clarissa's cook 'at this hour of the night'. The last reference in the novel to a specific time is a clock 'striking the hour, one, two, three' as Clarissa notices the old lady across the street putting out her light. There is no reference to clock time in the twelfth section.

The proofs Woolf sent to Harcourt Brace in New York were marked differently by Woolf than those she subsequently sent back to her printer for the Hogarth Press edition. Owing to these differences, together with the American compositor failing to indicate where space breaks fell at the foot of a page, the Harcourt edition appeared with only eight sections. When a second English edition appeared as part of the 'Uniform Edition' of Woolf's works in 1929, a break was missed between sections seven and eight, resulting in a version with eleven sections. Various editors have made decisions over the ensuing years that have resulted in a kind of free-for-all, with some versions of *Mrs Dalloway* having ten, others eight, others eleven sections, and so on. One editor of a recent lavishly illustrated annotated edition of the novel even decided to create her own hybrid version, retaining 'He made her feel the beauty; made her feel the fun' from the American edition but also inserting the section break that exists only in the English edition.[27] Many readers probably will not notice these differences, unless they are studying the novel or are scholars devoted to such supposedly negligible matters. (Such differences are among the reasons I have about twenty editions of the novel on my shelves!) The fact remains that the experience of reading *Mrs Dalloway* is somewhat different depending on which edition one happens to have. The rhythm of Woolf's sentences, after all, can be changed by the variant position of a comma. And the question of why the suicide of a young man whom she had never met or even knows the name of should make Clarissa Dalloway feel the 'beauty' and 'fun' of life is one that only American readers might have considered for the first few decades of the novel's existence.

13 Author's stack of *Dalloway* editions

First readers

As Leonard Woolf explained in his autobiography many years later, Woolf's reputation grew very slowly. From 1919 to 1924 she earned £228 from her first three novels, an average of £38 per year that was augmented by her journalism. The publication of *Mrs Dalloway* marked the start of what Leonard described as an 'astronomical increase' in her earnings, but this was only relative to the previous years. Woolf's sales were eclipsed, for example, by those of Vita Sackville-West. Soon after they first met, in December 1922, Woolf asked Sackville-West if she would write a book for the Hogarth Press. 'Darling', Sackville-West wrote to her husband, Harold Nicolson, on 10 January 1923, 'I love Mrs. Woolf with a sick passion'.[28] Beginning with *Seducers in Ecuador* (1924), dedicated to Woolf, Sackville-West would prove to be a lucrative author. When she delivered the manuscript of *Seducers* in person to Monk's House, Woolf marvelled at her industry: 'for is she not mother, wife, great lady, hostess, as well as scribbling ... I must lack some central vigour'.[29] On *Dalloway*'s publication day, however, Woolf admitted to her diary that she was not looking forward to talking all summer about her latest novel: 'I'm now all on the strain with desire to stop journalism & get on to *To the Lighthouse*'.[30] Before she started her next novel she would write eight stories of people at Clarissa Dalloway's party, only one of which would be published in her lifetime.

Despite Woolf's wish to move on to another project, she was of course anxious to hear the opinion of her friends about *Mrs Dalloway*. She was relieved to hear from E. M. Forster that he admired it. Forster would put that admiration in print the following year, writing in *The New Criterion* about this 'exquisite and superbly constructed book'[31] in which Woolf had managed 'to convey the actual process of thinking'[32] in a way no other writer had. In the weeks after publication, Woolf collected various opinions from friends and acquaintances, telling Gerald Brenan that 'when all is quiet, I shall creep out of my hole, and piece them together'. Brenan disappointed her by saying Septimus had 'no function in the book', although, as she told him, Roger Fry had thought Septimus 'the most essential part'.[33] A much more welcome response came from Vita Sackville-West, who told Woolf she had read both the novel and *The Common Reader*. The novel's beauty for her lay 'in its brilliance chiefly; it bewilders, illuminates, and reveals'. That brilliance 'made it unnecessary ever to go to London again, for the whole of London in June *is* in your first score of pages'.[34] The next day Woolf wrote coyly, 'I thought you wouldn't like Mrs Dalloway'.[35] Sackville-West reminded her of this later that year when Woolf claimed, 'I write prose; you poetry'.[36] Nonsense, replied Vita: 'There is 100% more poetry in one page of Mrs. Dalloway (which you thought I didn't like) than in a whole section of my damned poem [*The Land*]'.[37]

Woolf responded politely to C. P. Sanger, one of the older generation of Cambridge men whom she had known since the earliest days of Bloomsbury, when he wrote to say he thought her creation of characters in *Mrs Dalloway* was 'too analytic and not sufficiently sympathetic'.[38] He advised her to try to be more like Chekhov in her next book. This was ironic given Woolf's use in 'Modern Fiction' of that very writer's story 'Gusev' as an illustration of the kind of literature that English novelists should be writing. Starting in 1917, Woolf had written several essays on Russian writers. In 'Modern Fiction', published in *The Common Reader* just a month before *Mrs Dalloway*, she stated that the 'most elementary remarks upon modern English fiction can hardly avoid some mention of the Russian influence, and if the Russians are mentioned one runs the risk of feeling that to write of any fiction save theirs is waste of time'.[39] Perhaps, she suggested to Sanger, it was 'the queerness of the method' in her novel that led him to miss the emotion in it.[40]

Woolf was clear about her aims in *Mrs Dalloway*, as well as in stating her views on how the form of the novel should change to capture the experience of modern life. Her old Greek tutor, Janet Case, irritated her by saying she admired the technique but not the content of *Mrs Dalloway*: 'I don't believe you can possibly separate expression from thought in an imaginative work', Woolf replied.[41] Case's remark continued to annoy her a year later: 'Odd how I'm haunted by that damned criticism of Janet Case's "it's all dressing ... technique"'.[42] The remark probably nagged at her because it was something Woolf had herself worried about while writing *Mrs Dalloway*, that readers would not understand her experiment. Indeed, a few minutes' perusal of comments about

14 Cover by Vanessa Bell for the Hogarth Press first edition of *Mrs Dalloway*

Mrs Dalloway on Goodreads.com today will show that readers in the 1920s, trained to expect plot and sequence, and guidance from a narrative voice, differed little from readers in the 2020s.

No writer can really control how readers react to their inventions, but Woolf was amazed to hear from Philip Morrell that he believed himself 'to be the sort of model of all the dullest characters—a kind of combination of Hugh Whitbread and Richard Dalloway'.[43] Woolf acknowledged (in her diary) sometimes drawing from life—she once accidentally called Keynes's wife, Lydia Lopokova, 'Rezia'—but looking to particular real-life models for help in interpreting characters is always risky. 'By the way', she wrote to Philip Morrell, 'I meant Richard Dalloway to be liked, Hugh Whitbread to be hated. You hate them both I gather'.[44] Clarissa's husband's faults are nothing in comparison to Peter Walsh's judgement that 'the rascals who get hanged for battering the brains of a girl out in a train do less harm on the whole than Hugh Whitbread'. As in the passage about Bradshaw's worship of Proportion and Conversion, there are places in *Mrs Dalloway* where Woolf's bitter criticism of the social system is hard to miss.

A conversation with Lytton Strachey returned Woolf to the doubts she had had about the character of Clarissa Dalloway.

Strachey thought she was 'disagreeable & limited, but that I alternately laugh at her, & cover her, very remarkably, with myself'.[45] There had been a time, Woolf recalled, that she almost abandoned the novel because she thought her main character was 'in some way tinselly', but she had compensated for this by inventing Clarissa's memories, giving her more substance. Woolf discerned that some of the distaste she had felt for Kitty Maxse and her superficial, high society world had inevitably coloured her creation of Clarissa, but 'one must dislike people in art without its mattering'. Strachey had pointed out what he experienced in reading the novel as 'a discordancy between the ornament (extremely beautiful) & what happens (rather ordinary—or unimportant)'.[46] Her old friend thus brought up what would be a common theme in reviews of the novel: on the one hand, beautiful writing; on the other, not much of any interest seemed to happen.

Several reviewers took Clarissa and Peter Walsh to be the principal characters, overlooking Septimus, perhaps in search of some version of a conventional heterosexual romance plot. It was common, too, for early reviewers to remark on the novel's taking place within a single day, although some noted the precedent set by *Ulysses*. The 'speed' of the narrative and its apparently unbroken stream of impressions unsettled readers who wanted a resting-place. As the reviewer for the *Western Mail* put it, 'we like to have places which we can dog-ear when we go to bed, with the certainty of restarting at the exact line'.[47] Cinematic techniques had already been identified as a feature of modernist fiction—flashbacks, for example—but for many reviewers these were unwelcome innovations. Certain words recur in the early reviews of *Mrs Dalloway*, sometimes with negative, sometimes with positive connotations: sensation, sensibility, sensitiveness, sentimentality and impression. Book reviews are inherently ephemeral, but they do provide a snapshot, albeit a blurred one, of a novel's initial reception.

An unusually perceptive review that Woolf probably did not see for some time appeared in the New York-based *Saturday Review of Literature*. Twenty-five-year-old Richard Hughes had not yet written the novel that would bring him fame in 1929, *A High Wind in Jamaica*, but his review of *Mrs Dalloway* was well attuned to the context in which Woolf had written it.* Hughes likened Woolf's experiment with the form of the novel to Cézanne's manipulations of form in painting. He understood that she was, like a philosopher, concerned with 'the problem of reality':

> In contrast to the solidity of the visible world there rises throughout the book in a delicate crescendo *fear*. The most notable feature of contemporary thought is the wide recognition by the human mind of its own limitation ... it cannot 'find out' anything about the universe because the terms of both question and answer are terms purely relative to itself ...[48]

Woolf's characters—Hughes singled out Clarissa, Peter and Septimus—'together are an illustration of that bottomlessness on which all spiritual values are based'. Woolf does not mention having seen Hughes's review, but if she did she might have heard the echo there of what she had written about the Russian novelists who had influenced her: 'if honestly examined life presents question after question which must be left to sound on and on after the story is over'.[49]

It was more common for reviewers to want answers, conclusions. Judgements of novels often seem to be largely a matter of taste, one reader loving what another disdains. In the *New Statesman*, P. C. Kennedy wrote that Woolf excelled in 'description of mood or sudden scene; but the mood might always be anybody's; anybody might occupy the scene ... She understands a mood; she analyses

---

* Some years earlier, the Woolfs had turned down a long short story by Hughes but invited him to dinner at Hogarth House. Woolf found him charming (*L2* 454, 2 January 1921 to Vanessa Bell).

it; she presents it; she catches its finer implications; but she never moves me with it, because she never makes me feel that the person credited with it is other than an object of the keenest and most skilful study'.[50] We are back at the difference of opinion between Woolf and Arnold Bennett over Conan Doyle's Watson. For an opposing view we can turn to a review of *Mrs Dalloway* by Edwin Muir. In *We Moderns* (1918), Muir had been among the earliest to use the term 'modernism' to characterise the ongoing revolution in arts and letters. His *First Poems* had been published by the Hogarth Press in April 1925. In an article on Woolf in the *Nation & Athenaeum* the following year, Muir commented on a passage he quoted from Peter and Clarissa's conversation: 'How much more exact that is than analysis could be! It is more exact, for the ebb and flow of the imagery, the rhythm of the sentences, follow the course of the emotion'. This was what Woolf had told Roger Fry was the heart of her experiments with the form of fiction: emotion put into the right relations. Muir seemed to have grasped what she was attempting: 'The mood that Mrs Woolf catches here is quite beyond the reach of the psychological, analytical method; yet how perfectly it is conveyed'.[51]

Perhaps the difference in early responses to the novel was generational. After all, Woolf had told Janet Case that everyone over forty preferred *The Common Reader*, 'everyone under 40 Mrs D'.[52] Arnold Bennett could not even finish *Mrs Dalloway*. Woolf had 'told us ten thousand things' about her protagonist, but he 'got from the novel no coherent picture' of her.[53] And yet, Woolf noted the day after publication, a young man from Earl's Court had written to tell her, 'This time you have done it—you have caught life & put it in a book'.[54] For some, Clarissa Dalloway was (and remains) a straw-filled dummy; for others, she was a complex and realistic woman about whom it was difficult to come to a conclusion.

A letter from a 'common reader' would often outweigh a hurtful review (such as that by J. F. Holms in the *Calendar of Modern Letters*, which dismissed the novel as 'aesthetically worthless'[55]).

One that Woolf saved arrived in 1932 from Bloomfield Hills in Michigan. Marion Elden Bemis had admired *Mrs Dalloway* so much that she used it as a way to evaluate potential friends:

> I loan it to an acquaintance, and in his comment, when he returns it, is drawn, usually, the chart of our future course. I know him then for a stranger or an intimate, and in the back fly leaf of my copy are written the names of ten people ... and only two of these caught you—your style that so perfectly—more than poetry—catches the rhythm, the ebb and flow, the thought that fringes every act, and the past that is always an overtone. It pleased me that my half-brother, at twenty, delighted in you; knowing you a little helped us to know each other better.[56]

As Woolf had written in 'Character in Fiction', the ability to judge character is an essential human skill.

A modern novel

It is likely that Woolf's readers in the American Midwest in the 1930s purchased the Modern Library edition of *Mrs Dalloway*. The aim of this series of reprints was to bring the 'World's Best Books' to a wider audience than could be reached by their original publishers. The Modern Library published both Woolf's novel and Joyce's *Portrait of the Artist as a Young Man* in 1928, two examples of contemporary fiction with a reputation for challenging the average reader's abilities. As the print culture scholar Lise Jaillant has explained, the Modern Library was part of a wave of similar inexpensive editions that brought modernist texts to new markets throughout the world. That Woolf agreed to write an introduction to *Mrs Dalloway* for the Modern Library might seem surprising, given her often-repeated stance that books should stand on their own, but, as Jaillant surmises, she probably saw the Modern Library edition as an opportunity to reach a large American readership.

From its modest beginnings on the dining table in Richmond in 1917, the Hogarth Press had grown steadily alongside Woolf's

15 The Modern Library edition of *Mrs Dalloway*, 1928

own reputation. The Press's final profit in 1927 was £64 2s 0d. In 1928 it jumped to £380 16s 0d.[57] A year later, Woolf could write with satisfaction that she was making enough by her writing to 'look say at blue lustre cups in a shop & decide, well, why not buy them?' Beyond the improvement in her personal circumstances, she also noted 'with pride that 7 people depend, largely, on my hand writing on a sheet of paper. That is of course a great solace & pride to me. Its not scribbling; its keeping 7 people fed & housed'.[58] *Mrs Dalloway* marked a new phase in Woolf's widening fame; that she chose to write an introduction to this novel alone of all her works is a curious aspect of its story.

Characteristically, Woolf used her introduction for the Modern Library edition of *Mrs Dalloway* to argue that introductions are of little use. Once a novel is published 'it ceases to be the property of the author' and belongs entirely to readers.[59] Even were a reader to know a lot about a writer's life, she continued, the question of 'what was relevant and what not' to a particular work would still need to be decided. She casually throws out a scrap of possibly interesting information: that 'in the first version Septimus, who later is intended to be her double, had no existence; and that Mrs. Dalloway was originally to kill herself, or perhaps merely to die at the end of the party'.[60] Maybe by 'first version' Woolf had in mind the short story 'Mrs Dalloway in Bond Street'; there is not really any discrete version of the novel she might have been referring to here, but in any case nothing in any of the drafts or in her notebooks (or anywhere else!) ever suggested that Clarissa was to commit suicide. Septimus, too, occurred early in her process (on 14 October 1922 in her diary: 'Septimus Smith?—is that a good name?'). Her description of him as Clarissa's 'double', however, set off an exploration of what this might mean that continues to this day. The two characters were, indeed, always linked in their creator's mind; despite anything Woolf might say about the preeminence of the reader over the author, when it came to deciding what the novel is 'about' her comments had a weight she could not relinquish.

In 'How Should One Read a Book?', the talk that she gave to a London girls' school in 1926 and later revised for her second *Common Reader*, Woolf, in typical paradoxical manner, told the pupils that the best advice she had to offer was 'to take no advice, to follow your own instincts, to use your own reason, to come to your own conclusions'.[61] Always suspicious, usually derogatory, about professors—'heavily furred and gowned authorities' who 'tell us how to read, what to read, what value to place upon what we read'—Woolf championed the freedom of readers to choose their way through books without anyone looking over their shoulder. She echoed this in the Modern Library introduction, but also returned there to what she had described in her talk to the girls at Hayes Court school as the necessary second half of the process of reading. If the first half was receiving myriad impressions, building up an image of the book as a whole as one reads, the second was to make some judgement about books. In other words, mature readers should also become critics. They thus provide an important service to writers: 'The standards we raise and the judgments we pass steal into the air and become part of the atmosphere which writers breathe as they work'.[62]

It is telling that Woolf does not mean by 'critic' people who publish their views in any formal manner; rather she has in mind 'common readers', people who read and talk about books in no professional capacity. The atmosphere she had breathed since *Mrs Dalloway* was published was formed by readers such as Janet Case, who tried to separate her form from her content; or C. P. Sanger who, Woolf told Gerald Brenan, lamented 'the fact that I "contemplate the lives of the idle rich"'.[63] Woolf informed her Modern Library readers that she had heard her novel described as 'the deliberate offspring of a method', an idea she would like to rebut: 'The little note book in which an attempt was made to forecast a plan was soon abandoned'. In this manner she used the 1928 introduction to 'speak more explicitly to the reader who has put off his innocence and become a critic'. But, as she knew—as she stated—books belong to their readers no matter what their authors might intend.

Sixty-one thousand copies of the Modern Library edition of *Mrs Dalloway* were sold in the twenty years it remained in print. Between May 1942 and October 1943 *Mrs Dalloway* sold 4,271 copies;[64] by contrast, the Hogarth Press had sold only about three thousand copies of its own edition by the time it went out of print in 1929. (Even so, Woolf reported to Vita Sackville-West 'we are having two water-closets made, one paid for by Mrs. Dalloway the other by the Common Reader: both dedicated to you'.[65]) In 1929, Leonard decided to publish a 'Uniform Edition' of Woolf's works, beginning with *Jacob's Room*, *The Common Reader* and *Mrs Dalloway*. Priced lower than the 1925 edition, by 1933 the Uniform

Edition of *Mrs Dalloway* had sold twice as many copies as the first.[66] Historians of print culture have pointed out that the publication of a Uniform Edition positioned Virginia Woolf 'as a canonical author whose work deserved to be collected and preserved',[67] as well as enabling readers who first discovered her through *To the Lighthouse* or the very popular *Orlando* to 'easily and inexpensively begin retracing their steps through her career'.[68]

Before the Second World War, translations of *Mrs Dalloway* appeared in German (1928), French (1929), Catalan (1930) and Spanish (1939). Foreign editions in English also were published in the Tauchnitz Collection of British and American Authors and the Albatross Modern Continental Library, increasing the circulation of the novel throughout Europe. By the 1930s, *Mrs Dalloway* was frequently adduced as an exhibit for or against the reputation of

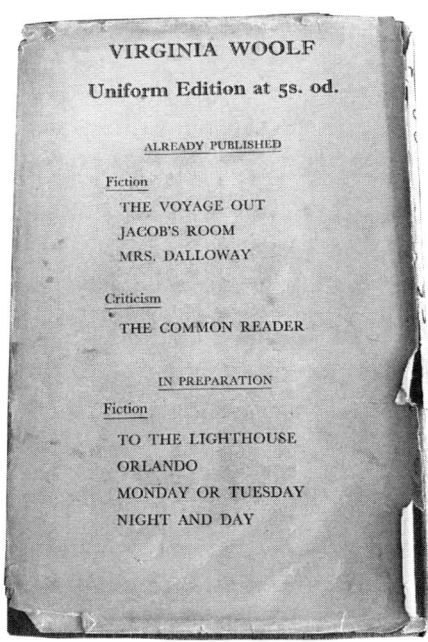

16   Advertisement for the Uniform Edition of Woolf's works, on back cover of first edition of *A Room of One's Own* (1929)

Virginia Woolf in the courts of public opinion or in scholarly wrangles over the place of modernist literature in the broader cultural scene. The reception of the English and American versions of the novel—and, indeed, of Woolf herself—diverged almost as soon as they were published, each absorbed into a quite different environment of readers and critics. And as Woolf continued to publish new works, *Mrs Dalloway* took its place among them. Readers of the novel in 1930 might think of it in relation to *To the Lighthouse* (1927), *Orlando* (1928) or *A Room of One's Own* (1929), each or all of these creating new contexts within which to read *Mrs Dalloway*.

For the writer of a brief review in *The New Yorker*, *Mrs Dalloway* was 'not a hammock novel'. One might need to 'attend a school of some sort established to educate readers for the works of this

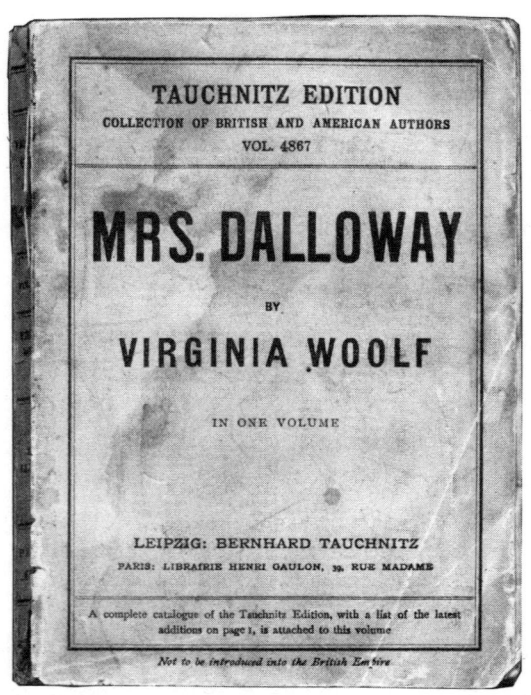

17 Tauchnitz edition of *Mrs Dalloway*, 1929

astonishingly clever writer', but it was 'worth any effort' a reader might feel necessary to reap the rewards of Woolf's fiction. The same reviewer noted that *The Dial* magazine deserved credit for the work it had done in America on Woolf's behalf. When 'Mrs Dalloway in Bond Street' was published in *The Dial* in July 1923 it had a circulation of about 18,000. The same issue included a positive review of *Jacob's Room* by David Garnett. The magazine's tagline was 'A Gift of Distinction for People of Discrimination', signalling to its readers that appreciation of writers such as Virginia Woolf identified them with a certain kind of cultural sophistication.[69] The ground was further prepared for *Mrs Dalloway* in America by a long article surveying Woolf's writing to date by her brother-in-law, the art critic Clive Bell, which appeared in the December 1924 *Dial*.

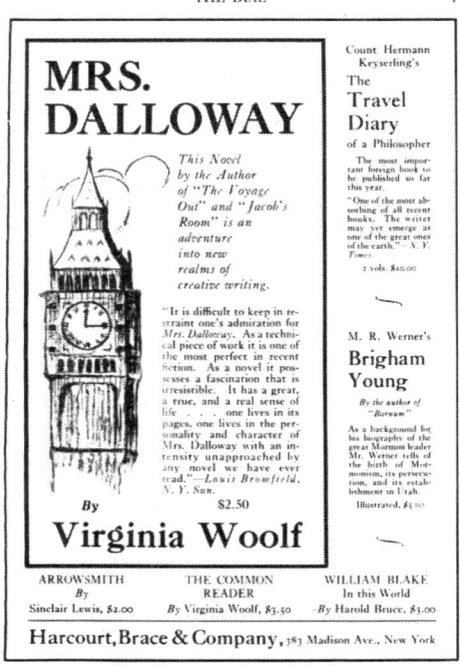

18 Advertisement by Harcourt Brace in *The Dial* magazine

Woolf was associated not only with 'stream-of-consciousness' writers (most often Joyce, Proust and Dorothy Richardson); glossy magazines such as *Vanity Fair* and *Vogue* also identified her as a member of the Bloomsbury Group. These identities evoked different responses on either side of the Atlantic, reflecting not only different understandings of social class (that would sometimes manifest themselves in critical discussions of Clarissa Dalloway or Doris Kilman) but also the ways in which modernist literature was deployed in debates about education, culture and reading in Britain and in the USA.

Across the United States, Woolf's novels were included in library discussion groups, as well as in book study groups that met in private homes. In Chicago, Florence Warren Seymour and her husband founded the Order of Bookfellows, for which she edited its monthly magazine, *The Step-Ladder*. The January 1926 issue included a 'Study Outline for *Mrs Dalloway* and *The Common Reader*', recommending that both be discussed 'as one throws much light on the other'. A programme for women's clubs organised by the Bureau for Public Discussion employed a lecturer from the University of Carolina's Extension division to give a series of presentations titled 'Adventures in Reading Current Books 1926–1927'. Professor Russell Porter included *Mrs Dalloway* as 'an example of stream-of-consciousness technique undiluted'. And at the first joint meeting of the California and Pacific Northwest Library Associations in June 1927, 'Modern Tendencies in Fiction' were outlined by Mrs Virginia Cleaver Bacon, the adviser in Adult Education for the Library Association of Portland, Oregon. On 12 January 1930, Elizabeth Cox Wright, a lecturer at Swarthmore College, wrote to Woolf from Moylan, PA:

> I am a little daft about London, and being an American, probably rather sentimental about it: *Mrs. Dalloway*, ever since I first read it, has been a great help when the nostalgia becomes too painful. The beauty and

penetration of the theme always strikes me with fresh admiration. It is a musical book.⁷⁰

Her letter echoed what the reviewer for *Commonweal* (30 December 1925) had said about Woolf's novel catching 'the very soul and essence of London', a significant aspect of its enduring popularity.

Harmon H. Goldstone (a name that might have been invented by the creator of J. Alfred Prufrock) was a twenty-one-year-old senior at Harvard when he wrote to Woolf in 1932 posing a number of questions he hoped would help him develop an essay he had written about her into a book. 'As far as I remember', she told him, 'the character of Septimus in Mrs Dalloway was invented to complete the character of Mrs Dalloway; I could not otherwise convey my whole meaning about her'.⁷¹ Woolf continued to correspond with Goldstone, graciously commenting on his outline (though adding that she would certainly read his book 'with great pleasure if it were about somebody else'⁷²), but he abandoned his plan when he heard about Winifred Holtby's *Virginia Woolf* (1932) and when Woolf told him of the imminent appearance in France of *Le roman psychologique de Virginia Woolf* by Floris Delattre, a professor at the University of Lille.

Holtby's was the first monograph in English devoted to Woolf. Although its subject told their mutual friend Ethel Smyth that the book made her 'roar with laughter',⁷³ Holtby, a novelist herself, wrote with insight about Woolf's life and work. Delattre's book appeared early enough in 1932 for Holtby to give an account of it in her own, noting that he believed that Woolf 'must at least be acquainted' with Henri Bergson's widely discussed theories about time. Woolf told Harmon Goldstone that she had never read anything by the French philosopher, but Delattre pointed out that her sister-in-law, the psychoanalyst Karin Stephen (married to Woolf's brother Adrian), had written a book about Bergson. It was, therefore, highly unlikely that Woolf was unaware of his theories, even had she not actually read his books. In a way, it does not matter whether she actually read the works of such thinkers or not: it would be surprising if a novelist who explicitly announced her intention to reform the novel to better reflect reality as it was experienced by herself and her contemporaries proceeded as if Einstein, Freud, Marx and others had not existed. In the case of Bergson, she almost certainly would have heard about his ideas from Roger Fry even if not from Karin Stephen.*

By the late 1920s, American students were submitting dissertations for Master's degrees that discussed Woolf and other modernist writers. The handling of time, both as experienced by their characters and as structured by their narrative techniques, was a frequent topic for students writing about Joyce, Proust, Richardson and Woolf. Several such theses were submitted in the 1920s and 1930s to the graduate school of the University of Minnesota, where Joseph Warren Beach taught for many years. A poet, novelist and literary critic, Beach was one of several academics in the 1930s who took notice of Woolf's introduction to the Modern Library edition of *Mrs Dalloway*. In *The Twentieth Century Novel* he characterised the introduction as leaving 'us pretty free to speculate upon her idea in the book', noting that the plan Woolf described of having Clarissa kill herself 'was happily abandoned'.[74] Woolf, as

---

* Jeff Wallace provides a useful summary of why Bergson is so relevant to Woolf: 'In *Matter and Memory* (1911) ... Bergson had begun to question the concept of recollection itself, tied as it was to a model of memory as a set of images in the brain, selected for projection in the private cinema of consciousness. Rather, Bergson theorized, memory was an *actualization* of the past in the body, a complex physical event or evocation through which the individual does not "have" memory but "is" memory. Thus, for example, the opening pages of Woolf's *Mrs Dalloway*, with their subtle manipulation of tense and careful ambiguity surrounding the question of "now", vividly suggest a sense in which Clarissa Dalloway is simultaneously a menopausal and a teenage woman'. Jeff Wallace, 'Modernists on the Art of Fiction'. In Morag Shiach, ed. *The Cambridge Companion to the Modernist Novel*. Cambridge University Press, 2007: 15–31, 26.

19 Alternative cover for Modern Library edition of *Mrs Dalloway*

already mentioned, worried that readers would find the twin narratives of Clarissa and Septimus confusing. Often, those fears were confirmed. Beach, for example, wrote

> One may guess that Virginia Woolf, in writing 'Mrs. Dalloway,' had in mind, as her real subject, something like this: what life seems like on a fine day in London. Or perhaps, more broadly, the sensation of being alive. She must proceed from a center, and she has chosen for that a cultivated middle-aged woman of fashion planning to give a party. ... But the author realizes how narrow a range of experience is implied in Clarissa Dalloway, her family and friends. She needs the Septimus Smiths to bring in the tragic note.[75]

Dorothy M. Hoare made a similar point: 'The parts about Septimus, one suspects, were put in almost purely for the sake of contrast'.[76]

Most reviews in the years immediately following publication tended to focus exclusively on Clarissa, either overlooking Septimus entirely or dismissing him as extraneous to the major concerns of the novel. In the *TLS*, for example, Arthur McDowall, author of a 1918 book, *Realism: A Study in Art and Thought*, took Clarissa and Peter to be the 'two chief figures', with Septimus only 'a block in the tideway now and then'.[77] The writer Gerald Bullett did take note of Septimus, but thought that Woolf's 'technical and intellectual bias' made his suicide 'trivial compared with the bright ferment of consciousness', even though it was 'the most startling action' in a novel whose 'cinematic' speed left readers little opportunity for reflection.[78] The earliest reviewers, writing without the benefit of Woolf's 1928 introduction, might be forgiven for their confusion, but it is surprising that American academics wrote in the 1930s as though they had never come across the notion of a doppelganger, despite its being such a common trope in Gothic fiction, to say nothing of its presence in Dostoevsky, a writer Woolf greatly admired and about whom she had published several essays by the time the Modern Library edition of *Mrs Dalloway* came out.

Modernist novels were 'difficult reading for the "tired business man," sitting down in his easy-chair for an evening's entertainment', said Beach,[79] a notion echoed in much of the commentary on *Mrs Dalloway* at the time. Burton Rascoe, literary editor of the *New York Herald Tribune*, wrote in *Arts & Decoration* magazine that Woolf's book did not have much to offer anyone 'who is uninterested in the technical problems of the writer'. His 'intelligent friends' were baffled because there seemed to be no 'rounded out story'. Novels were supposed to provide 'a conclusion, a plot and possibly a moral'.[80] Ralph Boas, a professor of English at Wheaton College, sounded the same note in *The Study and Appreciation of Literature*: 'readers like to be stirred emotionally. They like to laugh; they like to weep'.[81] The reviewer for the *New Statesman* would have agreed: P. C. Kennedy wanted 'to weep with Peter Walsh and leap to death with poor Septimus Warren Smith; and my trouble is that I can't'.[82] On the other hand, book-lovers in Chicago discussing *Mrs Dalloway* at a meeting guided by *The Step-Ladder* of

January 1926 would have read that Woolf had 'written a book that holds you breathless with interest from the first page ... Mrs Woolf can write a breathlessly interesting novel without any love scene in it and write a love story leaving the love scene to be inferred'.

Bloomsbury's enemies

Although it is usually difficult, if not impossible, to retrieve the experience of 'non-professional' readers—at least until the advent of book blogs and social media—the continuing popularity of *Mrs Dalloway* suggests that academics' and reviewers' perspectives on it often diverged sharply from those of the 'common reader'. As it is today, higher education was a cultural battleground after the First World War, a period that saw significant changes in universities both in Britain and the United States. Efforts to professionalise the study of English literature with a view to giving it a prestige similar to that enjoyed by the sciences led eventually to the 'New Criticism' that dominated the discipline for several decades after the Second World War. This doctrine derived in great part from the critical writings of T. S. Eliot, I. A. Richards and others who eschewed any attention to an author's biography or to the historical circumstances of when a work was produced in favour of close readings that treated any literary text as a discrete object.

In *A Room of One's Own*, Woolf argued that in fiction as in real life the values of men tended to prevail: 'Speaking crudely, football and sport are "important"; the worship of fashion, the buying of clothes "trivial"'. Consequently, a book dealing with war would be deemed important, but one that concerned 'the feelings of women in a drawing-room' was likely to be dismissed as 'insignificant': 'A scene in a battle-field is more important than a scene in a shop'. *Mrs Dalloway* is famously concerned with shops and shopping. The battlefield upon which Septimus saw his dear Evans blown to bits did not register for many readers, accustomed to more conventional modes of representation in fiction. Woolf might be heralded in *Equal Rights*—the 'Official Organ of the National Woman's Party' in Washington DC—for having 'understood so clearly and phrased so brilliantly every aspect of women's life',[83] but such lives were held to be less important than those of men. Long before Betty Friedan wrote in *The Feminine Mystique* about 'the problem that has no name', Woolf was praised in *The New Age* of 11 March 1926 for her realisation in *Mrs Dalloway* of 'the strange restlessness that is the demon of many women'.

It is possible even today to come across commentary that lumps together anyone associated with the Bloomsbury Group as though they were all of one mind. Such attitudes are reminiscent of Woolf's description for Gwen Raverat of Lady Sibyl Colefax, who gathered intellectuals at her Argyll House salons 'as a parrot picks up beads, without knowing Lord Balfour from Duncan Grant'.[84] Those who disparaged Woolf were even sometimes among her close friends. She was depressed by Desmond MacCarthy's 'usual sneer' about *Mrs Dalloway*, for example.[85] In a 1931 lecture, which he published in *Life and Letters*, the magazine he edited, MacCarthy complained that in the novels of young writers, 'events have become merely interruptions in a long wool-gathering process, a process that is used chiefly to provide occasions for little prose poems ... as when the tiny gathers in some green silk Mrs Dalloway is sewing on to her belt remind her of summer waves ... waves described in a passage of delicate and rhythmical prose'.[86] With friends like this, one might ask, who needs enemies? But enemies there certainly were, as there continue to be. Often, antagonism towards Woolf, and more broadly towards Bloomsbury, ran along lines inflected by class and gender.[87]

One of the arch-enemies of Bloomsbury was that talented precursor of today's laddish critics, Percy Wyndham Lewis. In *Men Without Art*, Lewis presented Woolf's argument with Arnold Bennett as no more than 'the old incompatibility of the eternal feminine, on the one hand, and the rough footballing "he" principle—the eternal masculine—on the other'.[88] With barely disguised homophobia, Lewis criticised Lytton Strachey and 'the way of life of Marcel Proust' before sneering that it 'has been with considerable shaking in my shoes, and a feeling of treading upon a carpet of eggs, that I have taken the cow by the horns in this chapter, and broached the subject of the part that the feminine mind has played—and minds as well, deeply feminized, not technically on the distaff side—on the erection of our present criteria'.[89] There was a great deal of anxiety over the criteria of judgement in the interwar period. In the wake of increasing literacy fostered by educational reforms came debates about what was worthwhile for people to read.

Q. D. Leavis published the dissertation she had written under the supervision of I. A. Richards as *Fiction and the Reading Public* in 1932. She and her husband, F. R. Leavis, represented 'all that is highest & dryest at Cambridge', Woolf quipped to Margaret Llewelyn Davies.[90] In her book, Q. D. Leavis worried that the newly educated masses were unable to resist the lure of 'the cheap and easy pleasures offered by the cinema, the circulating library, the magazine, the newspaper, the dance-hall, and the loud-speaker'.[91] The style of a writer like Woolf was 'especially calculated to baffle the general public of the twentieth century'. Leavis was referring to *To the Lighthouse* but could just as easily have had *Mrs Dalloway* in mind. Woolf was definitely a 'highbrow' writer, but she was the wrong kind of modernist for people like F. R. Leavis and Wyndham Lewis, champions of those whom Lewis named 'the Men of 1914'—himself, Joyce, Eliot and Ezra Pound. In *Scrutiny*, the journal F. R. Leavis co-founded to promulgate his views, a 'Manifesto' in the inaugural issue claimed that 'to-day there are anti-highbrow publics and "modernist" publics, but there is no public of Common Readers with whom the critic can rejoice to concur'.[92] Four months later, Woolf published *The Common Reader: Second Series*.

More attentive readers at the time might have noticed that Woolf actually embedded in *Mrs Dalloway* allusions to debates about literacy and education, in addition to her more overt criticism of doctors and politicians. When Clarissa runs her eye across the wares displayed in Hatchards' window, the titles she sees illustrate the explosion of reading matter that caused Cambridge dons to clutch their pearls. Yes, there is Shakespeare, but there is also the rambunctious *Jorrocks's Jaunts and Jollities* of R. S. Surtees, as well as his *Soapy Sponge*. Also displayed are the sensational memoirs of Margot Asquith, and a title invented by Woolf, *Big Game Hunting in Nigeria*. Woolf believed in the freedom of readers to choose their own path: 'we owe a great deal to bad books', she wrote in 'Hours in a Library'.[93] She reiterated this idea in 'Gothic Fiction': 'as literary critics are too little aware, a love of literature is often roused and for the first years nourished not by the good books, but by the bad. It will be an ill day when all reading is done in libraries and none of it in tubes'.[94] While critics such as Eliot, Richards, Lewis and F. R. Leavis came to dominate the ethos of English departments in the English-speaking world (which, of course, at that time included many countries in Africa as well as India, Australia and New Zealand), Woolf maintained a deeply critical attitude towards the academic study of literature throughout her life.

The 'manliness' that Septimus Warren Smith's employer, Mr Brewer, finds lacking in him is said to have been 'produced instantly' in the trenches of the First World War. Septimus was 'one of the first to volunteer' in 1914 because he wanted to fight for 'an England which consisted almost entirely of Shakespeare's plays and Miss Isabel Pole in a green dress walking in a square'. The teaching of literature in England, as Melba Cuddy-Keane observes, 'became permeated with the ideal of recovering a lost organic society'.[95] Woolf was keenly aware of the connection between how literature was taught and how values are thereby inculcated. Her own work during her lifetime and well into the second half of the twentieth century was often disparaged as 'feminine' (and therefore unaligned with the 'manly' values that send Septimus to war). Muriel Bradbrook, a student at Girton College, Cambridge, who attended one of the lectures Woolf developed into *A Room of One's Own* (as did Q. D. Leavis), wrote in the first number of *Scrutiny* that 'To demand "thinking" from Mrs. Woolf is clearly illegitimate: but such a deliberate repudiation of it and such a smoke screen of feminine charm is surely to be deprecated'.[96]

In the New York *Nation* of 8 June 1925, Joseph Wood Krutch called Woolf 'a sort of decorous James Joyce'. This was a dominant image of her for many decades, only giving way in the 1960s and 1970s—though in no way disappearing entirely—under the pressure of feminist readings of her work, as well as of better-informed understandings of her particular narrative methods. Leonard Woolf published *A Writer's Diary* in 1953, allowing readers for the first time to discover Woolf's intention of showing 'the sane & the insane side by side' in *Mrs Dalloway*, and to read about the 'tunnelling process' that enabled her to realise her vision for the novel's design. Still, a year later Walter Allen wrote in his influential survey *The English Novel* that 'At present the reaction against her work is probably at its greatest, and I must admit to sharing in it'.[97] Those moments of revelation, such as were to be found in *Mrs Dalloway*, seemed to Allen no more than 'a succession of short, sharp female gasps of ecstasy'.

Signs of a turning tide, however, could be observed. Edward A. Hungerford, who earned a PhD from New York University soon after the Second World War with a thesis on Woolf's literary criticism, referred to *A Writer's Diary* to argue that Woolf herself never described her own technique as 'stream-of consciousness', initiating more serious attention to her work. In a 1957 article in *Modern Fiction Studies*, Hungerford urged attention to her own metaphor, 'the tunnelling process as a descriptive term for the style of *Mrs. Dalloway*'.[98] He pointed out that the image of tunnelling occurred both in a 'Foreword' Woolf wrote for the catalogue to an exhibition of her sister Vanessa Bell's paintings, as well as in a 1925 essay, 'Pictures'. This method allowed Woolf to 'tunnel behind the façade of objective appearance'[99] and reveal the consciousness of a character like Septimus Smith. Critical debate about Woolf's achievement in *Mrs Dalloway* slowly gained substance in the second half of the twentieth century, opening new avenues of enquiry to place the novel into more nuanced contexts that revealed a prismatic array of meanings.

Part IV

Mrs Dalloway out in the world

When the man from the company moving the Woolfs' belongings from Richmond to Tavistock Square shook Leonard's hand, Virginia commented that the gesture was 'because we are real people & own a press'.[1] Although her remark was partly humorous, Woolf undoubtedly felt on the cusp of a new life of possibility and pleasure, responsibility and achievement. She commissioned Vanessa Bell and Duncan Grant to decorate their new living room, persuading Leonard to agree to this 'outrageous extravagance'.[2] (She had been inspired by the murals Bell and Grant had made for John Maynard Keynes's rooms in Cambridge.) A month after moving in to Tavistock Square she was able to tell Janet Case that her room was now 'all vast panels of moonrises and prima donna's bouquets'.[3] The decorations were featured in *Vogue* that November, and some elements of Bell and Grant's scheme can be glimpsed in the background of photographs taken of the Woolfs by Gisèle Freund in 1939, shortly before they moved to Mecklenburgh Square. In 1940 a Nazi bomb destroyed the Tavistock Square flat where Woolf wrote so many books.

The day that *Mrs Dalloway* was published felt like the beginning of summer, the trees of Tavistock Square already beginning to leaf. The novel inaugurated a period of immense industry and creative innovation in Woolf's life. Her stature as novelist, reviewer,

20 Vanessa Bell arranging flowers at Charleston, Duncan Grant standing nearby

essayist, public intellectual and publisher continued to grow. She and Leonard participated in both print and radio broadcast discussions about the book trade—the role of reviewers, the consequences of book pricing, relations between publishers and bookshops—and she always kept a keen eye on how her books were faring.

Woolf wrote several essays specifically about reading, one of which—'How Should One Read a Book?'—she chose to conclude her *Common Reader: Second Series*. That essay ends with a fantasy of readers arriving at the pearly gates of heaven 'with books under our arms'. Turning to Saint Peter, Woolf imagines, God would say 'Look, these need no reward. We have nothing to give them here. They have loved reading'.[4] Her 'common readers' tended not to read literary criticism, other than a book review perhaps. Nowadays, by contrast, readers of 'classic' fiction are often likely to have been influenced by the views of their teachers.

In her bibliomemoir *All the Lives We Ever Lived*, for example, Katharine Smyth recalls a tutor at Oxford who, 'miffed' by Woolf's treatment of Joyce, 'never missed an opportunity to ridicule her snobbishness and eccentricity'. Smyth entered university with Woolf already consigned by her high school teachers to 'the prim ranks of Women Writers'[5] but was able to come to her own conclusions, in good Woolfian fashion—assisted, no doubt, by the lectures of Hermione Lee which she also attended at Oxford. Many people will encounter visual and verbal representations of Woolf before having any experience of her writing because they circulate so widely in popular culture. In her contribution on *Mrs Dalloway* to the 'Bookmarked' series, Robin Black recalls noticing quotations from and images of Woolf throughout the Sarah Lawrence College campus when she became a student there in the early 1980s, sparking an identification with her as a woman well before she had read a word she wrote.

Ulysses

James Joyce's *Ulysses* has shadowed *Mrs Dalloway* since the 1920s. The two modernist masterpieces inevitably were compared because both take place within a single day in a major city. Both also play with the notion of the double—Stephen Dedalus and Leopold Bloom, and Clarissa Dalloway and Septimus Smith. It has often been the case that comparisons with Joyce are made at the expense of Woolf, though few have been as vituperative as Wyndham Lewis, who claimed in *Men Without Art* that the motor car scene in *Mrs Dalloway* was a 'sort of undergraduate imitation'[6] of the viceregal procession in the 'Wandering Rocks' section of *Ulysses*. Less antagonistic commentators were content to point out that the two writers—often in tandem with Dorothy Richardson and Proust—were examples of a new literary movement characterised by the 'stream-of-consciousness' technique, a term so broad it obscured the quite profound differences among these writers' experiments with the narrative representation of human consciousness.

Woolf's disparaging remarks about Joyce were included in the selections made by Leonard Woolf when he published *A Writer's Diary*. Woolf had written in 1922 that *Ulysses* seemed to her the effort of a 'self-taught working man' (which was not at all accurate). She also recorded, more damningly in the eyes of those who took her opinion to be a kind of patrician disdain, that reading *Ulysses* brought to mind 'a queasy undergraduate scratching his pimples'.[7] For decades, her early praise in 'Modern Novels' forgotten, these snooty comments stood for the whole story of Woolf's response to *Ulysses*, confirming for her detractors that *Mrs Dalloway* was her (failed) attempt to match her exact contemporary at his own game. When Richard Ellmann's magisterial biography of Joyce came out in 1959, he noted that the Woolfs had declined Harriet Shaw Weaver's invitation to publish *Ulysses* because it would have taken two years to produce on their handpress. (They knew, too, that they would be liable as publishers to prosecution under the Obscene Publications Act.) Ellmann also pointed out that they had told Weaver that 'they were very much interested in the first four episodes' which they had read in the *Little Review*.[8] In an account of the initial reception of *Ulysses*, Ellmann quoted some of Woolf's comments from *A Writer's Diary*, but also added the 'more violently hostile view' expressed by the writer Edmund Gosse, who told French art historian Louis Gillet that 'no English critics of weight' considered Joyce of any importance.[9]

It is likely that Woolf's impressions of Joyce (whom she never met) were coloured by her brother-in-law Clive Bell's tales of encountering him in Paris. T. S. Eliot's high praise for the writing not only of Joyce but also of Ezra Pound and Wyndham Lewis was a frequent topic of baffled conversation at Charleston gatherings frequented by the Woolfs. When Clive Bell ran into Joyce at

Michaud's restaurant in Paris late one night in May 1921, he told Mary Hutchinson that he found him 'pretentious, underbred and provincial beyond words'.[10] Such was the gossip Woolf undoubtedly would have heard. Vanessa Bell was renting a studio in Paris in February 1922 when Shakespeare and Co. published *Ulysses*. 'For Gods sake make friends with Mr Joyce', Woolf wrote. 'I particularly want to know what he's like'.[11]

Two months after this, Woolf decided it was 'necessary' to read *Ulysses* and ordered a copy from David Garnett and Francis Birrell's bookshop in Bloomsbury. Her language concerning *Ulysses* at this time, just months before she began to put down her first thoughts about *Mrs Dalloway*, consistently suggests that she was reading it as a chore, an obligation for someone in her line of work. To make things worse, *Ulysses* cost the enormous sum of £4,* leaving her 'no money to buy clothes' until she had sold some books from her own library to defray the expense.[12] She made a point of letting Eliot know that she had laid out £4 for the book about which the usually buttoned-up American had been 'rapt, enthusiastic' when he told her about it.[13]

Eliot's enthusiasm for Joyce certainly shaped Woolf's response to *Ulysses*. We have seen already that a visit from him while she was at work on *Jacob's Room* led her to worry that what she was attempting was being more successfully achieved by Joyce. That *Ulysses* was 'prodigious'[14] in the opinion of a writer she not only admired but had published at her own press inevitably influenced Woolf's expectations. On the same day that she let Eliot know she was cutting the pages of her copy of *Ulysses*, she told Clive Bell that only Leonard had begun to read it: 'I look, and sip, and shudder'. Asking Bell if he had seen Wyndham Lewis's hostile

---

* 'To buy a copy of the first edition of *Ulysses* ... was not an action that can be readily compared with the everyday purchase of a book'. Lawrence Rainey, *Institutions of Modernism: Literary Elites and Public Culture*. Yale University Press, 1998, 64.

review of his book *Since Cézanne*, Woolf wondered 'what scurvy of the soul' people like Lewis were afflicted with 'that they must scratch in public?'[15] It was the same metaphor she would use a few months later in her diary when she put down her first impressions of *Ulysses*. No doubt Bell repeated to her what he told Mary Hutchinson and Vanessa Bell about the grand dinner in honour of Diaghilev's Ballets Russes given that May by Sydney and Violet Schiff at the Hotel Majestic in Paris: Joyce had arrived at 2 a.m. either too drunk or too shy to say a word. Marcel Proust, on the other hand, had been charming.

Woolf at first avoided reading her copy of *Ulysses* because she was once again being swept off her feet by Proust, whose second volume, *À l'ombre des jeunes filles en fleurs*, she plunged into in May 1922. In June, however, Gerald Brenan was coming to stay and had let her know that he looked forward to discussing *Ulysses*. 'Oh what a bore about Joyce!' Woolf told him; 'Just as I was devoting myself to Proust'.[16] She began to read *Ulysses* and got through the first two hundred pages by the middle of August: 'amused, stimulated, charmed, interested by the first 2 or 3 chapters—to the end of the Cemetery scene; & then puzzled, bored, irritated'.[17] She could not understand why Eliot thought it such a masterpiece. Eliot's high praise, she told Ottoline Morrell, had prepared her for a gigantic effort to read Joyce's book, but 'the poor young man has only got the dregs of a mind .... I mean if you could weigh the meaning on Joyces page it would be about ten times as light as on Henry James'.[18] Woolf seems to have stopped after those two hundred pages (just before the end of the ninth episode of *Ulysses*, 'Scylla and Charibdys', in which Stephen delivers his lecture on *Hamlet*). 'Never did I read such tosh', she told Lytton Strachey. The first two chapters were all right, but after that it was 'merely the scratching of pimples on the body of the bootboy at Claridge's'.[19]

The repeated note of disgust, of repulsion by the physical, long dominated discussion of Woolf's response to *Ulysses*, and clearly she did not think much of the book. 'I dislike Ulysses more & more', she went on that August; 'that is think it more & more unimportant'.[20] By September she had raced through to the end: 'I have not read it carefully; & only once'. She was prepared to admit that in her haste she might have 'scamped the virtue of it more than is fair',[21] but if she even read Molly Bloom's monologue, she left no trace of what she thought about it. The novel was 'a memorable catastrophe', she said in an article for the *TLS* in April 1923; 'immense in daring, terrific in disaster'.[22] That December, although she agreed with Brenan that *Ulysses* was 'underrated', she let him know that 'never did any book so bore me'.[23]

When she learned of Joyce's death in January 1941, Woolf thought back more than twenty years to Harriet Shaw Weaver bringing the manuscript of *Ulysses* to Hogarth House for her and Leonard to consider publishing. She remembered that Katherine Mansfield had visited while she had the manuscript on a table, and 'began to read, ridiculing'.[24] Mansfield shared Woolf's distaste for Joyce and had complained to Sydney Schiff about the 'horrors in the house of his mind. He's so terribly *unfein*'.[25] But that day in 1918, Mansfield had suddenly said 'But theres something in this' as she continued to read. Only weeks from her own death, Woolf recalled how she had read the novel in the summer of 1922 under the spell of Eliot's superlatives, 'with spasms of wonder, of discovery, & then again with long lapses of intense boredom'.[26] The fact is, *Mrs Dalloway* no more 'plagiarises' *Ulysses* than *Ulysses* plagiarises Homer's *Odyssey*.* More fruitful for reading *Mrs Dalloway* than to focus on distasteful comments and gossipy posturing are the notes Woolf made when she first encountered *Ulysses* in the

---

* Woolf is so often chastised for her remarks about Joyce that it is important to acknowledge that she was hardly alone in her views at the time. Even Wyndham Lewis, in *Time and Western Man*, called Joyce 'the poet of the shabby-genteel, impoverished intellectualism of Dublin. His world is the small middle-class one'. D. H. Lawrence also criticised Joyce for his indecency.

pages of the *Little Review* in 1918, that magazine on the masthead of which Ezra Pound vowed to 'make no compromise with the public taste'.

Woolf's reading notes on the *Little Review* excerpts from *Ulysses* were not published until 1990, transcribed by Suzette Henke, who had come across them in the Berg Collection of the New York Public Library in the mid-1980s. The jottings made as she read each month's number give context to Woolf's offhand remarks in her diary, and also demonstrate her serious appraisal of Joyce made while she was preparing to write her manifesto, 'Modern Novels', for the *TLS*. We can, for example, see that her note, 'Question how far we now accept the old tradition without thinking',[27] makes its way into the development of the argument from 'Modern Novels' through 'Modern Fiction' into 'Mr Bennett and Mrs Brown' and 'Character in Fiction' about how difficult it is to overcome readers' conventional expectations.

We can also discern the first inkling of a criticism that would emerge in Woolf's diary in 1920 of 'the damned egotistical self' which she believed 'ruined' both Joyce and Dorothy Richardson, when she wrote of Joyce's method in *Ulysses* that it perhaps 'gets less into other people and too much into one'.[28] Mansfield made a similar criticism of Dorothy Richardson's *The Tunnel*, the fourth of her *Pilgrimage* series of novels, when she wrote in a review that there was no selection at work in the presentation of the content of the mind of Miriam Henderson, Richardson's 'soul-sister': 'until these things are judged and given each its appointed place in the whole scheme, they have no meaning in the world of art'.[29] 'Stream of consciousness' was only just beginning to come into focus in the 1920s as the term migrated from its origin in William James's 1890 *Principles of Psychology* to being used in literary criticism. A writer in the *Atlantic Monthly* in September 1926 wondered for how long a large part of the reading public might regard this new kind of fiction as only 'an eccentric fad'.[30]

In the classroom

For about thirty years after the end of the Second World War, literary critics were keenly interested in defining the varieties of how novelists used stream-of-consciousness techniques. Their efforts often confused rather than clarified things, unfortunately, owing to the imprecision of the terminology bandied about in books and articles. When discussing Woolf, critics most often called on *Mrs Dalloway* to illustrate her specific methods. But when Ralph Freedman, for example, labelled the method of that novel 'interior monologue', he used a term more fitting for Joyce's Molly Bloom. Robert Humphrey was closer to the mark when he identified 'the basic method of indirect interior monologue' as the mode in which Woolf introduced Clarissa to the reader in the novel's opening pages. A more common term for Humphrey's label is 'free indirect discourse'. That narrative mode had in fact been used by novelists before Woolf, Joyce and their contemporaries. In the nineteenth century it was called *erlebt Rede* by German linguists, and *style indirect libre* by French. In essence, as close readers of *Mrs Dalloway* can observe, the style weaves together a narrator's voice with the thoughts of a character. The expected signals that would be provided by 'she thought' or 'he remembered' are usually absent. In Woolf's case, the point of view also is often difficult to pin down, challenging readers to do without the direction supplied by a traditional third-person fictional narrative.[31] It is difficult for a reader to come to any conclusion about Septimus when he is introduced because, as Molly Hite has observed, the narrative offers a number of descriptions of the character 'that make the project of choosing one interpretation rather odd'.[32] The onus is on the reader to suspend any final judgement, the novel functioning more in the manner of a piece of music than as a plot.

Erich Auerbach's *Mimesis*, which appeared in English translation (from the German) in 1953, was a landmark in the study of how writers represent reality in fiction. Although he chose a passage from *To the Lighthouse* to analyse in his final chapter, the questions Auerbach posed about Woolf's narrative method might equally well have been asked about *Mrs Dalloway*: Who is speaking? or Who is looking? How a reader answers such questions determines the judgements they make about particular characters. Auerbach took Woolf's narrative technique in *To the Lighthouse* to be a development from the single point of view presented by a writer such as Dorothy Richardson to a 'multipersonal representation of consciousness' that dissolved reality 'into multiple and multivalent reflections'.[33] Perhaps because he wrote his book during the Second World War while exiled in Istanbul, Auerbach believed the experiments of writers such as Woolf and Proust to be a 'symptom of the confusion and helplessness' that followed the First World War: 'a certain atmosphere of universal doom', he wrote, pervades modernist fiction.[34]

Auerbach concluded that although *To the Lighthouse* was filled 'in its feminine way, with irony, amorphous sadness, and doubt of life', Woolf's exploitation of the ordinary, the random, revealed 'the elementary things which our lives have in common'.[35] Even relatively positive readings of Woolf in the post-Second World War period often diminished her achievements as 'feminine', especially in comparison to Joyce. Walter Allen accurately explained that in *Mrs Dalloway* Woolf uses not stream of consciousness but 'a very deft adaptation' of it. He does not doubt that Woolf can create convincing characters, and praises the solidity of the London within which *Mrs Dalloway* takes place. But as we saw above, he dismissed any 'revelation and illumination' in the novel as 'female gasps of ecstasy'. Ten years later, Allen more or less reiterated this judgement in *Tradition and Dream*, referring to *Mrs Dalloway* as 'a tiny *Ulysses*'.[36]

The question of point of view, of how Woolf might have intended her readers to judge her characters, was brought sharply into focus by John Carey's bitter attack on modernism in *The Intellectuals and the Masses*. Carey identified Doris Kilman as 'just the sort of woman' that Woolf, 'as a campaigning feminist, might be expected to champion'. He argued that due to her class prejudice, however, Woolf depicts Kilman 'as a monster of spite, envy and unfulfilled desire'.[37] Although extreme, Carey's tirade focuses attention on an important aspect of *Mrs Dalloway*, a novel, after all, in which its author explicitly intended 'to criticise the social system'.

Carey's line of attack was not unusual. Since the 1930s, when Dmitri Mirsky wrote in *The Intelligentsia of Great Britain* that 'Bloomsbury liberalism can be defined as a thin-skinned humanism for enlightened and sensitive members of the capitalist class who do not desire the outer world to be such as might be prone to cause them any displeasing impression',[38] and up to today, the charge of snobbery, of elitism, has been levelled against the Bloomsbury Group in general, and against Woolf in particular.* *Mrs Dalloway* has often been summoned as a witness for the prosecution, with the testimony of Doris Kilman offered as clinching the case.

In a review of *Mrs Dalloway* for the *Annual Register* of 1925, Clarissa was described as 'the mother of an exquisite daughter, Elizabeth, desperately grudged her by the pitiful, grotesque and vampirine governess Miss Kilman'. For a sizeable number of critics, this was the view Woolf took of her character, and therefore intended her readers to take. There is little question about how we are 'supposed' to feel toward Dr Holmes or Dr Bradshaw. The 'Proportion' and 'Conversion' passage is a rare intrusion by an 'objective' third-person voice into the typical free indirect discourse of the novel. That diatribe explains the relationship between the

---

* For example: 'She has benefited immensely from a gang of sycophants in the literary trade and academia talking her up for nearly a century, not so much for her own sake as for the sake of the cult of Bloomsbury that she incarnated so well'. Simon Heffer, 'The True Great 20th-Century Novelists who Irked the Bloomsbury Snobs'. *Daily Telegraph* 9 January 2010.

social power by which Bradshaw secluded 'lunatics', 'forbade childbirth, and penalised despair', and the similar desire of Christianity to 'impress, to impose', to offer help but desire power, and to feast 'most subtly on the human will'. It is at this aura of chilling power Clarissa shudders when she contemplates Sir William at her party after hearing about Septimus's death. But the directness of the social criticism here is unusual in the novel. Woolf may have told Philip Morrell that she intended Hugh Whitbread to be hated and Richard Dalloway to be liked, but his apparent dislike of both confirmed what she wrote in the Modern Library introduction: books belong to their readers, despite what an author might intend.

The critic A. David Moody singled out a moment late in the novel when he believed that Clarissa is 'unmasked': 'Her hatred of Miss Kilman shows her state to be worse than mere superficiality: her cultivated surface has masked something evil'.[39] In this 1963 article, Moody cuts off the text he quotes in support of his claim at 'how she hated her', thus obliterating what Woolf actually wrote so that it will not contradict his argument. Clarissa's 'revelation of herself in that moment relates her unmistakably to Sir William Bradshaw, who is certainly evil'. Ten years later, in the *New York Review of Books*, Elizabeth Hardwick brought up Kilman as a character who, by contrast with the 'complicated ... creatures of intricate feeling' Woolf usually presents, is 'a repellent person' who is 'the object of the author's insolent loathing'.[40] Go forward another twenty years, and we find Claire Tomalin asserting in her introduction to an Oxford World's Classics edition of *Mrs Dalloway* that 'Where Miss Kilman was drawn from, and why she gets this vicious treatment, remains mysterious, an uncomfortable blot on the book'.[41] It is possible still to come across the view that Kilman represents 'a rare failure of compassion' by Woolf.[42]

Literary criticism might be imagined as a sprawling conversation among professionals about reading. The conversation moves on or lingers, repeats itself or brings to light something new, confuses or clarifies, and at times can be difficult even for insiders to follow. At its heart, though, when all the theories and specialised terminology, the trends and assumptions, are put aside, literary criticism consists of people saying 'I thought this when I read that'. How we are 'supposed' to feel about Clarissa Dalloway, Peter Walsh or Doris Kilman is the wrong question. More interesting is to ask how *do* you feel, and why?

Doris Kilman does represent a social fact of the immediate post-First World War period in Britain when there was a backlash against women in the workforce, as well as an economic crisis that briefly affected the middle class. As we have already noted, Woolf likely drew on the plight of Louise Matthaei, Leonard Woolf's assistant at the *International Review*, for aspects of Kilman. The well-qualified Matthaei had lost her job at Girton College during the War because she was of German descent. Kilman, whose family name had been changed from Kiehlman, lost her job at Miss Dolby's school during the War 'because she would not pretend that the Germans were all villains'. Another figure who informed Woolf's conception of Kilman was her cousin Dorothea Stephen, daughter of Leslie Stephen's brother James Fitzjames. Dorothea had outraged Woolf and her sister, Vanessa, in 1921 when she expressed reservations about bringing her daughter to Charleston because she took umbrage at Vanessa's domestic arrangements. After this upset, Woolf described to Vanessa how Dorothea had 'devoured huge quantities of muffin and cake' on a visit, 'and so oppressed me with her moral depravity—her sheer repulsiveness and obtuseness and stodge—that I was practically fainting'.[43] The connection between Dorothea and Kilman comes into sharper focus when Woolf rants in a letter to Ethel Smyth against those who wish to convert others: they are 'impertinent, insolent, corrupt beyond measure'. She traced the root of her antipathy to the fact that 'our religious friends, some cousins in particular, the daughters of Fitzjames, rasped and agonised us as children by perpetual attempts at conversion. As they were ugly women, who sweated, I conceived a greater hatred for them than ever for anyone'.[44]

Some of the 'hatred' Woolf felt for proselytising women probably did, therefore, become an element of the characterisation of Doris Kilman. But there is always the danger in identifying models of assuming the fictional is a close recreation of the biographical. There is in Kilman something, too, of Jean Thomas, the proprietor of the 'home' in Twickenham to which Woolf was sent several times before her marriage to recover from breakdowns. Thomas's Christian proselytising irritated Woolf but did not elicit her 'hatred'. To discern a conclusive attitude toward Kilman in the prose through which she is created is to overlook the way in which Woolf's free indirect discourse creates a space that must be occupied by each reader, each time the novel is read, a space in which the reader is invited to become, as Woolf wrote in 'How Should One Read a Book?', the writer's 'accomplice'. In that spirit, I offer a possible reading of Miss Kilman, such as one might lead students through in a classroom.

Clarissa Dalloway, we know, 'would not say of anyone in the world now that they were this or were that'. Our introduction to Doris Kilman occurs within Clarissa's consciousness as she laments her daughter's being 'mewed' in a stuffy room with her tutor. Clarissa knows that Miss Kilman has been 'badly treated of course'; acknowledging her worry, Clarissa's husband has told her that their daughter's devotion to the older woman may be only a phase. Clarissa wishes that Elizabeth cared more about appearances, but she knows this is unlikely while she is under Kilman's influence.

The reader is immersed in Clarissa's consciousness as she continues thinking about Kilman. Clarissa acknowledges that Kilman does good works (for the Russians, the Austrians) but thinks that 'in private' her green mackintosh is a 'positive torture'. She is affronted because Kilman 'perspired'. Kilman also has a way of making one feel her superiority (a sensation echoed by Elizabeth later in the day at the Army & Navy Stores). Woolf gives us Clarissa's perspective, but this has been assumed by too many critics to be Woolf's own. Kilman was dismissed from her teaching post because she was of German descent, Clarissa thinks, so no wonder she is 'embittered'. Clarissa does not hate *her*, she tells herself, but 'the idea of her'. The narrative implies that Clarissa experiences some guilt about her antipathy toward Kilman.

As her train of thought continues, Clarissa reflects that it is only circumstances which cause her feelings for Kilman: 'with another throw of the dice' it would all have been different. What irritates Clarissa is her own *conscience*: Kilman reminds her of the world's injustices and she is not so shallow that she can dismiss them from her mind entirely; but their insistence troubles her 'pleasure in beauty, in friendship, in being well' (after her illness), as well as her enjoyment of her nicely appointed house. So, it is not *her* that Clarissa hated but 'the idea of her': Kilman is a kind of totem for Clarissa. In just a few paragraphs, Woolf reveals aspects of Clarissa's character by way of her thoughts about Kilman.

Kilman then disappears from the narrative for about a hundred pages. By the time Richard Dalloway returns from Lady Bruton's lunch and asks Clarissa about 'our dear Miss Kilman', a reader knows a vast amount of detail about Clarissa: her past, her history with Peter, her losses, her pain, her illness, her youthful love for Sally, her self-image … but nothing more yet about Kilman. Richard leaves—off to his committee on the Armenians, or was it the Albanians?—and suddenly, 'for no reason she could discover', Clarissa feels 'desperately unhappy'. She examines this feeling and determines that her unhappiness is due to her being misunderstood and mocked about her parties by her husband and by Peter, who both 'laughed at her'.

Therefore, when Elizabeth comes in to see her mother, and Kilman waits outside on the landing, Clarissa is feeling particularly sensitive about being judged as frivolous, shallow—'a perfect hostess'. At this point the narration enters Kilman's consciousness for the first time, through a free indirect discourse that explains why she always wears the mackintosh that so bothers Clarissa: 'First, it was cheap; second, she was over forty ... She was poor'. Kilman judges Clarissa, as so many literary critics (and even some of Woolf's friends) judged her: 'the most worthless' kind of woman. Kilman thinks to herself that she has 'a perfect right to anything the Dalloways did for her'. She reveals to the reader her private pain. Learning that 'her brother had been killed' might be a clue as to how 'with another throw of the dice' Kilman and Clarissa could have found something in common, because Clarissa's sister had also been 'killed'. But, a reader might reflect, 'here was one room, there another', and people fail to know one another: 'communication is health, communication is happiness', but it so often does not take place.

Kilman's religious *conversion* has led her from envy to pity with regard to 'women like Clarissa'. And like Clarissa with regard to her, Kilman seems to hate 'the idea' of Clarissa: she 'pitied and despised' women like that. As Kilman is a symbol for Clarissa, so Clarissa is a symbol for Kilman. She exhibits a generalised class bitterness: 'But Miss Kilman did not hate Mrs Dalloway'. Do we remember that a hundred or so pages earlier we read that Clarissa did not hate Kilman, that it was 'the idea of her' she hated? Is Woolf perhaps helping us to see something by requiring us to be her 'accomplice' in reading the text, rather than telling us what we should think?

Kilman's emotions lead her to wish to dominate—we might say to 'force the soul' of Clarissa. Her version of religion promotes anger toward Clarissa: she is *better* than Clarissa, Kilman thinks. Clarissa senses this and is 'really shocked'. When Elizabeth, who has run up to her bedroom because she cannot stand the tension, returns, Clarissa softens: she 'would have liked to help'

Miss Kilman. As her daughter and Kilman leave for their shopping expedition, Clarissa laughs as she says goodbye; we do not know for certain *why* she laughs. Kilman, we will soon learn, assumes that Clarissa was laughing *at* her; but perhaps Clarissa was laughing at herself, realising how silly her feelings about Elizabeth and Kilman's closeness are. The 'monster' she imagined has dwindled to the merely human—shabby, unhappy, awkward.

Conversion, that clear enemy, is embodied in Kilman; to Clarissa, she is one of those who would destroy 'the privacy of the soul'. For her part, Kilman thinks Clarissa 'had insulted her': but had she? Just because Kilman *feels* laughed at does not make it true. But Kilman tells us that she feels self-conscious and ungainly, clumsy next to fashionable Clarissa. Her desire to be like Clarissa wrestles with her despising what Kilman imagines Clarissa's values to be. Is a reader supposed to agree with Kilman? Is the point not, perhaps, that Kilman is just as complex a character as Clarissa Dalloway, marked by ambivalence, by contradictions, by, in effect, humanity? For a critic who believes Woolf is an insufferable snob, a woman who, as Q. D. Leavis put it, would not know which end of the cradle to stir,[45] Kilman arrives as confirmation of those preconceptions. There is no reason, however, that Woolf's critical eye might not fall on people of all classes. There is no particular virtue in being poor.

What did Clarissa laugh at? Her own ridiculous feelings that Kilman is a 'monster'? We are immersed in Kilman's point of view as she goes through London streets with Elizabeth. We hear about her sexual loneliness at a time, after all, when the ratio of men to women, following the slaughter of the War, disfavoured women in the marriage market. She is a woman over forty with a large bald forehead and shabby clothes, and hair that won't look nice no matter how she does it: does this elicit sympathy for a woman who cannot compete with slender girls of the 1920s in their sheath dresses and elegant gloves? Kilman thinks that women 'like' Clarissa escape the agony she feels, but should a reader necessarily agree? (We are not told why, for example, Clarissa had her single child so relatively late in life.)

The free indirect discourse then merges into Elizabeth's consciousness at the tea room at the Stores: can Kilman *really* be hungry, she wonders. A shop assistant, we have been told by the narrator, thinks Kilman is 'mad' (because she buys a petticoat wildly at odds with the style she presents herself as having). Elizabeth thinks about how Kilman has made efforts to mentor her; how her mother gave Kilman flowers from Bourton; how Kilman cannot respond to this kindness and has no 'small talk'. Miss Kilman makes one 'feel so small', thinks Elizabeth. Kilman wishes to make Elizabeth hers 'absolutely and forever and then die'. The self-pitying words she blurts out make Elizabeth uncomfortable: 'people with parcels who despised her' *make* Kilman say these things, apparently. Is she not beginning to sound quite like mad Septimus?

In Westminster Abbey, after Elizabeth has escaped her clutches, Kilman is seen from another perspective, that of a Mr Fletcher. His view suggests that what Clarissa felt might not have been entirely due to her snobbery: he is 'a little distressed by the poor lady's disorder'. After Elizabeth's thoughts about Kilman as she gets on the 'pirate' bus, she disappears from the reader's view until later that evening, at the party, when she is brought back to our attention for the last time. Clarissa's once more glimpsing the painting on the landing where Kilman had waited that afternoon brings her back 'with a rush; Kilman her enemy. That was satisfying; that was real. Ah, how she hated her—hot, hypocritical, corrupt; with all that power; Elizabeth's seducer; the woman who had crept in to steal and defile (Richard would say, What nonsense!). She hated her: she loved her. It was enemies one wanted, not friends'.

Clarissa has just been thinking that the envy she assumes others feel—because the prime minister comes to her party—is hollow now, not satisfying as it once would have been. She has changed.

When she thinks that her friends must now seek her out because 'She was for the party!' is there a sense that her 'party' front is just another face she prepares, as she did earlier in the day when she looked into her dressing-table mirror? On this day of reflection, of the reappearance of those with whom she shared such profound experiences when she was eighteen, a day on which she has looked back on her life with the new perspective her serious illness has given her, the party no longer satisfies her. When she hears about the death of a young man, Clarissa responds in ways she might not have before. Would she say of Kilman she was one thing rather than another? If she can both hate and love Kilman, it is because Clarissa recognises her humanity in all its complexity. And after all, Woolf thought, 'one must dislike people in art without its mattering'.[46]

21 Mid-1950s Harcourt editions

Crossing borders

There are moments when the name 'Virginia Woolf' suddenly erupts into wider recognition, to circulate for a time in unexpected places before sinking down again. Such attention does not necessarily mean more people are reading her work: in the same way in which many people recognise 'to be or not to be' without having read *Hamlet*, or might talk about 'the unconscious' without having read Freud, so someone might respond to 'Virginia Woolf' with a quip such as 'no one's afraid of her any more' (or say, 'wasn't she insane?' or 'didn't she kill herself?') without having read a word she wrote. The movie version of Edward Albee's play *Who's Afraid of Virginia Woolf?* in 1966, starring Elizabeth Taylor and Richard Burton; Michael Holroyd's biography of Lytton Strachey in 1967–68; and Quentin Bell's biography of his aunt Virginia in 1972 are markers of such moments. Michael Cunningham's 1998 *The Hours* and its star-studded movie version in 2002 created waves whose ripples can still be discerned, and there is evidence to suggest these phenomena really did bring people to read Woolf for the first time, particularly *Mrs Dalloway* through its association with *The Hours*.

In the meantime, Woolf's fourth novel has thrummed along in university classrooms for nearly a century. At the University of California, Berkeley, where she taught from 1939 to 1978, the poet and critic Josephine Miles had her students read *Mrs Dalloway* alongside David Daiches' account of Woolf in his book *The Novel and the Modern World*. Daiches described *Mrs Dalloway* as 'constructed in terms of the two dimensions of space and time',[47] and represented Woolf's methods with ingenious diagrams. In 1947, a professor at the University of Wisconsin ordered 1,400 copies, whilst another at the University of Chicago placed an order for 800.[48] After 1945, *Mrs Dalloway* could reliably be found on any syllabus in the United States to do with modern English fiction, albeit often as a lesser example of what Joyce had achieved in *Ulysses*. That opinion would begin to change in the 1970s when new versions of Woolf were created by feminist readers. Many generations of American students read *Mrs Dalloway* in a paperback edition first published in 1981, with an insightful introduction by the novelist Maureen Howard. Woolf's achievement, wrote Howard, was 'heroic'.[49] In her own country, resistance in the universities derived from the long reach of dominant Leavisian readings that considered the world of Woolf's novels too constrained by her social class, rendered in 'tepid Bloomsbury prose'.[50] As F. R. Leavis's biographer put it, 'to be Leavisian was to be against Bloomsbury'.[51]

Outside the anglophone world, Woolf's reputation as a key modernist figure spread steadily before the Second World War in widening circles that began in Spain, Germany and France, and continued to ripple across continents. The records of Sylvia Beach's lending library at Shakespeare & Co. in Paris show that *Mrs Dalloway* (in English) was the most-borrowed of Woolf's titles (the American journalist Pauline Pfeiffer borrowed it in 1926 at the beginning of her relationship with Ernest Hemingway, whose second wife she would become the following year).[52] By 1930, the publication of *A Room of One's Own* had consolidated Woolf's 'reputation as a feminist public intellectual and novelist' in Australia, where a review in the Hobart *Mercury* of *The Voyage Out*, *Jacob's Room* and *Mrs Dalloway* acknowledged the challenges of her 'highly individual style' whilst praising her many innovations.[53] Woolf became a global literary figure, *Mrs Dalloway* but one facet of a complex legacy that had already begun to be created in her own lifetime.

In France, the first translation of *Mrs Dalloway* (by Simone David) appeared in 1929 with a preface by the popular novelist and biographer André Maurois. Maurois told the story of dropping by Birrell and Garnett's bookshop in Bloomsbury to ask what new works they could recommend. Francis Birrell gave him *Jacob's Room*, which he read with delight on his journey back to

Paris. After a quick biographical sketch of Woolf, Maurois places *Mrs Dalloway* in the context of her career so far. He poses the question that Woolf had asked herself when she began to think about *Jacob's Room* (although of course he could not have known this): was it possible to create at the length of a novel what she had achieved in short sketches such as 'The Mark on the Wall' and 'Kew Gardens'? In other words, could she make characters 'live' using such experimental narrative techniques? For all its great qualities, Maurois wrote, *Ulysses* was a failure (*échec*) as a novel, and Woolf knew that. Maurois believed that *Mrs Dalloway* was a victory, no less bold than *Ulysses* in its ambitions. Its simple plot belied how all of the past is contained in the present, how everyone in the great metropolis is linked by common emotions. In Maurois's judgement, Woolf, like Proust, had gone beyond impressionism with her vision of the beauty and grandeur of life contained in the simplest moment.

Maurois's preface first appeared in *Les Nouvelles Littéraires* in January 1929 as 'Première Rencontre avec Virginia Woolf'. Although a version of the 'Time Passes' section of *To the Lighthouse* was published in a French translation in a Paris-based journal, *Commerce*, in 1926, *Mrs Dalloway* was the first of her novels to appear in French. Maurois was unusual at the time in elevating it above Joyce's modernist masterpiece. Later in 1929, Louis Gillet (to whom Edmund Gosse had disparaged *Ulysses*) wrote in *La revue des deux mondes* that all Woolf's work bore the imprint of Joyce's genius, although with her refinement she had 'tamed the bear'.

Throughout the 1920s and 1930s articles and book chapters devoted to Woolf were published in Europe and in Latin America, often pairing her with modernist peers such as Joyce, Aldous Huxley and D. H. Lawrence. In addition to Floris Delattre's *Le roman psychologique*, published in France in 1932, a monograph on Woolf appeared that year in Germany, Ingeborg Badenhausen's *Die sprache Virginia Woolf: Ein Beitrag zur Stilistik Des Modernen*

22 French edition of *Mrs Dalloway*, 1929

Englischen Romans (Virginia Woolf's Language: A Contribution to the Stylistics of the Modern English Novel).[54] In 1928, a translation of *Mrs Dalloway* into German by Therese Muntzenbecher was published by Insel Verlag. Woolf had been pleased to receive an inquiry from Tauchnitz, who specialised in English editions for markets outside Britain and the USA, about both *The Common Reader* and *Mrs Dalloway*. Tauchnitz brought out an edition of *Mrs Dalloway* in 1929. Daniel Göske and Christian Weiß have explained how Woolf's reputation began to spread in Germany, despite an unpromising start:

> in the *Weltbühne* [World Stage], the radical and influential Berlin weekly, the British writer and musicologist Eric Walter White much preferred the 'cinematic' technique of Woolf's slender city novel to the 'prolonged massiveness' ('Langwierigkeit') of Joyce's *Ulysses* …. German reviewers followed suit. In the *Deutsche Allgemeine Zeitung* (Berlin), Kaethe Miethe called Woolf 'in all seriousness a poet' and *Mrs Dalloway* 'one of those rare books which teach you how to read. Slowly,

drop by drop, does the world it builds sink in'; and Thomas Mann's son Klaus later praised the book as a new type of novel, 'composed with an exactness that is masterly. It is nothing but a fugue, a fugue of interlocking fates, feelings, tones'.[55]

By January 1929 Insel Verlag was able to report that 1,380 copies of Muntzenbecher's translation had been sold.

There was particular interest in Woolf in Spain in the 1930s, with the translation of *Mrs Dalloway* into Catalan reflecting a burgeoning interest in experiments with the novel form among writers.[56] Alberto Lázaro has explained the central position of *Mrs Dalloway* in Spanish literary scholarship, with discussions of it 'vastly outnumbering those of any other novel'.[57] Many writers throughout the world, both before and immediately after the Second World War, regarded Woolf as a kind of paradigm of how fundamentally the novel could be reformed, opening up new possibilities for fiction even in languages whose structures did not find easy parallels to Woolf's. Translators continued to rise to those challenges with

23 German edition of *Mrs Dalloway*, 1955

24 German edition of *Mrs Dalloway*, 1964

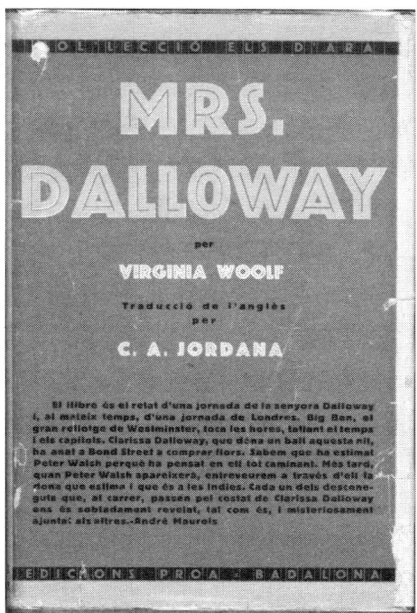

25 Catalan translation of *Mrs Dalloway*

very uneven results, and as time went on, new translations were made to replace the early ones.

Before returning to the story of *Mrs Dalloway* in English, it is worth looking at the novel's fate behind the Iron Curtain. It is well known now that Virginia and Leonard Woolf were on a secret list of intellectuals and writers to be rounded up after a Nazi invasion of England. She was officially banned in Germany as an enemy author in 1942.[58] Being seen as anti-fascist (as she was) might have made Woolf acceptable to the Communists who met in Moscow in 1934 for the Soviet Writers Congress, where Socialist-realism was declared to be the only desirable form for fiction, but modernist writers' treatment of reality was considered 'decadent'. A change in Woolf's standing in Communist countries occurred concurrently—and coincidentally—with the revision of her image that was the result of the women's movements in the USA and in Britain in the 1970s.

26 Bulgarian translation of *Mrs Dalloway*

The 1928 German translation of *Mrs Dalloway* was among the works by which Woolf was introduced to the post-Stalinist German Democratic Republic ('East Germany') in the late 1970s. As Wolfgang Wicht explains, such work had to be approved by the Ministry of Culture, which would review a scholar's recommendation commissioned by the publisher. To be successful, the recommendation would have to stress the novel's 'humanistic' tendencies, and point out that 'the writer had sympathies with the working class though belonging to an elite coterie'; also, that the narrative was 'a critique of capitalist alienation'.[59] To the probable astonishment of Woolf's antagonists who only see her as an 'elitist', Wicht cites reviews of the time 'stressing Woolf's criticism of English class bigotry' that appeared in such places as *Junge Welt* (Young World), the 'daily of the Socialist Youth Organization'.[60] It has not been unusual for readers unburdened by English class prejudice to 'hear' clearly the social critique in Woolf's fiction.

Even before their appearance in the GDR, Woolf's novels circulated in other Communist countries. Whereas the official line might have been that Woolf was a 'nihilistic' modernist, her works lived 'a different life among readers' behind the Iron Curtain who appreciated the liberating effects of her individualism.[61] In Communist Romania, the dictator Nicolae Ceaușescu allowed translations of writers such as Woolf in order to demonstrate that his country was independent of the Soviet Union. Adriana Varga surmises that contemporary Romanian interest in Woolf is 'arguably, the continuation of a process that began in 1968 with the publication of translations of *Orlando* and *Mrs Dalloway*'.[62] It was in the Soviet Union, of course, that the condemnation of modernist writers as decadent first emerged in the postwar period. In 1965, *Mrs Dalloway* was singled out by the critic Dilyara Zhantieva as the only one of Woolf's novels to protest, even if indirectly, against the 'brutal reality' of western authority. Zhantieva's article viewed

27 Livre de Poche edition of *Mrs Dalloway*, 1982

Septimus Warren Smith's madness as 'taking a stand against the callous and carefree bourgeoisie, the final word there being used as profanity by most Soviet literary critics'.[63]

Feminist revaluations

The Bloomsbury Group seemed 'dead and stinking' in England when Quentin Bell began his short book about them in 1967.[64] However, it was on the cusp of a revival. Across the Atlantic, a professor of English at Columbia University described her tentative introduction of the Bloomsbury Group to a graduate seminar in which a young Englishman 'accused them all of being shrill, arty, escapist, aristocratic and insufficiently talented (was *Mrs Dalloway*, after all, as great a book as *Ulysses*?)'.[65] Carolyn Heilbrun's 1968 article on the Bloomsbury Group began by pointing out 'how

like they were, when young, to the rebellious youth of today'.*
Heilbrun described those young people, 'seen almost anywhere in
the world today—their long hair and costumes making uneasy, in
both senses of the word, the immediate identification of gender', as
representing a 'new homage to androgyny'.[66] Her graduate student
admitted that his passionate antipathy toward Bloomsbury was
rooted in homophobia. It is important to bear in mind that only
a single American state (Illinois) had decriminalised homosexual
activity by 1968; in Britain homosexual acts in private between
consenting adults over the age of twenty-one were illegal until 1967
(and in Ireland until 1993).

Why is this relevant to *Mrs Dalloway*? Sally Seton and Clarissa
Dalloway's kiss did not draw the attention of the censors in 1925,
despite their zeal. In 1921, an amendment to the Criminal Law
Amendment Bill that would have made illegal 'acts of gross indecency between female persons' was quashed by the House of Lords.
The Conservative MP for Chatham, John Moore-Brabazon, would
have preferred the death sentence for lesbians, but the Lords
rejected the amendment on the grounds that attention to the very
existence of lesbianism (which they did not name) would 'lead to
unlooked to and evil results'. What is now seen unquestionably as
a particularly evocative description of orgasm in *Mrs Dalloway* was
not remarked upon by critics for decades. But that description—of
a 'tinge like a blush which one tried to check and then, as it spread,
one yielded to its expansion, and rushed to the farthest verge and
there quivered and felt the world come closer, swollen with some
astonishing significance, some pressure of rapture, which split its
thin skin and gushed and poured with an extraordinary alleviation
over the cracks and sores'—was singled out by Ellen Hawkes Rogat

---

* A point echoed recently by Nino Strachey: 'A family of choice, they created
ties of love that lasted a lifetime, embracing queerness, acknowledging difference, defying traditional moral codes'. *Young Bloomsbury*. John Murray,
2022, 4.

in the first published challenge to Quentin Bell's depiction in his biography of Woolf as sexually frigid:

> Erotic tone is unmistakable; sexual desire rises to the surface, crests and falls in explicit imagery. Her metaphors intensify rather than veil sexuality. Again, this is not the writing of a cold woman. Immersion in the experience, not a frightened escape, moves the language. Then why has this passage failed to correct the predominant impression of Woolf? Aside from the basic suspicion that Woolf's use of imagery signifies withdrawal from experience, it is also difficult for readers to accept homosexual overtones as valid sexual feelings. Here Woolf describes Clarissa Dalloway's response to women when 'she did undoubtedly then feel what men felt'.[67]

Rogat was one of the founders of the *Virginia Woolf Miscellany* in 1973, a newsletter 'for the common reader as well as the scholar' at a time when Woolf was being read 'with a new energy, intensity and sympathy', as the inaugural issue put it. At the time, she was writing a doctoral dissertation titled 'The Lifted Veil: Virginia Woolf and Women's Consciousness'.

For women who were trying in the 1970s to influence what was taught in universities, and, more importantly, *how* it was taught, Woolf's *A Room of One's Own* provided a 'set of questions, a way of asking them, a possible vision of what lay behind and beyond women's silence'.[68] Surveying the new feminist literary criticism in 1975, Elaine Showalter remarked on 'the extreme diversity of the current approaches to literature which involve women, sex roles, the family, or sexual politics in any of their permutations and combinations'.[69] In their groundbreaking book *The Madwoman in the Attic*, Sandra Gilbert and Susan Gubar argued that women's fiction was often 'palimpsestic, works whose surface designs conceal or obscure deeper, less accessible (and less socially acceptable) levels of meaning'.[70] Elizabeth Abel explained in an essay on *Mrs Dalloway* how 'the plot of female bonding began to vie repeatedly with the plot of heterosexual love' in fiction written in the 1920s.[71]

For a time Woolf became central to feminist literary criticism not only as a subject for analysis but also as a guide and inspiration. Showalter drew a picture of the Berg Collection of the New York Public Library 'filled day after day with women scholars from all over the world, each one raptly reading a volume of Woolf's unmistakable Florentine-paper-covered manuscript diary, each one locked into an encounter both intimate and collective, smiling a private smile over a joke between Virginia and herself'.[72] Indeed, Rogat wrote in the first number of the *Miscellany* about the 'pilgrimage' she made to the Berg to read Woolf's unpublished diaries and letters. Making her way through a throng of proselytisers gathered at the library steps each morning, she remembered Woolf's 'antagonism toward the world's egotistical fanatics who think that everyone should be badgered into submissive conversion'. Just in case the allusion to *Mrs Dalloway* was too subtle, Rogat reminded her readers of Woolf's anger at 'those who stamp their feet on others' souls'.[73]

The 1970s saw, in addition to Bell's biography, the beginning of the publication of Woolf's diary (eventually in six volumes) and of her letters, as well as the first edition of *Moments of Being*, a collection of previously unpublished autobiographical writings that included Woolf's fragmentary memoir 'A Sketch of the Past'.* In attempting 'to describe Virginia's madness from her point of view', Quentin Bell had drawn on *The Voyage Out* and *Mrs Dalloway* (as well as Leonard Woolf's account in *Beginning Again*), but *Moments of Being* provided Woolf's own record of traumatic events in her life, such as sexual abuse at the hands of her two half-brothers. From now on, Woolf would be a polarising figure in debates about incest, trauma, memory and women's testimony. This would lead, in time, to a recognition of her achievement in creating Septimus

---

* A revised edition of *Moments of Being* was published in 1985 after more drafts of 'A Sketch' were discovered at the British Library.

28 Spanish edition of *Mrs Dalloway*, 1975

Warren Smith as a figure who spoke to the concerns of generations blighted by other wars.

Another researcher who made her way to the Berg Collection in the 1970s was Stella McNichol, who was interested in the manuscripts of *Mrs Dalloway*. In the course of her work in that fabled archive, McNichol came across drafts of several short stories which she saw were related to the novel. McNichol arranged seven of these stories into a volume published as *Mrs Dalloway's Party* in 1973, numbering the stories as 'chapters' and arguing in her introduction to the slim volume that the form she had imposed on these manuscripts fit Woolf's 6 October 1922 plan in her writing notebook for a 'short book consisting of six or seven chapters'.[74] McNichol was criticised by other scholars at the time for muddying Woolf's composition processes, and also missing two other stories that were clearly related to the ones she had published.

When Woolf's *Complete Shorter Fiction* was published in 1983, the editor of that volume explained that when Woolf finished *Mrs Dalloway* she quickly began to write eight stories that were set at Clarissa Dalloway's party, beginning with 'The New Dress'. 'The New Dress' was published in the New York magazine *Forum* in 1927, and reprinted along with three other 'Dalloway' stories in *A Haunted House and Other Stories*, a collection put together by Leonard Woolf in 1944. 'Mrs Dalloway in Bond Street' and the unpublished 'Prime Minister' preceded *Mrs Dalloway*. Woolf came to think of the stories she wrote after the novel, still exploring the 'party consciousness', as a 'corridor' leading to another book. Unfortunately, publishers have sometimes either disregarded or been unaware of scholarship on Woolf, and the shape given by McNichol to the stories published as *Mrs Dalloway's Party* remained in print long after its shortcomings had been pointed out.

Fundamental to the second-wave women's movement was consciousness-raising through the sharing of stories. The importance of telling the stories of women's lives is central to Woolf's arguments in *A Room of One's Own*—'Anon.', she wrote there, 'was often a woman'. The mission she gives to the young women listening to her lecture is to give 'anonymous' a name. Clarissa's meditation when she feels herself disappearing in the morning crowd on Bond Street resonated with many women who were reflecting on their circumstances in a rapidly changing society. Clarissa feels

> unseen; unknown; there being no more marrying, no more having of children now, but only this astonishing and rather solemn progress with the rest of them, up Bond Street, this being Mrs Dalloway; not even Clarissa any more; this being Mrs Richard Dalloway.

Acknowledging the place *Mrs Dalloway* holds in 'feminist imagination', Sara Ahmed defines an 'outpouring of feminist sympathy for Mrs. Dalloway's predicament':[75] this was made possible only by the work of scholars who, beginning in the 1970s, talked back to those who had consigned Woolf to the category of minor lady novelist. In her short story 'Buckets of Blood', Tessa Hadley has a character, Hilary, helping her sister, Sheila, through a miscarriage when she is a student at Oxford. Hilary takes Sheila's bloodied sheets to the launderette and reads Woolf while she waits for the machine to finish. Hadley has explained that when her character 'reached for a cultural marker, to begin to find models of female identity that could save her from becoming her mother (or her sister?), it would inevitably be Woolf that she'd be guided towards' in 1972, when the story takes place.[76]

Paul Bailey, a novelist himself, wrote in 1973 that 'for all her talk of Mrs Brown, Virginia Woolf rarely persuades one of Clarissa Dalloway's existence. At her most interesting she is a snobbish, vain, repressed Lesbian who has dabbled in culture, but for the greater part of the novel she is only a shadow, poetically enshrined'. He was reviewing *Mrs Dalloway's Party* for *The Observer*, but took the opportunity to damn the novel. Although he allowed that Quentin Bell's biography was 'splendid', it had had the unfortunate effect, in his opinion, of making Woolf 'fashionable' amongst young people: 'It is time', wrote Bailey, 'that her dangerous influence came to an end'. Presumably, he felt no need to spell out in what the danger lay of reading Woolf, but the persistent association of this writer with an uncanny fear has been documented in great detail by Brenda Silver in *Virginia Woolf Icon*. By the centenary of Woolf's birth in 1982, those who wrote about her work and celebrated her life were characterised by Helen Dudar as a 'cult'.[77] Dudar was unlikely to have known that she echoed *The Literary Digest International Book Review* of May 1925, where the author of *Mrs Dalloway* was described as 'one of the most expert performers among the newly "arrived" British writers, with a large enough body of admirers to form something of a cult'.

Trauma

As discourses of trauma have become pervasive over the last forty years, those who teach *Mrs Dalloway* may have noticed that young people find Septimus Warren Smith a more 'relatable' character than Clarissa. This is not to say that Clarissa's doubts, her struggles with the past and with her identity do not continue to resonate, but the traumatised veterans of wars around the globe, as well as the traumatised residents of cities struck by terrorist attacks, offer contemporary 'doubles' of Woolf's creation. Septimus exemplifies 'not only the psychological injuries suffered by victims of severe trauma, such as those endured by soldiers in combat, but also the need for survivors to give meaning to their suffering in order to recover from post-traumatic stress disorder', in the words of one critic.[78] Furthermore, the way that Woolf's free indirect discourse allows readers access into what Septimus experiences 'mimics the trauma survivor's perception of time'.[79]

In 1980, the third edition of the *Diagnostic and Statistical Manual of Mental Disorders* included post-traumatic stress disorder (PTSD) for the first time. American veterans of the war in Vietnam had lobbied for several years for recognition of PTSD, a circumstance that in some ways echoed the situation immediately following the First World War when the British Parliament established its Committee of Inquiry into 'shell-shock'. The 1980s also witnessed the onset of a flood of books about sexual abuse and incest that informed the context of Louise DeSalvo's *Virginia Woolf: The Impact of Childhood Sexual Abuse on Her Life and Work* in 1989. One of the most influential of these was Judith Lewis Herman's *Trauma and Recovery*—subtitled 'The Aftermath of Violence, from Domestic Abuse to Political Terror'—in which she explicitly alluded to a famous passage from Woolf's *Three Guineas*. Herman's stated intent was to 'restore connections' between the public and private worlds, between the individual and community, between men and women. It is a book about commonalities between rape survivors and combat veterans, between battered women and political prisoners, between the survivors of vast concentration camps created by tyrants who rule nations and the survivors of small, hidden concentration camps created by tyrants who rule their homes.[80]

Mrs Dalloway is barely mentioned in DeSalvo's controversial book, warranting only a passing mention of Clarissa's strained relationship with her daughter in a chapter on adolescence, but it became part of a wave of attention in the 1990s to sexual abuse as a paradigm for women's oppression. The figure of Woolf as a survivor of incest caused elements of her life story to be blended with other narratives that sought to establish that the sexual abuse of girls and women was, as Herman argued, traumatic in ways that shared *structural* similarities with the psychological experiences of combat veterans. Several novels of the past twenty or so years that demonstrate some degree of relationship to *Mrs Dalloway* are set against a background of traumatic violence, or its threat. Septimus's terrified question, 'The world has raised its whip; where will it descend?', echoes loudly in the twenty-first century.

Part V

Mrs Dalloway's legacies

Like its protagonist's sense of her own life, *Mrs Dalloway* has 'spread ever so far', carried through the years on the breath of thousands of readers, mingling with uncountable other stories, resonating in myriad ways with individual experiences and memories. 'Influence' is a treacherous word, too limiting, too blunt to capture the ways that writers have woven their readings of Woolf's novel into their own creations, deliberately or unconsciously. The novel continues to travel widely—new Arabic translations were published in Syria in 1994, in Lebanon in 1998; three Polish feminist writers published works inspired by *Mrs Dalloway* in 2012 alone.[1] New editions in English seem to appear almost monthly. The novel has been likened to 'an invitation to a party', as if demanding a response, a return again and again to revise or reshape its features, to add one's own take, to contribute to the conversation.[2]

Many novels have been written that bear some degree of relation to *Mrs Dalloway*. Elizabeth Abel has identified perhaps the earliest echo in Nella Larsen's *Passing* (1929), when Irene Redfield wanders the streets of Harlem '*long after she had ordered the flowers which had been her excuse for setting out*'.[3] Whether the relation to Woolf's novel is explicitly acknowledged by an author or only assumed by readers or critics, such works create a rich legacy, especially in fiction written since the 1960s. For writers in the post-9/11, post-pandemic, post-George Floyd era, it has often been the trauma and anxiety coursing through *Mrs Dalloway* that is refracted in their own work. The framework of a single day—not, of course, unique to *Mrs Dalloway*—sometimes provides nothing more than a structure within which a reader might detect some Woolfian resonances, whereas in other instances it is deployed in fully realised homage. Sometimes all it takes is a self-reflecting woman and a party to lead critics to comparisons with *Mrs Dalloway*, as is the case with Natasha Brown's *Assembly*.[4] Lost men experiencing some kind of mid-life crisis (as in John Lanchester's *Mr Phillips* or James Hynes's *Next*) or women confronting unsettling memories from their youth (as in Asali Solomon's *The Days of Afrekete* or Zadie Smith's *NW*) might be viewed as existing to some extent in updated versions of the world imagined by Woolf.

These contemporary works can change how we 'see' *Mrs Dalloway* when writers emphasise what has been most relevant or useful in it for their own concerns. Perhaps *Mrs Dalloway* has been so generative because it invites readers, if not to complete the 'story', at least to participate in its creation. But *Mrs Dalloway* can never really be completed: 'For there she was' continues to be interpreted differently by every reader, Clarissa being 'there' only for that moment. Then we go back to the beginning and recreate the moment differently.

'Books continue each other'

By the 1990s, Woolf had become synonymous with 'the woman writer'. She had chafed at the idea of being pigeonholed as 'one of our leading female novelists',[5] but despite her admonition in *A Room of One's Own* that it is 'fatal for anyone who writes to think of their sex', her global reputation by the late twentieth century was very much entangled with the persona of spokesperson for a particular kind of second-wave feminism. Eighty years after the publication of *A Room* (and half a century after Simone de Beauvoir's *The Second Sex*), according to Rachel Cusk this identification was no longer tenable: 'It may be that today's woman writer doesn't have much to do with the concept of "women's writing". Feminism as a cultural and political crisis is seen to have passed. ... Were a woman writer to address her sex, she would not know who or what she was addressing'.[6] Despite the plausibility of Cusk's claim, the ways in which *Mrs Dalloway* has been refracted, adapted, reworked and echoed in fiction demonstrates that, with some exceptions, it remains usually within the ambit of 'women's writing' about women's lives.

As an example, in Kate Walbert's 'Sick Chicks', one of the linked stories that make up her novel *Our Kind*, a group of well-heeled women gather for a book group in a Connecticut hospice early in the twenty-first century to discuss *Mrs Dalloway*. Though they were young married women in the 1950s, the book does not speak to them. Mrs William Lowell is baffled by the lack of a plot. Cynthia Patrick loves it, and Bebe McShane is fascinated by Woolf's handling of time, but the overall mood of the group is 'at best confusion, overlaid by a thick quilt of boredom'.[7] The group leader, Viv, who chose the book, despairs. Another of the women, Betsy Croninger, says that Woolf's description of the sound of Big Ben makes her think 'of the word *cancer*. Musical at first, then irrevocable'.[8] Clearly, for this group, the 'seven ages of woman' represented in *Mrs Dalloway*, from Elizabeth to ancient Miss Helena Parry, do not resonate with their own experience.[9]

It would be possible to write a book about the many descendants of *Mrs Dalloway*.* From the pastiche of David Lodge's *The British Museum Is Falling Down* (1965) to twenty-first century

---

* Indeed, Monica Latham has done just that, though by now a second volume may be warranted: *A Poetics of Postmodernism and Neomodernism: Rewriting Mrs Dalloway*. Palgrave Macmillan, 2015.

poetic meditations on loss, grief and memory such as Gail Jones's *Five Bells* (2011), *Mrs Dalloway* is a continuing presence in contemporary fiction. The novel had a walk-on part in Nancy Mitford's *Love in a Cold Climate* when Lady Montdore asks Fanny Wincham 'Who is this Virginia Woolf you mentioned to me?' Because she declares that she prefers 'books about society people, not being myself a highbrow', Fanny recommends she read *Mrs Dalloway*, 'a fascinating book about a society person'. A week later, Lady Montdore has to confess that the book was so boring that she 'never got to the society person you told me of'.[10]

Clarissa herself appears in David Lodge's comic tale, in which he parodies several modern novelists. Adam Appleby is on his way to the British Museum when an 'expectant hush' falls over the traffic which is being held up by a policeman. To signal just what he is up to, Lodge continues: 'From nearby Westminster, Mrs Dalloway's clock boomed out'.[11] The crowd begins to speculate about what royal personage is causing the traffic jam (it is in fact the Beatles), and as it begins once more to flow, Adam is suddenly startled by 'an old lady, white-haired and wrinkled' waiting to cross the road. At the Museum he tells a friend he has had 'a queer experience ... I met Mrs Dalloway grown into an old woman'.[12]

Zadie Smith's quip that 'when you have London in a novel you don't need much else'[13] opens onto a vista that takes in works set on a single day in that city as different as Smith's own *NW*, Ian McEwan's *Saturday*, Rachel Cusk's *Arlington Park* and John Lanchester's *Mr Phillips*, all of which share some family resemblance to *Mrs Dalloway*. Lanchester has said that he had not read Woolf's novel, but *Mr Phillips* exemplifies how it circulates in the cultural atmosphere nonetheless. The object of Mr Phillips's desire is a television personality named Clarissa Colingford whom he spots from his seat on a bus as she walks past Harrods. Mr Phillips disembarks to follow her, bringing to mind Peter Walsh on Cockspur Street. The bus route itself seems to implicate *Mrs Dalloway*:

> The bus went through all the glamorous parts of London. First it went down past the Trocadero, down Haymarket, then back up Regent Street to Piccadilly, then along past the Royal Academy, past the Ritz, past Green Park, round Hyde Park Corner, and along Knightsbridge. By and large these were all parts of London that Mr Phillips never visited. They belonged to other kinds of people.[14]

A further Woolfian echo might be heard when Mrs Phillips contemplates death: 'The awfulness of nothing. To lose all this'.[15]

Although London's cartography is an essential aspect of Smith's *NW*, as it is of *Mrs Dalloway*, it functions primarily as a contrast between the two novels because their respective worlds have little else in common. Smith's Caldwell is an invented housing estate, but her characters traverse the same London as Woolf's, albeit on very different routes. Like Solomon's Liselle and Selena in *The Days of Afrekete*, *NW* revolves around the relationship of two women, Leah and Natalie, whose lives diverged but whose shared past retains a hold on them in the present. Leah and Natalie's reunion is set in motion by the murder of Felix, a young man whose psychological struggles echo in a different register those of Septimus. Felix and Septimus do intersect on the map of London. Septimus crosses through the junction of Oxford and Regent Streets after his consultation with Dr Bradshaw, and Felix goes through the same intersection with a man selling a vintage car. 'London's map', as Amy Elkins explains, 'becomes something networked—between characters within these novels but also across them'.[16]

Two circadian novels that are centred, like Lanchester's *Mr Phillips*, entirely within the consciousness of a male character, but whose authors make explicit their work's relationship to *Mrs Dalloway*, are Christopher Isherwood's *A Single Man* and James Hynes's *Next*. Isherwood—who knew Woolf well and was one of the Hogarth Press's best-selling authors—re-read *Mrs Dalloway* as he prepared to write *A Single Man*. His novel relates the last day in the life of George, a recently bereaved gay Englishman who teaches at a university in California. Isherwood described *Mrs Dalloway* as 'prose written with perfect pitch, a perfect ear. You could perform it with instruments'. He wondered if he could write something 'like that and keep it within the nature of my own style'.[17]

A very different creation is Kevin Quinn, the dissatisfied editor in Hynes's *Next* who lands in Austin, Texas, for a job interview on a day when the United States is on edge after a coordinated rocket attack on six European cities the previous week. Flashbacks throughout the day bring memories to Kevin's mind of failed relationships, his thwarted or fulfilled sexual desires and confrontations at his job. Hynes announces his debt to Woolf in two epigraphs: her 1915 diary entry about an exploding tyre prompting fears of an imminent attack, and the passage in *Mrs Dalloway* where Clarissa feels 'that it was very, very dangerous to live even one day'.

Several recent novels with an acknowledged relation to *Mrs Dalloway* borrow from it the figure of a woman planning a party when the world might burst into flame. Asali Solomon has referred to the mood of preparation for 'a dinner party at the end of the world' as one resonance between her novel and Woolf's.[18] A similar idea occurred to Anna Korkeakivi while she wrote her first novel, *An Unexpected Guest*. *Mrs Dalloway* provided a model for her story involving the planning of a party against a background of global conflict.[19] Yet another version of today's dis-ease can be found in Deborah Levy's *August Blue*, which was written 'in conversation ... with a generalized contemporary anxiety'.[20] Levy has said that she was 'looking for a narrative for the end of the world': in *August Blue* Elsa, the virtuoso pianist who has sabotaged her career, encounters her double in a narrative haunted by *Mrs Dalloway*.

Monica Ali's bestowing the name 'Mr Dalloway' on her character Chanu's boss in *Brick Lane* allows us, the critic Susan Stanford Friedman has argued, to see that novel as a 'cultural translation' of *Mrs Dalloway*. Ali transposes to her society of Bangladeshis in London such familiar Woolfian elements as 'issues of masculinity and social standing, motifs of depression and suicide, and mysteries of human character'.[21] *Brick Lane* is a different novel for someone who has read *Mrs Dalloway* than it will be for someone who has not read it. The resonances of shapes and patterns, motifs and incidents, across these two very different works provide yet another example of how Woolf's novel continues to be recycled in new idioms, new contexts.

Despite its epigraph from *To the Lighthouse*, Miranda Darling's *Thunderhead* is overtly indebted to *Mrs Dalloway*, not least in the name of the woman whose first-person narrative recounts the events of a day during which she is preparing a dinner party—Winona Dalloway. In this tour de force, Darling merges Woolf's doubles into a single character: although Winona shares many of Clarissa's characteristics, the extremity of her anxieties also recalls Septimus's trauma. Winona wakes in the morning with a racing heart because she is gripped by fear, by uncertainty. She has a heart problem from which she has 'grown paler', and experiences 'the relentless heat of the sun' as she goes from appointments with a cardiologist and a psychiatrist to other errands, such as buying flowers for the party. Her Australian suburb vibrates with a sense of ever-present danger: tanks appear in the streets at the opening and close of the school day, and as she prepares dinner she hears on the radio that a suicide bomber 'has detonated himself in a market'. We learn that her mental anguish dates to the Lockerbie bombing of 1988, but her situation is exacerbated by the menace of her controlling husband, whom she will escape at the end of the day, taking their two young sons with her into the night.

The above are but a few examples of the many ways in which writers have refashioned and reimagined elements of *Mrs Dalloway*—its structure, its mood, its themes—in a world where the anxieties and fears of Clarissa, as well as the trauma and terrors of Septimus, have become common psychological currency. Towards the end of summer 2024, filming wrapped up on an adaptation of Tatiana de Rosnay's novel *Les fleurs de l'ombre* ('Flowers of Darkness'), in which Clarissa Katsef is assisted by an artificial intelligence program called Dalloway to write her next book. The fertility of *Mrs Dalloway* in the imaginations of other artists shows no signs of abating. What Woolf hoped her novel would achieve continues to be realised over and over again in multiple languages, multiple modes: to 'criticise the social system'; to show the world 'seen by the sane & the insane side by side'; as well as to celebrate 'life, London, this moment'.

Adaptation

It is fair to say that familiarity with the opening sentence of *Mrs Dalloway* owes more now to Michael Cunningham than to Virginia Woolf (just as the currency of the name 'Virginia Woolf' once owed more to Edward Albee than to her). 'Buying the—[fill in the blank]—herself' has become a meme, an update for the social media age of that other catchphrase initiated by Woolf: 'A—[fill in the blank]—of one's own'.* In terms of commercial success, *The Hours* has eclipsed other fictions written in the wake of *Mrs Dalloway*, its influence multiplied in untold ways by the star power of its movie version. In 2016, when the *New York Times Book Review* commissioned US-based Nigerian novelist Chimamanda Ngozi Adichie to write a short story about that year's election, her opening line made plain the cultural capital enjoyed by *Mrs Dalloway*: 'Melania decided to order the flowers herself'.

---

* On 'X' from menswear writer Derek Guy: 'pretending im mrs dalloway walking home with flowers as I carry eight family sized bags of jalapeno kettle chips for dinner'. @dieworkwear 10 March 2024.

Twenty-five years after *The Hours* was published, an article on the BBC Culture website described it as 'the book that changed how we see Virginia Woolf'. If Edward Albee's play, and subsequent film adaptation, had brought the name 'Virginia Woolf' to circulate in the cultural imagination of the 1960s, an era riven by profound social upheaval, Cunningham's novel, and later movie adaptation, shifted those former associations to resonate with the concerns of another time. *The Hours* had an enormous and continuing impact on Woolf's cultural presence, as well as on sales of *Mrs Dalloway*. It also spawned what might be regarded as grandchildren of Woolf's novel, as writers incorporated Cunningham's response to Woolf into their own fiction.

Some examples of this phenomenon include Anna Solomon's *The Book of V*, whose flap copy promises that it will appeal to fans of *The Hours* and of Lauren Groff's *Fates and Furies*. Solomon, who has spoken of how she closely observed Cunningham's methods of using *Mrs Dalloway*, follows three intertwined stories of women, in the era of the Old Testament's Book of Esther, 1970s Washington DC and twenty-first-century Brooklyn, New York. Vee and Lily are both preparing parties in the course of the day on which their stories are set, and the Biblical Esther also is preparing for a grand event at which she will be presented to the king.

A more direct incorporation of *The Hours* occurs in Ann Packer's *Songs Without Words*. Women who have enjoyed discussing Cunningham's novel, and then the movie, in their book group in the late 1990s, reassemble at a theatre to watch a play by one of the group's members, Miranda, who believes that fictional characters are always aspects of their creators: 'What had Miranda been saying? ... Mad Septimus Smith and all the characters of literature ... they *were* their makers, painful parts of their makers'. In the lobby after the performance someone is overheard saying they wanted the Woolf on stage to meet Mrs Dalloway.

In Elina Hirvonen's *When I Forgot* (translated from the Finnish by Douglas Robinson) the main character, Anna, deals with her brother's mental illness as well as the post-traumatic stress disorder of her boyfriend's father, a veteran of the war in Vietnam. The story is set against the backdrop of the terrorist attacks of 11 September 2001 (events that occurred between the publication of Cunningham's novel and the release of the movie version). At a café, Anna reads *The Hours* and reflects on Woolf's suicide, echoing *Mrs Dalloway*: 'This moment in April. This moment, she has thought, and stroked the book's surface. How sad if someone were to kill herself without knowing that moments like this exist'.

Just months before *The Hours* was published, a film adaptation of *Mrs Dalloway* was released, directed by Marleen Gorris with a screenplay by Eileen Atkins. It received a glowing review from Andrew Sarris, who wrote in *The Observer* that 'every member of the cast down to the tiniest bit player projects the authority and confidence only British ensembles seem consistently capable of managing'. Reviewing the film for the *New York Times*, Edward Rothstein noted its affinities with other 1990s films of novels, such as *Remains of the Day* and *The Wings of the Dove*, that in his view reflected the time's 'dismay and bewilderment, loss and disorientation, expectation and uncertainty'.[22] We are, he claimed, Elizabeth Dalloway's grandchildren, living at a time of unsettling cultural and political change. Gorris and Atkins's *Mrs Dalloway* was, in fact, a quite conventional period film. Its own production notes described it as 'a romantic drama with deep psychological insight into the world of urban English society in the summer of 1923'. Aside from some reorganisation of the novel's timeline and the direct representation of what is conveyed through memories—for example, the opening scene shows Septimus on an Italian battlefield in 1918, crying out 'Evans! Don't come!'—the film stays fairly close to the outline of the novel's bare plot, using voiceover for Clarissa's innermost thoughts as she walks on Bond Street.

Several of the principals had never read Woolf before being engaged on the film. Even Eileen Atkins, whose one-woman show of *A Room of One's Own* and performance in her play *Vita & Virginia* had already closely identified her with Woolf, said that she assumed Woolf 'was gloomy and difficult to read' before she was approached with the adaptation of *A Room*.[23] Vanessa Redgrave, who plays the Clarissa of 1923, also only began to read Woolf when she appeared as Vita Sackville-West in Atkins's play (subsequently coming to believe 'she's on the level of Shakespeare—she's a genius'). Natascha McElhone, who portrays young Clarissa at Bourton, also 'had never read any Virginia Woolf before taking the role but immediately fell in love with the novel'. The actors recognised that Woolf was far better known in the United States than in Britain. Despite its Dutch, feminist director, *Mrs Dalloway* was a very English production, with familiar actors such as Rupert Graves, playing Septimus. Graves prepared by immersing himself in First World War literature and talking to psychiatrists who worked with PTSD sufferers, as well as delving into the literature about Woolf's own madness. Robert Hardy, well known from the popular television series *All Creatures Great and Small* and several roles as an irascible paternalistic figure with an underlying goodness, portrays William Bradshaw with none of that sense of 'evil' discerned by Clarissa.

A producer of the film, Stephen Bayly, spoke about its intentional focus on the story of a woman who is reflecting on the course her life has taken due to choices she made some thirty years earlier: 'Everyone can relate to Mrs. Dalloway and the question, "What have I done with my life?" Everyone can look back at crossroads and decisions that have not worked out exactly as planned'. The realist mode, the use of voiceover and flashbacks (to Bourton) and the transformation of Clarissa's party into a dance all contributed to the sense that Woolf's novel was a rather conventional romantic tale, in effect a marriage plot worthy of Austen.

Atkins has spoken of how her role as one of the creators of the period drama *Upstairs, Downstairs*, which takes place between 1903 and 1930, gave her insight into the time in which *Mrs Dalloway* is set. Her *Mrs Dalloway* led (inevitably) to a reissue of Woolf's novel with Vanessa Redgrave and Natascha McElhone on the cover. It also prompted a new Japanese translation by Ai Tanji. At first-run showings of the movie at Tokyo's iconic Iwanami Hall cinema, a travel agency distributed pamphlets advertising tours to England where participants could experience 'the Manor House life' and partake in flower arranging and afternoon tea. From late 1998 until early 1999 'about 500 women over 40, most of whom had seen the film, joined the tour'.[24]

The origin story of Michael Cunningham's discovery of *Mrs Dalloway*, which he has told wittily many times in versions that vary only in small details, involves a challenge to his callow teenaged self from the 'pirate queen' of his California high school:

> I found myself standing next to her, and I thought, "Uh oh, uh oh … Think fast, be suave, say something that will make her love you forever." So I said something that I thought then—and I think today—was very winning, about the poetry of Bob Dylan and Leonard Cohen. She was kind to me. She sucked in her entire Marlboro in one drag, but the ash didn't fall, and exhaled an immense cloud of smoke, and said, "Well, yes, they're very good, but how do you feel about T. S. Eliot and Virginia Woolf?"
> Now, I wasn't completely illiterate—I had heard of T. S. Eliot and Virginia Woolf, and I knew Virginia Woolf was very tall and insane and lived in a lighthouse and jumped in the ocean, but I never expected I'd have to read either one of them.[25]

Mrs Dalloway turned out to be as memorable for Cunningham as a first kiss. He has spoken often of Woolf's novel in terms of music—that he considered what it does with prose to be akin to what Jimi Hendrix did with his guitar; that his own celebrated novel *The Hours* relates to *Mrs Dalloway* in the way 'a jazz musician might play improvisations on a great piece of music'. His first idea for what would become *The Hours* was to have been a rewriting of *Mrs Dalloway* for the contemporary moment, but he abandoned that plan for a more complex response to Woolf's art. Cunningham has said that his initial impulse was to write 'a book about reading a book. About how a book could matter to someone as much as a love affair'.[26]

The Hours opens with a 'Prologue' wherein the reader watches as Woolf walks to her suicide in the River Ouse. It includes a transcription (preserving the line breaks) of a letter she left for Leonard on the mantelpiece at Monk's House. Turning the page after the prologue, one might notice the book's headers. On the left-hand page is 'The Hours', and on the right 'Mrs. Dalloway', the title of the first of those sections that will alternate among the three women a single day of whose lives Cunningham's narrative follows. The three narrative strands follow Clarissa Vaughan, nicknamed 'Mrs. Dalloway' by her friend Richard; 'Mrs. Brown', the Los Angeles housewife Laura Brown in 1949, who is reading *Mrs Dalloway*; and 'Mrs. Woolf', Virginia Woolf in Richmond in 1923, writing the novel that inspired Cunningham's own. The page headers at the start of the main narrative—'The Hours'/'Mrs. Dalloway'—create an image of the two novels mirroring one another, or even speaking to one another, across a divide of space and time, generations and geography.

Cunningham redeploys elements from *Mrs Dalloway* into the different contexts and for the unique purposes of his own narrative. When Richard Brown tells the eighteen-year-old Clarissa Vaughan that she has all the makings of a 'good suburban wife',[27] this is Peter Walsh damning Clarissa Dalloway as a 'perfect hostess', but Cunningham's Richard is not Woolf's Peter.* Woolf's Sally

---

* There is perhaps an autobiographical Easter egg to be discovered by those who know Cunningham's anecdote, when Richard refers to Clarissa's 'pirate-girl veneer'.

Seton appearing three decades past her youthful rebelliousness at Clarissa's party as the wife of an industrialist and mother of 'five enormous boys' is replaced by Cunningham with a Sally who produces an interview programme on public television and lives with Clarissa as her life partner in early twenty-first-century New York. The kiss between Richard and Clarissa, two queer characters, echoes the kiss between Sally and Clarissa in Woolf's novel. Kisses become a leitmotif in *The Hours* similar to roses in *Mrs Dalloway* (as do clocks and mirrors). Such reimagining is not confined only to the 'Mrs. Dalloway' sections of *The Hours*. When Laura Brown kisses and holds her neighbour, Kitty, who has just divulged her cancer diagnosis, she thinks, 'This is how a man feels, holding a woman',[28] an echo of Clarissa's reflection on her own feelings about women. Throughout *The Hours*, Cunningham uses ingredients from *Mrs Dalloway* to concoct a very different dish than that served by Woolf.

Since the success of *The Hours*, Cunningham has come to be regarded by publishers as something of an authority on Woolf. In his introduction to a Modern Library reprint of *The Voyage Out*, he comments on Woolf's 'tea-table delicacy' around sex: 'While Woolf was fully aware of the power of sexuality she had little interest in going into its particulars'.[29] Strangely, Cunningham sees Richard Dalloway's forcing a kiss on Rachel Vinrace in this first of Woolf's novels as the beginning and end of her recognition of 'the physically violent possibilities between women and men': the child Rose Pargiter's experience in *The Years* of a man exposing himself and stepping towards her as he unbuttons his fly, and the brutal rape of a young woman by soldiers in *Between the Acts* escape his attention. The other 'major sexual episode' in Woolf is, for Cunningham, Sally's kissing Clarissa. He notes that the two kisses both involve 'one of the Dalloways, those emblems of all that Woolf found terrible and compelling in English society', and describes Clarissa in *Mrs Dalloway* as 'more undone by the experience of being kissed' than is Rachel in *The Voyage Out* (this despite her ensuing nightmares of being pursued by 'barbarian men'[30]). For Woolf's Clarissa, in Cunningham's reading, Sally's kiss implies 'a fleeting promise, lost almost as soon as found, that runs to depths far greater than those implied by questions of hetero- versus homosexuality'.[31]

Adaptations refract their source texts in ways that can sometimes bring into the foreground elements hitherto buried or unnoticed. The many writers who have drawn inspiration from *Mrs Dalloway*, either simply as a model for a circadian narrative or in more complex relationships with Woolf's explorations of consciousness, reflect telling aspects of how her novel circulates in readers' imaginations at different times. Early interest in Woolf's methods often sought to determine how she provided 'unity' to her complex narrative, with its disruptions of memory and strange intimations of connection among its characters. This interest in pattern and in psychology, which dominated critical readings from the 1960s into the 1970s, gave way to more political interpretations of the novel, especially the politics of gender, as feminist criticism came to the fore in the 1980s. As more information about Woolf's life became available, a fuller picture of the genesis and development of *Mrs Dalloway* emerged. For lesbian-feminist critics of the 1970s and 1980s, for example, attention to the kiss bestowed by Sally upon Clarissa had tended to obscure other aspects of Clarissa's passionate relations with her friend. When Clarissa remembers how she would repeat to herself 'She is beneath this roof', thrilled by Sally's proximity at Bourton, Woolf lends her a feeling identical to her own about her early infatuation with Madge Vaughan, the eldest daughter of John Addington Symonds. Woolf recalled how she would stand in the night nursery at Hyde Park Gate 'saying to myself "At this moment she is actually under this roof"' when Madge came to stay.[32]

In the 'Mrs. Dalloway' parts of *The Hours*, Cunningham illuminates aspects of *Mrs Dalloway* that had become familiar in scholarly readings of the novel since the 1980s. Among the few sources he lists is a single work of literary criticism, Joseph Allen Boone's *Libidinal Currents*. There Cunningham would have read Boone's analysis of the passage in *Mrs Dalloway* that leads to a description of orgasmic ecstasy, when Clarissa reflects on how she had 'failed' her husband through the lack of 'something central which permeated; something warm which broke up surfaces and rippled the cold contact of man and woman, or of women together. For *that* she could dimly perceive'. Boone writes, 'An immense psychological and narrative weight is brought to bear on Woolf's italicized word'.[33] The same-sex love that is so vital a part of both Clarissa and Septimus in Woolf's novel is given more prominence by Cunningham through his tender exploration of Clarissa Vaughan's and Richard Brown's lives, Clarissa's memories of their emotional, and briefly sexual, entanglement coursing through her mind as she prepares a party in his honour.

The AIDS crisis replaces the First World War as the source of trauma and suffering in the 'Mrs. Dalloway' sections of *The Hours*. Just as Woolf subtly incorporated contemporary elements that would have been at the forefront of her 1920s readers' minds, so Cunningham has his Clarissa allude to the insistent presence of AIDS in late twentieth-century New York.* Clarissa tells Richard's former lover, Louis, that he 'was a little too far gone for the protease inhibitors to help him the way they're helping some people'.[34] Among those being helped is Evan, the young lover of Walter Hardy (Cunningham's echo of Woolf's Hugh Whitbread), whom

---

* A report in the *New York Times* in December 1993 of a presidential shopping expedition on Fifth Avenue drew upon *Mrs Dalloway*'s juxtaposition of power and powerlessness in its description of a 'car with darkened windows and the flags fluttering' which stirred wonder in a crowd of 'ordinary people' brought to a standstill. After the president's car had moved on and the crowd dispersed, the reporter lingered. He noticed a young man lying on the pavement, a cardboard sign on his chest, 'illegible in the fading light' but most likely saying 'Homeless' or 'AIDS' ('Shopping').

Clarissa has encountered earlier on her way to buy flowers: 'How can she help resenting Evan and all the others who got the new drugs in time; all the fortunate ("fortunate" being, of course, a relative term) men and women whose minds had not yet been eaten into lace by the virus'.[35] This aspect of the continuity between *Mrs Dalloway* and *The Hours* was remarked upon in a review by Christopher Lane. Both novels seemed to him to be asking, 'How can we endure such challenges to our humanity? ... And should literature try to protect us from these difficulties? Can it teach us how we might outlast them?' At 'a time when much of our community is experiencing a similar kind of numbness', Lane continued, Cunningham depicted an 'aftershock' similar to that which Woolf had shown gripping postwar English society in his comparison of the AIDS epidemic 'to the haunting afterlife of military conflict, "as if the war were still on"'.[36]

The Hours won the Pulitzer Prize in 1999, beating out Russell Banks's *Cloudsplitter* and Barbara Kingsolver's *The Poisonwood Bible*. Even before it won the prestigious prize, the novel had been optioned by the producer Scott Rudin, who then approached David Hare to write a screenplay. The release of Hare and director Stephen Daldry's movie adaptation of Cunningham's novel in 2002, with three Hollywood stars portraying the three women, led to an immense amount of attention paid not only to Cunningham's novel but also to the novel that haunted it. This attention intensified when the film received nine nominations at the 2003 Oscars, where Nicole Kidman won the award for Best Actress for her portrayal of Virginia Woolf. Kidman won other accolades, as did Meryl Streep as Clarissa Vaughan, and Julianne Moore as Laura Brown. Both the film and the novel had an immediate effect on sales of *Mrs Dalloway*, despite the widely held view of Woolf as a 'highbrow' writer. The two novels were promoted side by side in bookshops. The existing Harcourt paperback was reissued with a sticker announcing that it was 'the book that inspired *The Hours*' and including a reading group guide. A brief biographical note described Woolf as the 'victim of a lifetime of mental illness' and erroneously stated that Joyce had been published by the Hogarth Press. After the film's release, American sales of *Mrs Dalloway* increased to four hundred thousand. Fifty-three thousand copies were sold in all of 2002; in January 2003 alone that number soared to fifty-six thousand. In 2022, Picador published *The Hours* and *Mrs Dalloway* in a combined edition. Which novel comes 'first' depends upon which way up the volume is held, each having its own front cover. In a new introduction, Cunningham tells yet another version of his first encounter with the novel to which his own stands in the relation of 'a variation, an homage, a new interpretation that testifies to the potency and scope of the original'.[37]

The Hours was a phenomenon, one of those cultural events that produces such a cacophony of chatter and reaction, argument and opinion, that it soon becomes difficult to keep abreast of all the claims being made, positions staked out and misrepresentations passed off as gospel. The noise around the 'Pulitzer Prize-winning novel' and 'Oscar-winning movie' drowned out for a time quieter conversations that were taking shape and have continued since the heady days of early 2003, when Woolf scholars' opinions of a 'major motion picture' were being quoted in daily newspapers. Although Louise DeSalvo, whose book Cunningham lists among his sources, went on record as saying that *The Hours* was 'one of the great books of the twentieth century' and that the movie was 'fabulous', much media attention was focused on the negative reaction to Kidman's wearing a prosthetic nose for her portrayal of Woolf: '"Ugh" huffed Jane Marcus', the author of many milestones of Woolf scholarship.[38]

The *New York Times* summed up some scholars' objections: *The Hours* reinforced 'long-held, insidious views of Woolf that they have spent their professional lives repudiating. For years the standard take on Woolf was as the invalid lady of Bloomsbury, a frail, snobbish madwoman'. Understandably, Cunningham defended the movie against what he characterised as 'a cranky and willful misviewing'. The question of who 'owns' Virginia Woolf—a writer, after all, for whom there are at least fifteen full-length biographies in addition to many other biographically inflected studies—was exacerbated by the media attention to *The Hours*. Even before his novel was published, Cunningham was aware that many people had 'a remarkably proprietary sense of Virginia Woolf, more than just about any other figure I know. We all seem to feel that we have our Virginia Woolf'.[39] This rather generous view on the eve of his novel's triumph became somewhat more bitter as time went on. In Cunningham's telling, Woolf scholars 'tend to insist on one single aspect of her life as explaining the whole thing: Woolf as incest survivor, Woolf as repressed lesbian, Woolf as this, Woolf as that'. In his novel, he preemptively exacted his revenge on these sorry creatures by having the queer theorist Mary Krull 'stand in for a kind of miniaturizing, overly-focused approach to Woolf that I'm aware of in some academics'.[40]

It was not solely academics who were troubled by Kidman's portrayal. Doris Lessing saw in Kidman's Woolf 'the very image of a sensitive suffering lady novelist ... It was inevitable that Woolf would end up as a genteel lady of letters, though I don't think any of us could have believed that she would be played by a young, beautiful, fashionable girl who never smiles, whose permanent frown shows how many deep and difficult thoughts she is having'.[41] The ancient idea expressed by English poet John Dryden that 'Great wits are sure to madness near allied' seemed to some influential critics a hallmark of Hare and Daldry's Woolf. Prominently placed print advertisements for *The Hours* (with the tagline 'Our Lives. Our Story') showed several stills of Kidman as Woolf surrounding a quotation from the *New York Times* review by Stephen Holden:

> Nicole Kidman tunnels like a ferret into the soul of a woman besieged by excruciating bouts of mental illness. As you watch her wrestle with the demon of depression, it is as if its torment has never been shown on the screen before. Directing her desperate, furious stare into the void, her eyes not really focusing, Ms. Kidman, in a performance of astounding bravery, evokes the savage inner war waged by a brilliant mind against a system of faulty wiring that transmits a searing, crazy static into her brain.

As Lessing commented, 'How we do love female victims; oh, how we do love them'.

Of adaptation, Cunningham has said that writers must do whatever they can 'to get over the notion of the sacred text. You cannot consider the source as some kind of holy finger of the saint'. In writing *The Hours*, he had to overcome his 'reverence' for Woolf's novel in order to free himself to realise his own vision.[42] His novel is not, however, an adaptation of *Mrs Dalloway* in the sense that Hare and Daldry's film is an adaptation of Cunningham's fiction. The filmmakers made a number of significant changes to what Cunningham had written. Hare has said that 'the great mystery of adaptation is that true fidelity can only be achieved through lavish promiscuity':[43] such promiscuity can, of course, be interpreted. For example, Louis in Cunningham's novel echoes Woolf's Peter Walsh closely when he unexpectedly appears at Clarissa's home on the day of her party: he is inappropriately in love with a former student; he thinks to himself that Clarissa looks older; he weeps. In the film, however, it is *Clarissa* who cries when Louis visits. This change seemed to some commentators an example of a generally regressive attitude to women that was not supported by Cunningham's novel (although the distinction between book and film quickly got blurred, as does, at times, that between what Woolf wrote and what was invented by David Hare). The implication of the change from Louis to Clarissa crying seemed to be that women are unable to cope. Writing for *Slate*'s 'culturebox', Meghan O'Rourke claimed that not only would Virginia Woolf have hated being depicted as 'a jaw-clenched nut-job', she would have objected to the film's 'sentimentality about women and suffering'. Daniel Mendelsohn interpreted Clarissa Vaughan's tears as evidence that 'what the makers of the film are doing, it occurs to you, is exactly what Woolf worried that men did in their fictional representations of women: seeing women from the perspective of men'.

The Hours was generally positively received as a fine piece of literary fiction. Cunningham's choice of an epigraph from Jorge Luis Borges's poem 'The Other Tiger' signalled his intention of exploring questions about the relations between art and life, just as his other epigraph, from the diary entry where Woolf described how the tunnels she dug behind her characters in *Mrs Dalloway* would come 'to daylight in the present moment',[44] intimated the structure of *The Hours*. In the 'Mrs. Woolf' sections, Cunningham stayed close to the biographical accounts he had read by Quentin Bell and Hermione Lee, although Lee found the experience of having her work redeployed as fiction 'peculiar'. In a review for the *TLS*, Lee pointed out that the novelist's freedom to invent had led Cunningham to some 'embarrassing' chats between Leonard and Virginia that were 'not always spot on in class terms'. She returned to the matter of class when she reviewed the film (beneath the subheading 'moody, suicidal Virginia Woolf'). The idea that Vanessa Bell would ever have bought a coat for her daughter at Harrods was just one of several false notes struck in the movie version.[45]

By naming his 1949 Los Angeles housewife 'Mrs. Brown', Cunningham gestured to Woolf's figure of the 'reality' novelists must seek to catch in their nets of words in her famous essay 'Mr Bennett and Mrs Brown'. She is also, for Woolf, an emblem of the lives of women whose stories have remained untold. It is in the 'Mrs. Brown' sections of *The Hours* that Woolf's own words are most present, in long quotations from *Mrs Dalloway* as Laura reads the book, first at home and then later in a hotel room to which she has escaped so that she can read without interruption. Laura wonders how someone capable of writing sentences whose sense of joy moves her so deeply could have killed herself. In the novel, Laura takes to the hotel 'her pocketbook, and her copy of *Mrs. Dalloway*'. There, in Room 19, Laura, who is pregnant with her second child, thinks 'It is possible to die', but says aloud 'I would never'.* In the film, however, Laura also takes sedatives with her to the hotel, making a concrete intention of what in the novel is only a momentary musing prompted by Laura's reflections on Woolf's suicide. In the novel, Laura is allied to Woolf as an artist when she thinks about the perfect cake she wishes to create 'out of the humblest materials' for her husband's birthday: 'Wasn't a book like *Mrs. Dalloway* once just empty paper and a pot of ink?' Clarissa Vaughan, too, echoes her namesake in regarding her party as a creation, but in the movie she is shown cleaning her bathroom and kitchen more than she is arranging her flowers.

Laura Brown's unhappiness, to say nothing of the fact that she desires both her neighbour, Kitty, and her husband, Dan, resonate with Woolf's Clarissa Dalloway. Gloria Steinem praised Julianne Moore's performance of Laura for helping an audience 'understand the price paid by everyone when women are allowed to give birth to others but not themselves'.[46] Sara Ahmed, too, singles out Laura as a means of explaining why *Mrs Dalloway* continues to exert such a hold on feminist readers: 'Laura's sense of companionship with Mrs. Dalloway derives from a desire not to be in her life, to be suspended from its time and rhythms'.[47] In an earlier work, Ahmed discussed how Clarissa Dalloway exemplifies Woolf's 'political consciousness of what women are asked to give up for happiness'.[48] Such a notion sometimes evokes virulent backlash.

---

* In Doris Lessing's short story 'To Room 19' a mother, Susan, escapes to a hotel room, where she does eventually take her own life. Presumably Cunningham was aware of this story and is alluding to it.

For the conservative Christian writer Rod Dreher, *The Hours* was 'pure poison', and Laura Brown's story in particular 'an apologia for evil': 'We are meant to sympathize with this existential heroine instead of seeing her for what she is: a selfish, cold-hearted bitch who walked out on a decent man and two little children to go off in search of herself'.[49]

The art historian Christopher Reed has said that the anger Bloomsbury often triggers 'suggests that the group continues to stand for something that threatens established beliefs'.[50] In Britain, the popularity of *The Hours* aroused misogynist comments similar to Dreher's that conformed to sentiments familiar from decades of disparagement of the Bloomsbury Group. 'Virginia Woolf Makes Me Want to Vomit', Philip Hensher informed readers of the *Daily Telegraph* on 25 January 2003 (Woolf's 121st birthday!). *The Hours* was, apparently, 'about Woolf's tragic and glamorous life' amidst the 'intellectually glamorous society in which she lived'. As a 'secular saint of early feminism and a martyr to those modern obsessions, child abuse and depression', Woolf was known more for her biography than for her novels which, Hensher opined, are 'inept, ugly, fatuous, badly written and revoltingly self-indulgent'. Channelling Arnold Bennett, Hensher said that the characters of *To the Lighthouse* 'remain completely dead'. As Cunningham—and many others—have observed, Woolf arouses strong feelings.

Whatever distortions of Woolf's life and work *The Hours* engendered—the film a far greater culprit in this regard than the novel—it resulted not only in much greater recognition of an iconic 'Virginia Woolf' but also in vastly increased sales of *Mrs Dalloway*.* Furthermore, it provided an introduction to

---

* In *Virginia Woolf Icon*, completed just as *The Hours* appeared, Brenda Silver documented the extraordinary transformation of Woolf into 'a powerful and powerfully contested cultural icon, whose name, face, and authority are persistently claimed or disclaimed in debates about art, politics, sexuality, gender, class, "the canon," fashion, feminism, race, and anger'. Silver 3.

Woolf for many readers who might not otherwise have read her. The reception of *The Hours* frequently divided along lines of age and sexuality. A reader attuned to Cunningham's representation in the 'Mrs. Dalloway' sections of people with AIDS, of New York's gay culture, of men's memories of being bullied at school, experienced *The Hours* quite differently than, say, someone who had spent years studying Woolf, had published articles about her, had struggled as a woman in the academy, aware of being paid less than her male colleagues or having been passed over for advancement, her work treated as less important than others' because she did not write about Joyce or Faulkner. The generational divide was encapsulated in a 2003 post to the VWoolf listserv by a Woolf scholar, who wrote of hardly thinking about Kidman's performance, while her eighteen-year-old daughter had been 'stunned' by the movie: it had, she told her mother, 'changed her life'.

Subscribers to the VWoolf list (who include students, Woolf fans and scholars—not always clearly distinguished—and common readers) were invited in 2024 to answer the question of whether *The Hours* in fact had 'changed the way we see Virginia Woolf'. Drew Shannon, now a literature professor in Ohio, was about to begin his graduate studies when *The Hours* was published. He happened to read a review in *The Advocate* in which Robert Plunket admitted, 'I've never been a Woolf devotee until now, and I see that the problem was that nobody had ever explained her properly. Cunningham has opened my eyes to her genius'.[51] Intrigued, Shannon read *The Hours* the next day, which then led him to read Woolf's diary, gifted to him by a friend but so far unopened. This initiated a love of Woolf, who became the focus of much of his subsequent scholarship. In New York, the writer Matthew Cheney was already a fan of Cunningham's work, having picked up his earlier novel *A Home at the End of the World* at A Different Light bookshop. A few years out of college when *The Hours* was published, Cheney was far enough away from my Woolf studies that I didn't nitpick, but rather threw myself into the imaginative, imagined world. It was one of those lucky moments of reading exactly the right book at exactly the right time. Its aesthetic and emotional structures enraptured me. I was just out of New York, AIDS was very much on my mind, life felt terribly uncertain, and the mix of Cunningham's mind and words with a fictive Woolf was the perfect recipe.

Laura Cernat recalled being in high school in Romania when *The Hours* was released: the film 'did a lot to shape Woolf for people of my generation, at least. I have to say that, growing up in a non-Anglophone country, watching this film when it came out was actually among my first moments of acquaintance with Woolf, even before reading *Mrs Dalloway*'. Whatever one's point of view on Cunningham's novel, or on its film adaptation, *The Hours* is an inescapable chapter in the biography of *Mrs Dalloway*. The Uruguayan writer Antonio Larreta had not read Woolf for sixty

29 Spanish edition of *Mrs Dalloway*, 1939

years when he saw *The Hours*. The film inspired him to pick up again the Sudamericana edition of *La Señora Dalloway* (translated by Ernesto Palacio) which he had bought in 1939. In a preamble to his play 'Virginia', and two short stories that he subsequently wrote, Larreta said of *Mrs Dalloway*:

> I confess that sixty years went by before I re-read it, and that it was the cinema (Daldry's film, Cunningham's novel) that sent me to find the green book, its Sudamericana colour well-preserved. This was a second revelation, or the real revelation. At 17 I was a snob as a reader. At over 80 I am a virgin reader. And I have now spent almost an entire year with Virginia Woolf.[52]

As Woolf explained in her introduction to the Modern Library edition of *Mrs Dalloway*, books belong to readers, not to their writers.

Cannily taking advantage of the success of *The Hours*, Woolf's American publisher brought out *The* Mrs. Dalloway *Reader* in 2003. This hardcover volume included not only the text of the novel but also reprinted Stella McNichol's *Mrs Dalloway's Party*, Woolf's 1928 Modern Library introduction, some diary entries and a letter from Woolf to Vanessa Bell written in late December 1918. In the letter, Woolf suggested several names for her niece, who had just been born, among which was 'Clarissa'; this must have struck the editor of this deeply flawed volume, Francine Prose, as relevant to *Mrs Dalloway*.

As a group of Woolf scholars informed the publisher, *Mrs Dalloway's Party* had for many years been known not to be in any sense at all what the *Reader*'s flap copy claimed it to be: 'a kind of writer's notebook, containing many outtakes from Woolf's initial attempt to write *Mrs. Dalloway*'. Although publishers of Woolf's works (who proliferate as her copyrights expire*) continue too often to remain innocent of the extensive scholarship on

---

* On 10 July 2024 Goodreads.com listed 1,934 editions worldwide.

the writer who provides their revenue, the *Reader*'s many errors were happily rectified for a paperback edition that appeared in 2004. The irrelevant letter to Vanessa was replaced by one to Gerald Brenan responding to his opinion of *Mrs Dalloway*; a new headnote was supplied for Katherine Mansfield's 'The Garden Party'—her 1922 short story about a party interrupted by death; and a Foreword explained the actual relation of Woolf's novel to the 'Dalloway' stories (three more of which were added to the paperback edition of the *Reader*). Amongst reprints of various short pieces, including some from a PEN American Center event with Michael Cunningham, Elaine Showalter, James Wood and Mary Gordon, the *Reader* included new essays by the writers Sigrid Nunez, Deborah Eisenberg, and Elissa Schappell giving accounts of their individual, and markedly different, experiences of reading *Mrs Dalloway*. In her introduction to the revised, and now useful, companion, Francine Prose trenchantly explained its enduring appeal:

> Among the most striking and admirable things about *Mrs Dalloway* is how far it reaches, how many characters, how much personal history and sheer experience it crams into a book that is—I suppose you could say—nominally about a woman getting ready for a party during a single day in London. But, in fact, it's all here: life, death, sex, love, marriage, parenthood, youth, age, the present and the past, memory, London, war, reason and unreason, loyalty, medicine, social snobbery, friendship, compassion, cruelty; the occasionally apt but more often unfounded snap judgments we make about ourselves, each other, loved ones, strangers, and the world in which chance and fortune have thrown us all together.

The Hours undoubtedly led many new readers to discover this richness for themselves.

Mrs Dalloway as muse

As it still does, *Mrs Dalloway* attracted the interest of artists in many fields even before the star power of *The Hours* for some time eclipsed all references to Woolf's novel.[53] In the year Michael Cunningham won the Pulitzer Prize, Sarabande Books, a non-profit small press in Louisville, Kentucky, published *Mr. Dalloway* by Robin Lippincott. Set in 1927, the novel 'stretches the queer elasticity of the Dalloways' marriage'[54] by imagining a queer Richard whose lover Robbie's uninvited appearance at the excursion Richard has planned in celebration of his and Clarissa's thirtieth wedding anniversary (for which, of course, he 'said he would buy the flowers himself') has the happy result of Richard's realising that Clarissa 'understood'.[55]

Lippincott liberally plunders Woolf's writings, providing an enjoyable scavenger hunt for her aficionados. A neighbour dislikes Clarissa because she is 'too tinselly'; the June day on which *Mr. Dalloway* takes place is grey and misty rather than filled with sunshine; the concentric rings of the sound of striking clock bells are 'golden' not 'leaden', not rising up into the air but settling into the earth. In a shop window, Richard sees Woolf's 'novel of two years ago'—which is to say, *Mrs Dalloway*—and thinks (rather cheekily) that she 'had not captured it all'. He remembers a girl he once kissed on a boat going to South America, and how he tried to withhold from his daughter, Elizabeth, the possibility that her former teacher Miss Kilman's death might have been a suicide. Woolf herself is glimpsed with her lover Vita Sackville-West in the crowd who have gathered in Yorkshire to observe the total eclipse of the sun—the event to which Richard has brought his guests together to celebrate his marriage with Clarissa. Woolf and Sackville-West indeed were together to witness the eclipse in 1927, a momentous event that Woolf described in her diary, in an essay titled 'The Sun and the Fish', and also in *The Waves*.

Lippincott is a magpie, taking from Woolf whatever catches his eye to weave his clever sequel to *Mrs Dalloway*. The novel is to some extent in the mode of works such as Lin Haire-Sargeant's *H: The Story of Heathcliff's Journey back to Wuthering Heights* (1992) or

Alexandra Ripley's *Scarlett* (1991), but his gay Richard Dalloway is an invention that relies on no hints in Woolf's original, a fact that does not detract at all from its success.

Several composers have been inspired by the language of *Mrs Dalloway* to create both choral and instrumental works. In 1991, director Lisa Peterson and composer David Bucknam's oratorio 'Mrs Dalloway and the Aeroplane' was sung at the first annual conference on Virginia Woolf at Pace University in New York, perhaps the only time it has been performed. Six voices—Clarissa, Septimus, Mrs Coates, Mrs Dempster, Mr Bowley and Maisie Johnson—weave together the music of Woolf's rendering of a crowd united by their observation of a skywriting aeroplane. A fuller musical treatment of the novel was given in a chamber opera by Libby Larsen, with a libretto by the poet Bonnie Grice, which premiered at the Cleveland Institute of Music in July 1993. A quite different approach was taken in 1997 by The Ashley Adams Trio, whose jazz interpretation of the whole narrative, *Flowers for Mrs. Dalloway*, is divided into three parts—Morning, Afternoon, Evening—with a different instrument assigned to each character over thirteen episodes. The London-based Oslo Twins released their single 'Sally' in November 2024, named after Woolf's Sally Seton. In 2025, a new *Mrs Dalloway* opera with book, music and lyrics by Lindsey Augusta Mercer will be staged by the Cincinnati Shakespeare Company, who describe their production as follows: 'It is 1923 and the pandemic and WWI have ravaged Europe, but Clarissa Dalloway is determined to throw the greatest party London has ever seen ... reimagined for the stage as a musical with a sweeping neo-golden age score underpinned with a contemporary folk pop.'

The Party, a play written for Kathleen Chalfant by Ellen McLaughlin that is based on four of the stories exploring 'party consciousness' that Woolf wrote after she had finished the novel, debuted in 1990. The project was 'a child of *Angels in America*', said Chalfant, who had become friends with McLaughlin when they were both appearing on Broadway in Tony Kushner's play. A 1994 performance in New York benefited SafeSpace, a service for homeless and street youth with AIDS or at risk for HIV.[56] McLaughlin has also developed a play, 'Septimus and Clarissa', in collaboration with the Ripe Time theatre company, led by its artistic director Rachel Dickstein. In this production, staged in 2011 at Baruch College in New York, a character's portrayal by one actor is supplemented by the voices of others 'looking on, supporting and questioning, adding dimension'. The collaboration's intent was 'to achieve a choral dynamic which creates more texture for passages that would otherwise be simple monologues', as well as providing 'a theatrical means of exploring the fracturing of consciousness that Woolf is doing in the novel'.[57]

Mrs Dalloway lends itself to adaptations employing the creativity of set and lighting designers, composers and choreographers, all of whom respond to Woolf's richly textured and braided narrative, as McLaughlin's collaborators did. In 2018, an ambitious staging of an adaptation of *Mrs Dalloway* was created by Jean-Rémi Lapaire for students at the Université Bordeaux Montaigne. Distilled into just 1,965 words for a performance of about twenty minutes, *Performing Mrs Dalloway* encouraged the students 'to engage physically in their work, using *vocal* and *kinetic* resources to *enact*—not just *describe*—characters, relationships, moods, situations, concepts, or narrative perspectives' in a work that incorporated both dance and a chorus.[58]

Woolf, as we know, wanted to incorporate a chorus in her novel, 'some nameless observer' who might comment on the action in a manner similar to that employed by the ancient Greek dramatists whose work she was re-reading and translating while working simultaneously on her *Common Reader* essays and *Mrs Dalloway*. In the work of composers and playwrights, choreographers and novelists, the aesthetic possibilities and implications of *Mrs Dalloway* have been reimagined in an ever-changing kaleidoscope of adaptations. *The Hours* has also given impetus to these forms of creative expression. With another turn of the kaleidoscope, the *Mrs Dalloway* refracted by Cunningham's novel and its filmed adaptation has recently been given yet another iteration in Kevin Puts's opera *The Hours*. As with the film, New York's Metropolitan Opera staging of this work brought three stars to the roles of Clarissa Vaughan, Laura Brown and Virginia Woolf: sopranos Reneé Fleming (making a much-applauded comeback) and Kelli O'Hara, and mezzo-soprano Joyce DiDonato.

In *Woolf Works, A Triptych*, choreographer Wayne McGregor set 'I Now, I Then', the *Mrs Dalloway* part of his ballet, to music composed by Max Richter that incorporates a recording of the sound of Big Ben tolling throughout. The Royal Ballet first performed the work in 2015. Dramaturg Uzma Hameed explained that Woolf is particularly apt for dance because 'she plunges us into a world in which events are strung together thematically rather than chronologically, and the fabric of emotion and sensation appears denser than the brittle world of objects. All of this might be seen as the natural territory of dance'.[59] The American Ballet Theater premiered *Woolf Works* at the Segerstrom Center in California in spring 2024 before taking the production to New York's Metropolitan Opera House that June.

The principal challenge for all adaptations of *Mrs Dalloway* in any genre is to capture its interiority, an aspect that many creators of works it has inspired have acknowledged. Hameed, for example, asked how one could, 'like Woolf, provide just enough detail to allow the viewer to orientate him/herself, yet remain in the sentient "undermind"—open to abstract, even mystical states'.[60] The generative power of Woolf's vision, its 'queer' design and her successful effort to light up all 'inner feelings' have carried the novel into unexpected forms, unanticipated interpretations that give readers abundant new ways of understanding it each time they return to that single day in which all of life's experience is contained.

Coda

Twenty-first-century *Mrs Dalloway*

In 2020 the publisher of Penguin's Vitae series posed the question, 'What classic books would you place together on a shelf to represent the course of your life?' *Mrs Dalloway* made it on to that shelf in 2022. Penguin keeps a close eye on opportunities to promote the novel. When Miley Cyrus released her song 'Flowers' in 2023, the publisher tweeted

> Mrs. Dalloway 🖤 Miley Cyrus
> Buying the flowers herself

More and more often nowadays, the novel crops up in unexpected places. Reviewing the Design Museum's 2023 exhibition *Weird Sensation Feels Good*, devoted to ASMR (autonomous sensory meridian response), Ben Walker noted that the writer Clemens Setz had identified as a very early instance of ASMR that moment in *Mrs Dalloway* when Septimus Warren Smith hears a nursemaid watching the skywriting aeroplane say '"Kay Arr" close to his ear, deeply, softly, like a mellow organ, but with a roughness in her voice like a grasshopper's, which rasped his spine deliciously and sent running up into his brain waves of sound which, concussing, broke'.[1] From the 'Dalloway Burger' on the menu each June at the Dalloway Terrace restaurant on Great Russell Street in London, to the bookshop Mrs Dalloway's in Berkeley, California, which

30 *Mrs Dalloway* comic by R. E. Parrish

offers not only books but, 'inspired by the novel's opening line', gardening merchandise and plants, *Mrs Dalloway* is afloat as a brand, an icon, in that ocean of cultural markers in which we all swim. Although she lost out to Picasso in the artists and writers category on BBC2's *Icons: The Greatest Person of the 20th Century* in 2019, Woolf herself continues, as Brenda Silver noticed in 1999, to be 'everywhere'.[2] Clarissa Dalloway, like Woolf's Orlando, seems likely to live forever.

Dalloway Day

Several London walking tour companies already offered customers the opportunity to follow in the footsteps of *Mrs Dalloway*'s characters when Elaine Showalter suggested in the *Guardian* that there should be an annual celebration of the June day immortalised by the novel. She wondered why London could not 'raise a glass' to *Mrs Dalloway* in the way that fans of *Ulysses* did on 'Bloomsday'.[3] Her article was illustrated with an image of Vanessa Redgrave portraying Clarissa in Marleen Gorris's film, unfortunately connoting a world of tea and gentility that *Mrs Dalloway* had largely escaped by 2016. Dominating the few comments—still visible—on the *Guardian*'s website (where pseudonymous people present their opinions and tastes as incontrovertible facts) was the old tug of war between Joyce and Woolf. The exact date of Clarissa's Wednesday in June has in fact been a matter of some dispute, though settled for most readers by the indefatigable David Bradshaw's research into the *Cricketers' Almanack*, which established—based on Septimus's and Peter Walsh's observations of newspaper reports of cricket scores—that Woolf had no specific June 1923 Wednesday in mind. Joyce famously claimed to have put into *Ulysses* 'so many enigmas and puzzles that it will keep the professors busy for centuries'. Woolf's fiction only rarely offers such lures.

In 2017 the first 'Dalloway Day' (sometimes shortened to Dallowday) took place under the auspices of the Virginia Woolf Society of Great Britain, who teamed up with Waterstones booksellers. The day began, as has since become customary, with a guided walk through the London of *Mrs Dalloway*. That first Dalloway Day walk was led by biographer Jean Moorcroft Wilson, wife of the late Cecil Woolf, Leonard's nephew. Moorcroft Wilson's *Virginia Woolf, Life & London: A Biography of Place* was among the earliest works to pay attention to the importance of location in Woolf's fiction. Following a discussion of *Mrs Dalloway* chaired by Woolf scholar Maggie Humm, the day concluded with a 1920s-themed party.

By the hundredth anniversary of Dalloway Day in 2023, similar events were occurring each June in a number of other countries, marked by readings, discussions and, of course, parties. The Italian Virginia Woolf Society's Festa per Virginia Woolf took place at the Spazia Sette bookshop in Rome on the centenary, and in Uppsala a celebration was held at The English Bookshop, where Görel Kristina Näslund discussed her new biography (in Swedish) of Woolf.

By 2023, the Royal Society of Literature, the British Library and Hatchards had also recognised the significance of what Showalter had initiated. At Hatchards that June a discussion titled 'Clothes maketh Bloomsbury' was held among Wendy Hitchmough, author of *The Bloomsbury Look*, Charlie Porter, author of *Bring No Clothes: Bloomsbury and the Philosophy of Fashion*, and Claire Nicholson, chair of the Woolf Society. That year's theme, 'Dressing the Part', was rounded off with a panel on 'Bloomsbury in Society: Parties and Hostesses'. Just months before a crippling cyber-attack took its offerings offline that October, the British Library hosted a conversation about Woolf on Dalloway Day between the writers Lisa Appignanesi and Zadie Smith.

Dalloway Day went ahead in 2020 amidst the uncertainty and fear of the COVID-19 pandemic. Lockdown measures were legally enforced in England from 26 March, but by 10 May some restrictions had begun to be lifted. On 17 June, the Royal Society of Literature launched 'There We Stop; There We Stand' with S. I. Martin, the founder of '500 Years of Black London', a series of narrated walks. Participants explored the Black cultural heritage of Clarissa Dalloway's route through the city. Later that day, the RSL joined with Literature Hub editor Emily Temple, who hosted a Zoom discussion about how *Mrs Dalloway* related to readers' experiences during the pandemic. In the evening, Temple chaired a conversation with the writers Rowan Hisayo Buchanan and Kate Young to investigate 'the quotidian pleasures we've developed appreciation for since lockdown, how literature can support us in these confusing times, and how this experience compares to Clarissa Dalloway's own cerebral journey'.[4]

Pandemic

Mrs Dalloway's suddenly increased visibility in 2020 might at first have seemed an unlikely consequence of the pandemic. But as one teacher in Connecticut, forced like teachers everywhere to assimilate the technology of Zoom into her pedagogy at a week's notice, remarked, the novel 'became a lifeline for students': 'Death was all around us. But, unlike Clarissa and Septimus Smith, who are connected in *Mrs. Dalloway* by the dirge from *Cymbeline* encouraging the acceptance of death, we were all scared of death. We were all scared to death.'[5] That the novel had found a new audience in those days when the world had once again 'raised its whip' was given the imprimatur of a *New Yorker* article that April, when Evan Kindley published 'Why Anxious Readers under Quarantine Turn to *Mrs. Dalloway*'. Lockdown conditions had produced on Twitter (as it was then known) 'anxious variations on one of the most famous openings in English literature': 'mrs. dalloway said she would disinfect the doorknobs herself', or 'Mrs. Dalloway said she would buy the sanitiser herself'.[6]

The *New Yorker* writer drew at length on Elizabeth Outka's *Viral Modernism*, a book published in late 2019 whose argument that the presence of the profound effects of the 1918–20 influenza pandemic in many famous works of modernism had been largely overlooked came to seem uncannily prescient as the shadow of COVID-19 rapidly covered the planet. 'At a time when our most ordinary acts—shopping, taking a walk—have come to seem momentous, a matter of life or death,' Kindley wrote, 'Clarissa's vision of everyday shopping as a high-stakes adventure resonates in a peculiar way. We are all Mrs. Dalloway now.'

Outka's elegant readings of novels and poems written in the wake of the influenza pandemic led many to reconsider what they thought they knew about *Mrs Dalloway*. The pandemic's seamless sequel to the horrendous carnage of the First World War, Outka argued, led to a kind of grief-exhaustion, a limit to finding a language for this new trauma. She pointed out that the incessant tolling of bells was a feature in many pandemic survivors' accounts, giving a new understanding of the bells heard throughout *Mrs Dalloway*.

The postwar era was marked by a widespread interest in the return of the dead, a symptom of what the novel describes as 'this late age of the world's experience' that has bred in everyone 'a well of tears'. The pandemic gives a new significance to Clarissa's illness, to Richard's insistence that she must rest and to her weakened heart. By identifying Clarissa as a pandemic survivor, Outka claimed, Woolf made her and her double, Septimus, representatives of 'the era's two cataclysms'.[7] As a survivor, Clarissa is gripped by a 'paradoxical sense of astonishment, guilt, and joy at being alive at all in 1923, coupled with the hard-to-pinpoint atmospheric sense that death and the dead are ever close, intertwined with the living'.[8] Clarissa, therefore, is well positioned to intuit what Septimus might have suffered before his plunge.

For those re-reading *Mrs Dalloway* in 2020, or reading it for the first time because it was once again being referred to so widely, its sensations of invisible danger, the experiences of loss, of being cut off from other people—'here was one room, there another'—resonated profoundly. Outka explained how Woolf's narrative method itself was adapted to the novel's moods. Woolf had created 'a narrative perspective that could move as nimbly among bodies as a virus, a plot defined less by linear timelines and more by temporal and experiential fluidity, and a structure that could express the delirious, hallucinatory reality that infused the culture'.[9] The effect had been explained many decades earlier in strikingly similar terms by J. Hillis Miller, who in 1970 argued that in *Mrs Dalloway* 'narration is repetition as the raising of the dead'. The novel 'has the form of an All Souls' Day in which Peter Walsh, Sally Seton, and the rest rise from the dead to come to Clarissa's party'.[10]

Two weeks after *Mrs Dalloway* was published, Woolf wrote to the nineteen-year-old daughter of C. P. Sanger that she never expected people 'to agree with me in liking the books I like, because I rather want novels to depress me, and I don't much mind whether I like the people in them, or not. So I expect the books I write to be depressing and full of horrid monsters'.[11] Neither the flowers nor the sunshine, the exhilarating 'swing, tramp, and trudge ... the triumph and the jingle' of London in June, nor Clarissa's party itself can ultimately hide 'an emptiness at the heart of life'. In this world of revenants, Clarissa Dalloway pierces through the 'corruption, lies, chatter' she has known all her life and experiences a momentary communication with an unknown soldier that reveals 'a thing there was that mattered'.

In another country, one hundred years after the day on which the novel takes place, another teenager reflected on what *Mrs Dalloway* means to her generation following another pandemic. Los Angeles high school student Emily Li discerned in Clarissa's fears and sense of loss a pattern familiar in a time 'when many habitually communicate through social media or the internet and grow reluctant to connect with others face-to-face'.[12] Hearing that a young man has killed himself, Clarissa remembers that she was in love years ago with Sally Seton. 'If it were now to die', she had said to herself then, "twere now to be most happy'. Clarissa wonders whether the young man had plunged 'holding his treasure'. Across the divides of age, sex, class and experience, she 'felt somehow very like him', holding in her heart his gift as she turns away from the window so that her party can go on.

Abbreviations and a note on the text

D *The Diary of Virginia Woolf* (5 volumes cited by volume number, page and date)
E *The Essays of Virginia Woolf* (6 volumes cited by volume number and page)
L *The Letters of Virginia Woolf* (6 volumes cited by date, volume number and page)

Because there are so many available editions of *Mrs Dalloway*, page references for quotations from the novel have not been supplied. Unless otherwise indicated, quotations are from the 2005 Harcourt edition edited by Bonnie Kime Scott.

Notes

Preface

1 Virginia Woolf, 'Introduction'. *Mrs. Dalloway*. The Modern Library, 1928, vi.
2 Virginia Woolf to Violet Dickinson, October/November 1902, *L1* 60. (Woolf invariably omitted apostrophes in her letters and diary, and I have not corrected her when quoting.)
3 *D3* 128, 21 February 1927.
4 'Preparing for the Grand Style'. *Vogue* (London), early June 1922, 62–63.
5 *A Conversation* can be seen at London's Courtauld Gallery: https://gallery collections.courtauld.ac.uk/object-p-1935-rf-24.
6 Virginia Woolf to Vanessa Bell, 12 May 1928, *L3* 498.
7 Howard Ginsberg, 'The Mysterious Gift to Virginia Woolf'. *Bulletin of the Virginia Woolf Society of Great Britain*, January 2021, 55–57.
8 Jane Garrity, 'The Haunting of Mary Hutchinson'. In Erica Gene Delsandro, ed., *Women Making Modernism*. University Press of Florida, 2020, 55–96, 62.
9 Diane F. Gillespie, 'Virginia Woolf, Vanessa Bell and Painting'. In Maggie Humm, ed., *The Edinburgh Companion to Virginia Woolf and the Arts*. Edinburgh University Press, 2010, 121–139, 129.
10 Helen M. Wussow, ed. *Virginia Woolf "The Hours": The British Museum Manuscript of* Mrs. Dalloway. Pace University Press, 1996, 411.
11 Pamela C. Zhang, *Land of Milk and Honey*. Penguin, 2023, 120.
12 Dani Shapiro, 'Why My Fall Made Me Feel So Ashamed'. *New York Times*, 24 October 2023.

Part I: Drafting *Mrs Dalloway*

1 Leonard Woolf, *An Autobiography, vol. 2: 1911–1969*. Oxford University Press, 1980, 222.

NOTES

2 Virginia Stephen (Woolf) to Vanessa Bell, 12 August 1908, *L1* 351.
3 'Modern Fiction', *E4* 160.
4 The text of the notebook page in Figure 3 (for those who find Woolf's handwriting difficult to decipher) is as follows:

> October 6th 1922 Thoughts upon beginning a book to be called,
> perhaps, At Home: or The Party:
> This is to be a short book consisting of six or
> seven chapters, each complete separately,
> yet there must be some sort of fusion.
> And all must converge upon the party at the end
> My idea is to have some ~~very [ ]~~ characters,
> like Mrs Dalloway much in relief: then to have
> interludes of thought, or reflection, or short digressions
> (which must be related, logically, to the rest)
> all compact, yet not jerked.
>   The Chapters might be,
>
> 1. Mrs Dalloway in Bond Street.
> 2. The Prime Minister.
> 3. Ancestors.
> 4. A dialogue.
> 5. The old ladies
> 6. Country house?
> 7. Cut flowers.
> 8. The Party.
>
> One, roughly, to be done in a month: but this
> plan is to allow of some very short ~~pages~~:
> intervals, not whole chapters.
> There should be some fun—

5 *D2* 186, 26 July 1922.
6 *D2* 65, 15 September 1920.
7 Virginia Woolf, '22 Hyde Park Gate'. *Moments of Being*, ed. Jeanne Schulkind. 2nd edition. Harcourt, 1985, 165.
8 Virginia Woolf, 'Am I a Snob?' *Moments of Being*, ed. Jeanne Schulkind. 2nd edition. Harcourt, 1985, 207.
9 Virginia Woolf, 'A Sketch of the Past'. *Moments of Being*, ed. Jeanne Schulkind. 2nd edition. Harcourt, 1985, 81.
10 Ibid. 94
11 Ibid. 105.
12 Woolf, '22 Hyde Park Gate', 169.
13 *D3* 13, 27 April 1925.
14 *D2* 250, 28 June 1923.

15 Virginia Woolf, *A Passionate Apprentice: The Early Journals, 1897–1909*. Ed. Mitchell A. Leaska. Harcourt, 1990, 169.
16 Virginia Woolf, *The Voyage Out*. (1915) Penguin, 1992, 47.
17 Ibid. 33.
18 Leon Edel, *Henry James: The Master: 1901–1916*. Avon, 1953, 392.
19 Virginia Woolf, 'Old Bloomsbury'. *Moments of Being*, ed. Jeanne Schulkind. 2nd edition. Harcourt, 1985, 191.
20 Virginia Stephen to Leonard Woolf, 1 May 1912, *L1* 496.
21 Hermione Lee, *Virginia Woolf*. Chatto & Windus, 1996, 175.
22 Jacqueline Rose, 'Smashing the Teapots'. Review of *Virginia Woolf* by Hermione Lee. *London Review of Books* 23 January 1997, 6–7.
23 *D2* 206, 4 October 1922.
24 Virginia Woolf to Ethel Smyth, 22 June 1930, *L4* 180.
25 *D1* 32, 1 February 1915.
26 Virginia Woolf to Margaret Llewelyn Davies, 23 January 1916, *L2* 76.
27 *D1* 92, 14 December 1917.
28 Virginia Woolf to Ottoline Morrell, 15 August 1917, *L2* 174.
29 'Two Soldier-Poets', *E2* 269–272, 269–270.
30 *D2* 51, 29 June 1920.
31 'Modern Novels', *E3* 30–37.
32 *D2* 14, 26 January 1920.
33 Virginia Woolf, 'Modern Novels (Joyce)'. In Suzette Henke, 'The Modern Tradition'. In Bonnie Kime Scott, ed., *The Gender of Modernism: A Critical Anthology*. Indiana University Press, 1990, 622–645, 642.
34 Ibid. 643.
35 Virginia Woolf to Jacques Raverat, 3 October 1924, *L3* 135–136.
36 *D2* 189, 16 August 1922.
37 Woolf, 'Modern Novels (Joyce)' 644.
38 *D2* 200, 7 September 1922.
39 *D2* 189, 16 August 1922.
40 *D2* 203, 26 September 1922.
41 T. S. Eliot to Virginia Woolf, 4 December 1922. *The Letters of T. S. Eliot. Vol. 1: 1898–1922*. Revised edition. Ed. Valerie Eliot and Hugh Haughton. Yale University Press, 2011, 799.
42 *D2* 106, 8 April 1921.
43 *D2* 168, 18 February 1922.
44 *D2* 178, 23 June 1922.
45 Ibid.
46 Arnold Bennett, *Our Women: Chapters on the Sex Discord*. George H. Doran, 1920.
47 John Middleton Murry, 'Romance'. *Nation & Athenaeum*, 10 March 1923. *Virginia Woolf, The Critical Heritage*. Ed. Robin Majumdar and Allen McLaurin. Routledge & Kegan Paul, 1975, 109.

NOTES

48 Virginia Woolf to Gerald Brenan, 25 December 1922, *L2* 598.
49 Arnold Bennett, 'Is the Novel Decaying?' *Cassell's Weekly*, 28 March 1923. In Majumdar and McLaurin, 112–114.
50 *D2* 248, 19 June 1923.
51 Ibid.
52 *D2* 227, 16 January 1923.
53 *D2* 45, 31 May 1920.
54 Katherine Mansfield, *The Dove's Nest and Other Stories*. Alfred A. Knopf, 1923, 15.
55 Ibid. 22.
56 *D2* 248, 19 June 1923.
57 Ibid.
58 'Mr Bennett and Mrs Brown', *E3* 387.
59 'Character in Fiction', *E3* 504.
60 'Character in Fiction', *E3* 426.
61 Ibid. 430.
62 Ibid. 429.
63 Ibid. 435.
64 Ibid. 421.
65 Ibid. 436.
66 'Simon Pure' [Frank Swinnerton], review of 'Character in Fiction'. *Bookman*, October 1924. In Majumdar and McLaurin, 131.
67 Helen M. Wussow, ed. *Virginia Woolf "The Hours": The British Museum Manuscript of* Mrs. Dalloway. Pace University Press, 1996, 251.
68 *D2* 317, 17 October 1924.
69 Wussow 252.
70 Virginia Woolf, 'Mrs Dalloway in Bond Street'. *The Complete Shorter Fiction of Virginia Woolf*, ed. Susan Dick. 2nd edition. Harcourt, 1989, 152.
71 Ibid. 158–159.
72 Suzette Henke, 'From "The Prime Minister" Holograph'. In Bonnie Kime Scott, ed. *Gender in Modernism: New Geographies, Complex Intersections*. University of Illinois Press, 2007, 581–587, 581.
73 *D2* 207, 14 October 1922.
74 Virginia Woolf to Gerald Brenan, 14 June 1925, *L3* 189.
75 Virginia Woolf to Harmon H. Goldstone, 19 March 1932, *L5* 36.
76 Virginia Woolf, 'Introduction'. *Mrs. Dalloway*. The Modern Library, 1928, vi.
77 Virginia Woolf, 'The Prime Minister'. *The Complete Shorter Fiction of Virginia Woolf*, ed. Susan Dick. 2nd edition. Harcourt, 1989, 318.
78 Henke 585.
79 Ibid. 586.
80 Wussow 412.
81 'The Prime Minister' 322.

82 Virginia Woolf, *Roger Fry*. (1940) Ed. Diane F. Gillespie. Blackwell/Shakespeare Head, 1995, 124.
83 James Longenbach, 'The Women and Men of 1914'. In Helen M. Cooper, Adrienne Auslander Munich and Susan Merrill Squier, eds., *Arms and the Woman: War, Gender, and Literary Representation*. University of North Carolina Press, 1989, 115.
84 D2 93, 18 February 1921.
85 Ted Bogacz, 'War Neurosis and Cultural Change in England, 1914–1922: The Work of the War Office Committee of Enquiry into "Shell-Shock"'. *Journal of Contemporary History* 24, 2 (April 1989), 227–256, 227.
86 Ibid. 228.
87 Francis Younghusband. Letter. '"Shell-Shock" and Moral Control'. *The Times* 9 September 1922, 9.
88 Stephen Trombley, *All That Summer She Was Mad: Virginia Woolf, Female Victim of Male Medicine*. Continuum, 1982, 199–200.
89 D2 287, 20 January 1924.
90 E4 47–48.
91 W. H. R. Rivers, 'The Repression of War Experience'. In Fernald, ed. *Mrs Dalloway*. Norton, 2021, 254.
92 Trombley 175.
93 D1 204, 15 October 1918.
94 Clive Bell, *Peace at Once*. National Labour Press, 1915, 25–26.
95 Virginia Woolf to Margaret Llewelyn Davies, 30 September 1915, L2 65.
96 Clive Bell, *Peace* 20.
97 Wussow 418.
98 Ibid. 419.
99 Ibid. 418.
100 Virginia Woolf to Gwen Raverat, 1 May 1925, L3 180.
101 D2 283, 9 January 1924.
102 Wussow 425.
103 Virginia Woolf to T. S. Eliot, 4 June 1923, L3 45.
104 D2 243, 4 June 1923.
105 D2 244, 4 June 1923.
106 D2 248, 19 June 1923.
107 Virginia Woolf, 'Kew Gardens'. *The Complete Shorter Fiction of Virginia Woolf*, ed. Susan Dick. 2nd edition. Harcourt, 1989, 95.
108 D2 72, 25 October 1920
109 D2 272, 15 October 1923.
110 D2 314, 15 September 1924.
111 Hilary Spurling, *The Unknown Matisse. A Life of Henri Matisse: The Early Years, 1869–1908*. Knopf, 2000, 325.
112 Quoted by Woolf in *Roger Fry* 125.

113 J. B. Bullen, ed. *Post-Impressionists in England: The Critical Reception*. Routledge, 1988, 35n3.
114 Lia Giachero, ed. *Sketches in Pen and Ink: Vanessa Bell*. Pimlico, 1998, 130.
115 Virginia Woolf to Gerald Brenan, 25 December 1922, *L2* 598.
116 Vanessa Bell to Virginia Woolf, 19 October 1911. *Selected Letters of Vanessa Bell*, ed. Regina Marler. Pantheon, 1993, 109.
117 Julia Briggs, 'Hope Mirrlees and Continental Modernism'. In Bonnie Kime Scott, ed., *Gender in Modernism: New Geographies, Complex Intersections*. University of Illinois Press, 2007, 264.
118 *D2* 205, 4 October 1922.
119 'On Re-Reading Novels', *E3* 339.
120 Ibid. 340.
121 Virginia Woolf to Roger Fry, 22 September 1924, *L3* 133.
122 *D2* 272, 15 October 1923.
123 *D2* 313, 15 September 1924.
124 *D2* 272, 15 October 1923.
125 *D2* 263, 30 August 1923.
126 *D2* 272, 15 October 1923.
127 J. D. Beresford, 'The Successors of Charles Dickens', *Nation & Athenaeum*, 29 December 1923. In Majumdar and McLaurin, 123.
128 Wussow 416.
129 Ibid. 420.
130 Ibid. 422.
131 Ibid. 412.
132 Ibid. 414.
133 Ibid. 417.
134 Ibid. 419.
135 Ibid. 420.
136 *E4* 43.
137 *E4* 50–51.

Part II: *Mrs Dalloway*: content and influences

1 *D2* 251, 28 June 1923.
2 *D2* 291, 3 February 1924.
3 *D2* 283, 9 January 1924.
4 *D2* 298, 5 April 1924.
5 *D2* 301, 5 May 1924.
6 Letter. *Virginia Woolf Miscellany* 9 (Fall 1977), 3.
7 See for example, https://tinyurl.com/DallowayMap.
8 http://mrsdallowaymappingproject.weebly.com/.
9 As at https://western-civilization.providence.edu/mrs-dalloway-walking-tour/. A particularly sophisticated use of mapping technology to show the

patterns embodied in Woolf's narrative by the movements not only of the characters but also of the aeroplane, the car and even the sounds of Big Ben can be found in Melba Cuddy-Keane, 'Mapping *Mrs. Dalloway*: London as a Networked City', on-line essay, Powerpoint and PDF, University of Toronto, 2019: http://hdl.handle.net/1807/97406, Tspace Research Repository.
10 Sophocles, *The Antigone of Sophocles*. Edited with introduction and notes by Sir Richard Jebb. Cambridge University Press, 1891, ll. 353–360: www.perseus.tufts.edu/hopper/.
11 *D2* 47, 8 June 1920.
12 *D2* 79–80, 12 December 1920.
13 *D2* 48, 17 June 1920.
14 John Maynard Keynes, *The Economic Consequences of the Peace*. (1919) Penguin, 1971, 4.
15 David Bradshaw, 'Introduction'. *Mrs Dalloway* by Virginia Woolf. Oxford World's Classics. Oxford University Press, 2000, xxvi–xxviii.
16 Trudi Tate, '*Mrs Dalloway* and the Armenian Question'. *Textual Practice* 8, 3 (Winter 1994), 476–486, 484.
17 *D1* 136, 9 April 1918.
18 *D4* 103, 25 May 1932.
19 *D2* 63, 8 September 1920.
20 *D2* 320, 1 November 1924.
21 *D2* 322, 18 November 1924.
22 *D3* 12, 27 April 1925.
23 *D2* 322, 18 November 1924.
24 *D3* 91, 30 June 1926.
25 *D2* 239, 17 March 1923.
26 *D3* 21, 14 May 1925.
27 *D2* 322, 18 November 1924
28 Virginia Woolf to Jacques Raverat, 5 February 1925, *L3* 163.
29 *D2* 19–20, 13 February 1920.
30 *D2* 246, 13 June 1923.
31 Elaine Showalter, 'Introduction'. *Mrs Dalloway* by Virginia Woolf. Penguin, 1992, xxxi.
32 *D2* 166, 16 February 1922.
33 Virginia Woolf to Violet Dickinson, 30 November 1924, *L3* 146.
34 Bradshaw xxxiv.
35 *D2* 322, 18 November 1924.
36 Pericles Lewis, 'Proust, Woolf, and Modern Fiction'. *Romanic Review* 99, 1–2 (2008), 77–86, 85.
37 Virginia Woolf to Roger Fry, 6 May 1922, *L2* 525.
38 Virginia Woolf to Roger Fry, 3 October 1922, *L2* 566.
39 *D2* 234, 10 February 1923.

40 Marcel Proust, *Swann's Way*. Transl. C. K. Scott Moncrieff. (1922) Chatto & Windus, 1976, 22–23.
41 Virginia Woolf, *A Room of One's Own* and *Three Guineas*, ed. Michèle Barrett. Penguin, 1993, 93.
42 'Phases of Fiction', *E*5 67.
43 Ibid.

Part III: Publishing *Mrs Dalloway*

1 *D*2 325, 21 December 1924.
2 *D*3 4, 6 January 1925.
3 That would happen only once, in 1936, when Leonard feared the effect his blunt negative opinion on galleys of *The Years* might have on her fragile mental state.
4 Leonard Woolf, *An Autobiography, vol. 2: 1911–1969*. Oxford University Press, 1980, 241.
5 Donald Brace to Leonard Woolf, 16 December 1924: www.modernist archives.com/correspondence/letter-from-donald-brace-to-leonard-woolf-16121924-copy.
6 Virginia Woolf to Dorothy Bussy, 29 November 1924, *L*3 144.
7 William Pryor, ed. *Virginia Woolf & The Raverats: A Different Sort of Friendship*. Clear Books, 2003, 105.
8 Virginia Stephen to Vanessa Bell, 19 April 1911, *L*1 463.
9 Hermione Lee, *Virginia Woolf*. Chatto & Windus, 1996, 294.
10 Virginia Woolf to Gwen Raverat, 11 March 1925, *L*3 171–172.
11 Virginia Woolf to Jacques Raverat, 3 October 1924, *L*3 136.
12 Virginia Woolf to Jacques Raverat, 24 January 1925, *L*3 155.
13 Ibid. 156
14 Ibid. 154.
15 Pryor 102.
16 G. Patton Wright, 'Editorial Method'. In Virginia Woolf, *Mrs Dalloway*. (1925) The Definitive Collected Edition. Hogarth Press, 1990, 174.
17 Any discussion of Woolf's revisions to *Mrs Dalloway* is indebted to the scholarship of Anne E. Fernald, Jacqueline Latham, E. F. Shields, G. Patton Wright and Helen Wussow.
18 Pryor 153.
19 Virginia Woolf to Gwen Raverat, 11 March 1925, *L*3 172.
20 Pryor 175.
21 Ibid. 165.
22 Ibid. 174.
23 *D*2 249, 19 June 1923.
24 *D*2 323, 13 December 1924.
25 Virginia Woolf to Gwen Raverat, 1 May 1925, *L*3 180.

26 Anne E. Fernald, 'Introduction'. *Mrs Dalloway* by Virginia Woolf. Cambridge University Press, 2015, lxxxvi.
27 Merve Emre, *The Annotated* Mrs. Dalloway. Liveright, 2023, 229. Emre's edition also inadvertently omits an entire paragraph from the scene of Septimus being transfixed on Bond St (from 'Everything had come to a standstill' to 'But for what purpose') (Emre 28). This error was pointed out by 'M. C.' in the *TLS* 15 March 2024.
28 Nigel Nicolson, ed. *Vita and Harold: The Letters of Vita Sackville-West and Harold Nicolson.* Putnam's, 1992, 119.
29 *D2* 313, 15 September 1924.
30 *D3* 18, 14 May 1925.
31 E. M. Forster, 'The Early Novels of Virginia Woolf'. (1936) *Abinger Harvest.* Harcourt, 1964, 111.
32 Ibid. 113.
33 Virginia Woolf to Gerald Brenan, 14 June 1925, *L3* 189.
34 Vita Sackville-West, *The Letters of Vita Sackville-West to Virginia Woolf.* Ed. Louise A. DeSalvo and Mitchell A. Leaska. William Morrow, 1985, 26 May 1925.
35 Virginia Woolf to Vita Sackville-West, 27 May 1925, *L3* 184.
36 Virginia Woolf to Vita Sackville-West, 1 September 1925, *L3* 200.
37 Vita Sackville-West to Virginia Woolf, 2 September 1925.
38 *L3* 183n4.
39 *E4* 163.
40 Virginia Woolf to C. P. Sanger, 26 May 1925, *L3* 183.
41 Virginia Woolf to Janet Case, 1 September 1925, *L3* 201.
42 *D3* 109, 13 September 1926.
43 *L3* 195n1.
44 Virginia Woolf to Philip Morrell, 27 July 1925, *L3* 195.
45 *D3* 32, 18 June 1925.
46 Ibid.
47 Anonymous, 'A Long, Long Chapter'. *Western Mail,* 14 May 1925. In Fernald, ed. *Mrs. Dalloway.* Norton, 2021, 313.
48 Richard Hughes, 'A Day in London Life'. *Saturday Review of Literature* (New York), 16 May 1925. In Majumdar and McLaurin, 159.
49 'Modern Fiction', *E4* 163.
50 P. C. Kennedy, review of *Mrs Dalloway. New Statesman* 6 June 1925. In Majumdar and McLaurin, 167.
51 Edwin Muir, 'Virginia Woolf'. *Nation & Athenaeum* 17 April 1926. In Majumdar and McLaurin, 182.
52 Virginia Woolf to Janet Case, 1 September 1925, *L3* 201.
53 Arnold Bennett, 'Another Criticism of the New School'. *Evening Standard* 2 December 1926. In Majumdar and McLaurin, 190.
54 *D3* 21, 15 May 1925.

55 In Majumdar and McLaurin, 171.
56 Beth Rigel Daugherty, ed. 'Letters from Readers to Virginia Woolf'. *Woolf Studies Annual* 12 (2006), 25–212, 123.
57 J. H. Willis, *Leonard and Virginia Woolf as Publishers: The Hogarth Press 1917–1941*. University Press of Virginia, 1992, Appendix B.
58 *D3* 221, 13 April 1929.
59 Virginia Woolf, 'Introduction'. *Mrs Dalloway*. (1925) The Modern Library, 1928, v.
60 Ibid. vi.
61 *E5* 573.
62 *E5* 582.
63 Virginia Woolf to Gerald Brenan, 14 June 1925, *L3* 189.
64 Lise Jaillant, *Modernism, Middlebrow and the Literary Canon: The Modern Library Series 1917–1955*. Pickering & Chatto, 2014, 171n82.
65 Virginia Woolf to Vita Sackville-West, 17 February 1926, *L3* 241–242.
66 Lise Jaillant, *Cheap Modernism: Expanding Markets, Publishers' Series and the Avant-Garde*. Edinburgh University Press, 2017, 133.
67 Willis 121.
68 John Young, 'Canonicity and Commercialization in Woolf's Uniform Edition'. In Ann Ardis and Bonnie Kime Scott, eds. *Virginia Woolf Turning the Centuries: Selected Papers from the Ninth Annual Conference on Virginia Woolf*. Pace University Press, 2000, 236–243, 237.
69 Amanda Sigler, 'Expanding Woolf's Gift Economy: Consumer Activity Meets Artistic Production in "The Dial"'. *Tulsa Studies in Women's Literature* 30, 2 (Fall 2011), 317–342, 317.
70 Daugherty 74.
71 Virginia Woolf to Harmon H. Goldstone, 19 March 1932, *L5* 36.
72 Virginia Woolf to Harmon H. Goldstone, 16 August 1932, *L5* 90.
73 Virginia Woolf to Ethel Smyth, 6 October 1932, *L5* 108.
74 Joseph Warren Beach, *The Twentieth Century Novel: Studies in Technique*. Appleton-Century-Crofts, 1932, 431n1.
75 Ibid. 431.
76 Dorothy M. Hoare, *Some Studies in the Modern Novel*. Chatto & Windus, 1938, 23.
77 Arthur McDowall, 'A Novelist's Experiment'. *TLS* 21 May 1925. In Majumdar and McLaurin, 162.
78 Gerald Bullett, review of *Mrs Dalloway*. *Saturday Review*, 30 May 1925. In Majumdar and McLaurin, 164.
79 Beach 546–547.
80 Burton Rascoe, 'Contemporary Reminiscences'. *Arts & Decoration* September 1925, 40 + 76.
81 Ralph Philip Boas, *The Study and Appreciation of Literature*. Harcourt Brace, 1931, 130.

82 In Majumdar and McLaurin, 167.
83 Olivia Howard Dunbar, 'New Wings for Old Words'. *Equal Rights* 5 September 1925.
84 Virginia Woolf to Gwen Raverat, 1 May 1925, *L3* 181.
85 *D4* 42, 3 September 1931.
86 *D4* 57n7.
87 For one quite recent example, see Simon Heffer, 'Snobbish, Crude and Self-Obsessed: Has the Bloomsbury Group Lost Its Bloom?' *Daily Telegraph* 14 March 2019.
88 Percy Wyndham Lewis, *Men Without Art*. (1934) Black Sparrow, 1987, 133.
89 Ibid. 139–40.
90 Virginia Woolf to Margaret Llewelyn Davies, 6 September 1935, *L5* 425.
91 Q. D. Leavis, *Fiction and the Reading Public*. (1932) Russell & Russell, 1965, 225.
92 L. C. Knights and Donald Culver, 'Manifesto'. *Scrutiny* 1, 1 (May 1932), 2–7, 4.
93 *E2* 58.
94 *E3* 305.
95 Melba Cuddy-Keane, *Virginia Woolf, the Intellectual, & the Public Sphere*. Cambridge University Press, 2003, 84.
96 Muriel C. Bradbrook, 'Notes on the Style of Mrs Woolf'. *Scrutiny* 1, 1 (May 1932), 33–38, 38. Forty years later, Morris Beja noted in a selection of critical essays on *To the Lighthouse* that Bradbrook would not allow her essay to be reprinted because 'she no longer agrees with it'. Morris Beja, ed. *To the Lighthouse*. Macmillan, 1970, 20.
97 Walter Allen, *The English Novel: A Short Critical History*. (1954) Penguin, 1973, 351.
98 Edward A. Hungerford, '"My Tunneling Process": The Method of *Mrs. Dalloway*'. *Modern Fiction Studies* 3, 2 (Summer 1957), 164–167, 165.
99 Ibid. 167.

Part IV: *Mrs Dalloway* out in the world

1 *D2* 293, 23 February 1924.
2 Ibid.
3 Virginia Woolf to Janet Case, 12 April 1924, *L3* 97.
4 *E5* 582.
5 Katharine Smyth, *All the Lives We Ever Lived: Seeking Solace in Virginia Woolf*. Crown, 2019, 4.
6 Percy Wyndham Lewis, *Men Without Art*. (1934) Black Sparrow, 1987, 138.
7 *D2* 188–189, 6 August 1922.
8 Richard Ellmann, *James Joyce*. Oxford University Press, 1959, 457.
9 Ibid. 542.

NOTES

10 Mark Hussey, ed. *Selected Letters of Clive Bell: Art, Love & War in Bloomsbury.* Edinburgh University Press, 2023, 149.
11 Virginia Woolf to Vanessa Bell, 20 February 1922, *L2* 507.
12 *D2* 187, 3 August 1922.
13 *D5* 353, 15 January 1941.
14 *D2* 125, 7 June 1921.
15 Virginia Woolf to Clive Bell, 14 April 1922, *L2* 522.
16 Virginia Woolf to Gerald Brenan, 5 June 1922, *L2* 533.
17 *D2* 188, 16 August 1922.
18 Virginia Woolf to Ottoline Morrell, 18 August 1922, *L2* 548.
19 Virginia Woolf to Lytton Strachey, 24 August 1922, *L2* 551.
20 *D2* 195–196, 26 August 1922.
21 *D2* 200, 6 September 1922.
22 'How It Strikes a Contemporary', *E3* 356.
23 Virginia Woolf to Gerald Brenan, 1 December 1923, *L3* 80.
24 *D5* 353, 15 January 1941.
25 Ellmann 791n40.
26 *D5* 353, 15 January 1941.
27 Virginia Woolf, 'Modern Novels (Joyce)'. In Suzette Henke, 'The Modern Tradition'. In Bonnie Kime Scott, ed. *The Gender of Modernism: A Critical Anthology.* Indiana University Press, 1990, 622–645, 642.
28 Ibid. 643.
29 Mansfield, 'Three Women Novelists'. In Bonnie Kime Scott, ed. *The Gender of Modernism: A Critical Anthology.* Indiana University Press, 1990, 309.
30 E. W. Hawkin, 'The Stream of Consciousness Novel'. *Atlantic Monthly*, September 1926. In Fernald, ed. *Mrs. Dalloway.* Norton, 2021, 315.
31 I am drawing here on Anna Snaith's valuable discussion in *Virginia Woolf: Public and Private Negotiations.* Macmillan, 2000, 63–87.
32 Molly Hite, 'Tonal Clues and Uncertain Values: Affect and Ethics in *Mrs. Dalloway*'. *Narrative* 18, 3 (October 2010), 249–275, 257.
33 Erich Auerbach, *Mimesis: The Representation of Reality in Western Literature.* Transl. Willard R. Trask. (1953) Princeton University Press, 1968, 541.
34 Ibid. 551.
35 Ibid. 552.
36 Walter Allen, *Tradition and Dream: A Critical Survey of British and American Fiction from the 1920s to the Present Day.* (1964) Penguin, 1971, 41.
37 John Carey, *The Intellectuals and the Masses: Pride & Prejudice Among the Literary Intelligentsia, 1880–1939.* (1992) Academy Chicago, 2002, 19.
38 In S. P. Rosenbaum, ed. *The Bloomsbury Group.* University of Toronto Press, 1977, 384.
39 A. D. Moody, 'The Unmasking of Clarissa Dalloway'. *Review of English Literature* 3, 1 (1962), 67–79, 72.

40 Elizabeth Hardwick, 'Bloomsbury and Virginia Woolf'. *New York Review of Books* 8 February 1973.
41 Claire Tomalin, 'Introduction'. *Mrs Dalloway* by Virginia Woolf. Oxford University Press, 1992, xxxviii.
42 Robin Black, *Virginia Woolf's* Mrs. Dalloway—*Bookmarked*. Ig Publishing, 2022, 8.
43 Virginia Woolf to Vanessa Bell, 13 November 1921, *L2* 492.
44 Virginia Woolf to Ethel Smyth, 18 May 1931, *L4* 333.
45 Q. D. Leavis, 'Caterpillars of the Commonwealth, Unite'. In Majumdar and McLaurin, 415.
46 *D3* 32, 18 June 1925.
47 David Daiches, *The Novel and the Modern World*. University of Chicago Press, 1930. In Harold Bloom, ed. *Clarissa Dalloway*. Chelsea House, 1990, 31.
48 Lise Jaillant, *Modernism, Middlebrow and the Literary Canon: The Modern Library Series 1917–1955*. Pickering & Chatto, 2014, 99.
49 Maureen Howard, 'Introduction'. *Mrs Dalloway* by Virginia Woolf. (1925) Harvest/HBJ, 1981, xiii.
50 W. H. Mellers, review of *The Years*. *Scrutiny* June 1937. In Majumdar and McLaurin, 398.
51 Ian MacKillop, *F. R. Leavis: A Life in Criticism*. St. Martin's, 1995, 228.
52 Helen Southworth, Alice Staveley, Matthew Hannah, Claire Battershill and Elizabeth Willson Gordon, 'Virginia Woolf's Common Readers in Paris'. *Modernism/modernity* 28 May 2024: https://doi.org/10.26597/mod.0291. See also Shakespeare and Company Project: https://shakespeareandco.princeton.edu.
53 Suzanne Bellamy, 'The Reception of Virginia Woolf and Modernism in Early Twentieth-Century Australia'. In Dubino et al. 62–78, 68.
54 Jeanne Dubino et al., 'Introduction'. In Dubino et al. 7.
55 Daniel Göske and Christian Weiß, '"What a Curse These Translators Are!" Woolf's Early German Reception'. In Dubino et al. 25–41, 30.
56 Jacqueline A. Hurtley, 'Modernism, Nationalism and Feminism: Representations of Woolf in Catalonia'. In Caws and Luckhurst 297.
57 Alberto Lázaro, 'The Emerging Voice: A Review of Spanish Scholarship on Virginia Woolf'. In Caws and Luckhurst 247–262, 257.
58 Angsar Nünning and Vera Nünning, 'The German Reception and Criticism of Virginia Woolf: A Survey of Phases and Trends in the Twentieth Century'. In Caws and Luckhurst 68–101, 72.
59 Wolfgang Wicht, 'Installing Modernism: The Reception of Virginia Woolf in the German Democratic Republic'. In Caws and Luckhurst 102–126, 107.
60 Ibid. 111.
61 Urszula Terentowicz-Fotyga, 'From Silence to a Polyphony of Voices: Virginia Woolf's Reception in Poland'. In Caws and Luckhurst 127–147, 132.

62 Adriana Varga, 'The Translation and Reception of Virginia Woolf in Romania (1926–1989)'. In Dubino et al. 42–61, 48.
63 Maria Bent, 'Virginia Woolf's Literary Heritage in Russian Translations and Interpretations'. In Dubino et al. 132–151, 135.
64 Quentin Bell, *Bloomsbury*. (1968) New Edition. Weidenfeld & Nicolson, 1986, 7.
65 Carolyn Heilbrun, 'The Bloomsbury Group'. (1968) In Brenda Helt and Madelyn Detloff, eds. *Queer Bloomsbury*. Edinburgh University Press, 2016, 23–35, 24.
66 Carolyn Heilbrun, *Toward a Recognition of Androgyny*. W. W. Norton, 1982, xii.
67 Ellen Hawkes Rogat, 'The Virgin in the Bell Biography'. *Twentieth Century Literature* 20, 2 (April 1974), 96–113, 111–112.
68 Patricia Joplin, '"I Have Bought My Freedom": The Gift of *A Room of One's Own*'. *Virginia Woolf Miscellany* 21 (Fall 1983), 4.
69 Elaine Showalter, 'Literary Criticism'. *Signs* 1, 2 (Winter 1975), 435–460, 436.
70 Sandra M. Gilbert and Susan Gubar, *The Madwoman in the Attic: The Woman Writer and the Nineteenth-Century Literary Imagination*. Yale University Press, 1979, 73.
71 Elizabeth Abel, 'Narrative Structure(s) and Female Development: The Case of *Mrs. Dalloway*'. (1983) In Margaret Homans, ed. *Virginia Woolf: A Collection of Critical Essays*. Prentice-Hall, 1993, 93–114, 95.
72 Showalter, 'Literary Criticism' 439.
73 Ellen Hawkes Rogat, 'Visiting the Berg Collection'. *Virginia Woolf Miscellany* 1, 1 (Fall 1973), 1–2, 1.
74 Stella McNichol, 'Introduction'. Virginia Woolf, *Mrs. Dalloway's Party: A Short Story Sequence*. Harvest/HBJ, 1973, 15.
75 Sara Ahmed, *On Living a Feminist Life*. Duke University Press, 2017, 59.
76 Tessa Hadley email to Alice Lowe, quoted in Alice Lowe, *Beyond the Icon: Virginia Woolf in Contemporary Fiction*. Cecil Woolf, 2010, 19.
77 Helen Dudar, 'The Virginia Woolf Cult'. *Saturday Review* February 1982.
78 Karen DeMeester, 'Trauma, Post-Traumatic Stress Disorder, and Obstacles to Postwar Recovery in *Mrs. Dalloway*'. In Suzette Henke and David Eberly, eds. *Virginia Woolf and Trauma: Embodied Texts*. Pace University Press, 2007, 77–94, 77.
79 Ibid. 79.
80 Judith Lewis Herman, *Trauma and Recovery*. Basic, 1992, 2–3.

Part V: *Mrs Dalloway*'s legacies

1 Maria Nurowska's 'Requiem for a Wolf'; Marta Konarzewska's 'Doti'; and Sylwia Chutnik's 'Sly Women' are discussed by Paulina Pająk in 'Trans-Dialogues: Exploring Woolf's Feminist Legacy to Contemporary Polish Literature'. In Dubino et al. 332–353.

2 Richard Heppner, 'Mrs. Dalloway's Invitation:'. *Virginia Woolf Miscellany* 65 (Spring 2004), 17.
3 Elizabeth Abel, *Odd Affinities: Virginia Woolf's Shadow Genealogies*. University of Chicago Press, 2024, 25 (Abel's emphasis).
4 For example, Sara Collins, 'Assembly by Natasha Brown Review—A Modern Mrs. Dalloway'. *The Guardian* 12 June 2021.
5 *D2* 107, 8 April 1921.
6 Rachel Cusk, 'Shakespeare's Daughters'. *The Guardian* 11 December 2009.
7 Kate Walbert, *Our Kind*. Simon and Schuster, 2004, 105.
8 Ibid. 111.
9 Elaine Showalter, 'Introduction'. *Mrs Dalloway* by Virginia Woolf. Penguin, 1992, xxx.
10 Nancy Mitford, *Love in a Cold Climate*. (1949) Vintage, 2010, 170–171.
11 David Lodge, *The British Museum Is Falling Down*. (1965) Penguin, 1981, 38.
12 Ibid. 47–48.
13 Barbara Chai, 'How Virginia Woolf and London Inspire Zadie Smith'. *The Wall Street Journal* 8 June 2012.
14 John Lanchester, *Mr Phillips*. Putnam's, 2000, 219–220.
15 Ibid. 237.
16 Amy E. Elkins, *Crafting Feminism from Literary Modernism to the Multimedia Present*. Oxford University Press, 2022, 219.
17 Christopher Isherwood, *The Sixties. Diaries, vol. 2: 1960–1969*. Ed. Katherine Bucknall. HarperCollins, 2010.
18 Asali Solomon, '"For there she was": Writing About Now and Then with *Mrs Dalloway* and Virginia Woolf'. Presentation at 'Virginia Woolf and Ecologies' conference, Florida Gulf Coast University, 8–11 June 2023.
19 Sion Dayson. Interview with Anne Korkeakivi, 28 May 2012: https://parisimperfect.wordpress.com/2012/05/28/anne-korkeakivi.
20 Katy Waldman, 'Deborah Levy's Search for a Major Female Character'. *The New Yorker* 18 June 2023.
21 Susan Stanford Friedman, 'Migratory Modernisms: Novel Homelands in Monica Ali's *Brick Lane*'. *Asiatic* 11, 1 (June 2017), 102–118, 106.
22 Edward Rothstein, 'Critic's Notebook; A Cozy Familiarity Dissolves into an Unsettling Future'. *New York Times* 11 March 1998, E2.
23 All quotations regarding the Gorris and Atkins film are from the press kit distributed by First Look Pictures.
24 Masami Usui, 'Who's Afraid of Celebrating Virginia Woolf in Japan?' *Virginia Woolf Miscellany* 54 (Fall 1999), 7.
25 Michael Cunningham, 'First Love'. In *Prose* 136–137.
26 Michael Cunningham, 'The Biographical Novel and the Complexity of Postmodern Interiors'. In Michael Lackey, ed. *Truthful Fictions: Conversations with American Biographical Novelists*. Bloomsbury Academic, 2014, 89–100, 91.

27 Michael Cunningham, *The Hours*. Farrar, Straus, Giroux, 1998, 16.
28 Ibid. 109.
29 Michael Cunningham, 'Introduction'. *The Voyage Out* by Virginia Woolf. Modern Library, 2000, xxxiv.
30 Virginia Woolf, *The Voyage Out*. (1915) Penguin, 1992, 68.
31 Cunningham, 'Introduction' xxxv.
32 *D2* 122, 2 June 1921.
33 Joseph Allen Boone, *Libidinal Currents: Sexuality and the Shaping of Modernism*. University of Chicago Press, 1997, 188.
34 Cunningham, *The Hours* 131.
35 Ibid. 55–56.
36 Christopher Lane, 'When Plagues Don't End'. *The Gay & Lesbian Review* (January–February 2001): 30–32.
37 Michael Cunningham, 'Introduction', *The Hours*. (1998) Picador, 2022, xv.
38 Patricia Cohen, 'The Nose Was the Final Straw'. *New York Times* 15 February 2003, B9.
39 Michael Cunningham. Talk given at A Different Light, New York. 24 November 1998.
40 Cunningham, 'The Biographical' 97–98.
41 Doris Lessing, Foreword. *Carlyle's House and Other Sketches* by Virginia Woolf. Hesperus, 2003, ix.
42 Susan Salter Reynolds, 'Breakfast with Virginia Woolf'. *LA Times Book Review* 16 March 2003.
43 David Hare, *The Hours: A Screenplay*. Miramax Books, 2002, ix.
44 *D2* 263, 30 August 1923.
45 Hermione Lee, 'Ways of Dying'. *The Guardian* 8 February 2003.
46 Gloria Steinem. 'Self-Discovery: A Noble Journey'. *LA Times* 12 January 2003.
47 Sara Ahmed, *On Living a Feminist Life*. Duke University Press, 2017, 62–63.
48 Sara Ahmed, *The Promise of Happiness*. Duke University Press, 2010, 70.
49 Rod Dreher, 'Apologia for Evil'. *National Review Online* 24 January 2003.
50 Christopher Reed, 'Bloomsbury Bashing' (1991). In Brenda Helt and Madelyn Detloff, eds. *Queer Bloomsbury*. Edinburgh University Press, 2016, 36–63, 40.
51 Robert Plunket, review of *The Hours* by Michael Cunningham. *The Advocate* 8 December 1988.
52 Lindsey Cordery, 'Virginia Woolf's Enduring Presence in Uruguay'. In Dubino et al. 226–245, 234.
53 For a detailed account of how this star power operated in regard to *The Hours*, see Brenda Silver, 'Virginia Woolf: A Sound Investment'. In Clara Jones, ed. *Virginia Woolf and Capitalism*. Edinburgh University Press, 2024, 245–266.
54 Lane 31.

55 Robin Lippincott, *Mr. Dalloway*. Sarabande, 1999, 215.
56 *New York Times* 24 January 1994.
57 Ellen McLaughlin, 'Septimus and Clarissa'. Unpublished typescript, June 2014.
58 Jean-Rémi Lapaire, 'Performing *Mrs Dalloway* (1925)'. *Miranda* 17 (2018): https://doi.org/10.4000/miranda.14255.
59 Uzma Hameed, 'Woolfian Perspectives'. *Woolf Works* Programme. The Royal Ballet. The Royal Opera House 2016/17, 7–10, 7.
60 Ibid. 8.

Coda: Twenty-first-century *Mrs Dalloway*

1 Ben Walker, 'At the Design Museum'. *London Review of Books* 30 March 2023.
2 Brenda R. Silver, *Virginia Woolf Icon*. Chicago, 1999, xv.
3 Elaine Showalter, 'Bring out the Cardies and Cocktails: It's Time We Celebrated Dallowday'. *The Guardian* 13 June 2016.
4 British Library English and Drama blog, 17 June 2020: https://blogs.bl.uk/english-and-drama/2020/06/for-it-was-the-middle-of-june-dalloway-day.html.
5 Ellen C. Carillo, 'What I Learned About Teaching While Teaching *Mrs. Dalloway* During the Pandemic'. *Pedagogy* 23, 1 (January 2023), 1–9, 3.
6 Ibid. 2.
7 Elizabeth Outka, *Viral Modernism: The Influenza Pandemic and Interwar Literature*. Columbia University Press, 2019, 123.
8 Ibid. 140.
9 Ibid. 141.
10 J. Hillis Miller, '*Mrs. Dalloway*: Repetition as the Raising of the Dead'. In *Fiction and Repetition: Seven English Novels*. Harvard University Press, 1982.
11 Virginia Woolf to Daphne Sanger, 27 May 1925, *L*3 184.
12 Emily Li, 'The Clarissa Inside All of Us: A Literary Analysis of Virginia Woolf's *Mrs. Dalloway*'. *Los Angeles Times High School Insider* 13 November 2023.

Bibliography

Abel, Elizabeth. (1983) 'Narrative Structure(s) and Female Development: The Case of *Mrs. Dalloway*'. In Margaret Homans, ed. *Virginia Woolf: A Collection of Critical Essays*. Prentice–Hall, 1993: 93–114.
——. *Odd Affinities: Virginia Woolf's Shadow Genealogies*. University of Chicago Press, 2024.
Adichie, Chimamanda Ngozi. 'The Arrangements'. *New York Times Book Review* 28 June 2016.
Ahmed, Sara. *On Living a Feminist Life*. Duke University Press, 2017.
——. *The Promise of Happiness*. Duke University Press, 2010.
Ali, Monica. *Brick Lane*. Scribner, 2003.
Allen, Walter. (1954) *The English Novel: A Short Critical History*. Penguin, 1973.
——. (1964) *Tradition and Dream: A Critical Survey of British and American Fiction from the 1920s to the Present Day*. Penguin, 1971.
Auerbach, Erich (1953). *Mimesis: The Representation of Reality in Western Literature*. Transl. Willard R. Trask. Princeton University Press, 1968.
Bailey, Paul. 'Into the Waves'. *The Observer* 13 May 1973: 37.
Beach, Joseph Warren. *The Twentieth Century Novel: Studies in Technique*. Appleton-Century-Crofts, 1932.
Bell, Clive. *Peace at Once*. National Labour Press, 1915.
Bell, Quentin. (1968) *Bloomsbury*. New Edition. Weidenfeld & Nicolson, 1986.
Bellamy, Suzanne. 'The Reception of Virginia Woolf and Modernism in Early Twentieth-Century Australia'. In Dubino et al.: 62–78.
Bennett, Arnold. *Our Women: Chapters on the Sex Discord*. George H. Doran, 1920.
Bent, Maria. 'Virginia Woolf's Literary Heritage in Russian Translations and Interpretations'. In Dubino et al.: 132–151.
Black, Robin. *Virginia Woolf's* Mrs. Dalloway—*Bookmarked*. Ig Publishing, 2022.

Boas, Ralph Philip. *The Study and Appreciation of Literature*. Harcourt Brace, 1931.

Bogacz, Ted. 'War Neurosis and Cultural Change in England, 1914–1922: The Work of the War Office Committee of Enquiry into "Shell–Shock"'. *Journal of Contemporary History* 24.2 (April 1989): 227–256.

Boone, Joseph Allen. *Libidinal Currents: Sexuality and the Shaping of Modernism*. University of Chicago Press, 1997.

Bradbrook, Muriel C. 'Notes on the Style of Mrs. Woolf'. *Scrutiny* 1.1 (May 1932): 33–38.

Bradshaw, David. Introduction. *Mrs Dalloway* by Virginia Woolf. Oxford World's Classics. Oxford University Press, 2000.

Briggs, Julia. 'Hope Mirrlees and Continental Modernism'. In Bonnie Kime Scott, ed. *Gender in Modernism: New Geographies, Complex Intersections*. University of Illinois Press, 2007: 261–303.

Brown, Natasha. *Assembly*. Little, Brown, 2021.

Bullen, J. B., ed. *Post-Impressionists in England: The Critical Reception*. Routledge, 1988.

Carey, John. (1992) *The Intellectuals and the Masses: Pride & Prejudice Among the Literary Intelligentsia, 1880–1939*. Academy Chicago, 2002.

Carillo, Ellen C. 'What I Learned About Teaching while Teaching *Mrs. Dalloway* During the Pandemic'. *Pedagogy* 23.1 (January 2023): 1–9.

Caws, Mary Ann and Nicola Luckhurst, eds. *The Reception of Virginia Woolf in Europe*. Continuum, 2002.

Chai, Barbara. 'How Virginia Woolf and London Inspire Zadie Smith'. *The Wall Street Journal* 8 June 2012.

Cohen, Patricia. 'The Nose Was the Final Straw'. *New York Times* 15 February 2003: B9.

Cordery, Lindsey. 'Virginia Woolf's Enduring Presence in Uruguay'. In Dubino et al.: 226–245.

Cuddy-Keane, Melba. *Virginia Woolf, the Intellectual, & the Public Sphere*. Cambridge University Press, 2003.

Cunningham, Michael. 'The Biographical Novel and the Complexity of Postmodern Interiors'. In Michael Lackey, ed. *Truthful Fictions: Conversations with American Biographical Novelists*. Bloomsbury Academic, 2014: 89–100.

———. 'First Love'. In *Prose*: 136–137.

———. *The Hours*. Farrar, Straus, Giroux, 1998.

———. Introduction. *The Voyage Out* by Virginia Woolf. Modern Library, 2000.

———. Talk. A Different Light, New York. 24 November 1998.

Cusk, Rachel. 'Shakespeare's Daughters'. *The Guardian* 11 December 2009.

Daiches, David. *The Novel and the Modern World*. University of Chicago Press, 1930. In Harold Bloom, ed. *Clarissa Dalloway*. Chelsea House, 1990: 30–35.

Darling, Miranda. *Thunderhead*. Scribe, 2024.
Daugherty, Beth Rigel, ed. 'Letters from Readers to Virginia Woolf'. *Woolf Studies Annual* 12 (2006): 25–212.
Dayson, Sion. Interview with Anna Korkeakivi. 28 May 2012. https://parisim perfect.wordpress.com/2012/05/28/anne-korkeakivi/.
DeMeester, Karen. 'Trauma, Post-Traumatic Stress Disorder, and Obstacles to Postwar Recovery in *Mrs. Dalloway*'. In Suzette Henke and David Eberly, eds. *Virginia Woolf and Trauma: Embodied Texts*. Pace University Press, 2007: 77–94.
Dick, Susan, ed. (1985) *The Complete Shorter Fiction of Virginia Woolf*. 2nd edition. Harcourt Brace & Co., 1989.
Dubino, Jeanne, Paulina Pająk, Catherine W. Hollis, Celiese Lypka and Vara Neverow, eds. *The Edinburgh Companion to Virginia Woolf and Contemporary Global Literature*. Edinburgh University Press, 2021.
Dudar, Helen. 'The Virginia Woolf Cult'. *Saturday Review* February 1982.
Dunbar, Olivia Howard. 'New Wings for Old Words'. *Equal Rights* 5 September 1925.
Edel, Leon. *Henry James: The Master: 1901–1916*. Avon, 1953.
Eliot, T. S. *The Letters of T. S. Eliot. Vol. 1: 1898–1922*. Revised edition. Ed. Valerie Eliot and Hugh Haughton. Yale University Press, 2011.
Elkins, Amy E. *Crafting Feminism from Literary Modernism to the Multimedia Present*. Oxford University Press, 2022.
Ellmann, Richard. *James Joyce*. Oxford University Press, 1959.
Emre, Merve. *The Annotated* Mrs. Dalloway. Liveright, 2023.
Fernald, Anne E. Introduction. *Mrs. Dalloway* by Virginia Woolf. Cambridge University Press, 2015.
——, ed. *Mrs. Dalloway* by Virginia Woolf. Norton Critical Edition. W. W. Norton, 2021.
Forster, E. M. (1936) 'The Early Novels of Virginia Woolf'. *Abinger Harvest*. Harcourt, 1964.
Freedman, Ralph. *The Lyrical Novel: Studies in Hermann Hesse, André Gide and Virginia Woolf*. Princeton University Press, 1963.
Friedman, Susan Stanford. 'Migratory Modernisms: Novel Homelands in Monica Ali's *Brick Lane*'. *Asiatic* 11.1 (June 2017): 102–118.
Garrity, Jane. 'The Haunting of Mary Hutchinson'. In Erica Gene Delsandro, ed. *Women Making Modernism*. University Press of Florida, 2020: 55–96.
Giachero, Lia, ed. *Sketches in Pen and Ink: Vanessa Bell*. Pimlico, 1998.
Gilbert, Sandra M. and Susan Gubar. *The Madwoman in the Attic: The Woman Writer and the Nineteenth-Century Literary Imagination*. Yale University Press, 1979.
Gillespie, Diane F. 'Virginia Woolf, Vanessa Bell and Painting'. In Maggie Humm, ed. *The Edinburgh Companion to Virginia Woolf and the Arts*. Edinburgh University Press, 2010: 121–139.

Ginsberg, Howard. 'The Mysterious Gift to Virginia Woolf'. *Bulletin of the Virginia Woolf Society of Great Britain*, January 2021: 55–57.

Göske, Daniel and Christian Weiß, '"What a Curse These Translators Are!" Woolf's Early German Reception'. In Dubino et al.: 25–41.

Hameed, Uzma. 'Woolfian Perspectives'. *Woolf Works* Programme. The Royal Ballet. The Royal Opera House 2016/17: 7–10.

Hardwick, Elizabeth. 'Bloomsbury and Virginia Woolf'. *New York Review of Books* 8 February 1973.

Hare, David. *The Hours: A Screenplay*. Miramax Books, 2002.

Hawkin, E. W. 'The Stream of Consciousness Novel'. *Atlantic Monthly* September 1926. In Fernald, ed. *Mrs. Dalloway*. Norton, 2021: 315–317.

Heilbrun, Carolyn. (1968) 'The Bloomsbury Group'. In Brenda Helt and Madelyn Detloff, eds. *Queer Bloomsbury*. Edinburgh University Press, 2016: 23–35.

——. *Toward a Recognition of Androgyny*. W. W. Norton, 1982.

Henke, Suzette. 'From "The Prime Minister" Holograph'. In Bonnie Kime Scott, ed. *Gender in Modernism: New Geographies, Complex Intersections*. University of Illinois Press, 2007: 581–587.

Hensher, Philip. 'Virginia Woolf Makes Me Want to Vomit'. *Daily Telegraph* 25 January 2003.

Heppner, Richard. '*Mrs Dalloway*'s Invitation'. *Virginia Woolf Miscellany* 65 (Spring 2004): 17.

Herman, Judith Lewis. *Trauma and Recovery*. Basic, 1992.

Hirvonen, Elina. *When I Forgot*. Transl. Douglas Robinson. Tin House, 2009.

Hite, Molly. 'Tonal Cues and Uncertain Values: Affect and Ethics in *Mrs. Dalloway*'. *Narrative* 18.3 (October 2010): 249–275.

Hoare, Dorothy M. *Some Studies in the Modern Novel*. Chatto & Windus, 1938.

Humphrey, Robert. *Stream-of-Consciousness in the Modern Novel*. University of California Press, 1954.

Hungerford, Edward A. '"My Tunneling Process": The Method of *Mrs. Dalloway*'. *Modern Fiction Studies* 3.2 (Summer 1957): 164–167.

Hurtley, Jacqueline A. 'Modernism, Nationalism and Feminism: Representations of Woolf in Catalonia'. In Caws and Luckhurst: 296–311.

Hussey, Mark, ed. *Selected Letters of Clive Bell: Art, Love & War in Bloomsbury*. Edinburgh University Press, 2023.

Hynes, James. *Next*. Little, Brown, 2010.

Isherwood, Christopher. *A Single Man*. Methuen, 1964.

——. *The Sixties. Diaries, vol. 2: 1960–1969*. Ed. Katherine Bucknall. HarperCollins, 2010.

Jaillant, Lise. *Cheap Modernism: Expanding Markets, Publishers' Series and the Avant-Garde*. Edinburgh University Press, 2017.

——. *Modernism, Middlebrow and the Literary Canon: The Modern Library Series 1917–1955*. Pickering & Chatto, 2014.

Joplin, Patricia. '"I Have Bought My Freedom": The Gift of *A Room of One's Own*'. *Virginia Woolf Miscellany* 21 (Fall 1983): 4.
Keynes, John Maynard. (1919) *The Economic Consequences of the Peace*. Penguin, 1971.
Kindley, Evan. 'Why Anxious Readers Under Quarantine Turn to *Mrs. Dalloway*'. *The New Yorker* 10 April 2020: np.
Knights, L. C. and Donald Culver. 'Manifesto'. *Scrutiny* 1.1 (May 1932): 2–7.
Korkeakivi, Anne. *An Unexpected Guest*. Little, Brown, 2012.
Lanchester, John. *Mr Phillips*. Putnam's, 2000.
Lane, Christopher. 'When Plagues Don't End'. *The Gay & Lesbian Review* (January–February 2001): 30–32.
Lapaire, Jean-Rémi. 'Performing *Mrs Dalloway* (1925)'. *Miranda* 17 (2018). https://doi.org/10.4000/miranda.14255.
Latham, Jacqueline. 'The Origin of "Mrs. Dalloway"'. *Notes & Queries*, March 1966: 98–99.
Lázaro, Alberto. 'The Emerging Voice: A Review of Spanish Scholarship on Virginia Woolf'. In Caws and Luckhurst: 247–262.
Leavis, Q. D. (1932) *Fiction and the Reading Public*. Russell & Russell, 1965.
Lee, Hermione. 'Ways of Dying'. *The Guardian* 8 February 2003.
——. *Virginia Woolf*. Chatto & Windus, 1996.
Lessing, Doris. Foreword. *Carlyle's House and Other Sketches* by Virginia Woolf. Hesperus, 2003.
Levy, Deborah. *August Blue*. Hamish Hamilton, 2023.
Lewis, Percy Wyndham. (1934) *Men Without Art*. Black Sparrow, 1987.
Lewis, Pericles. 'Proust, Woolf, and Modern Fiction'. *Romanic Review* 99.1–2 (2008): 77–86.
Li, Emily. 'The Clarissa Inside All of Us: A Literary Analysis of Virginia Woolf's *Mrs. Dalloway*'. *Los Angeles Times High School Insider* 13 November 2023.
Lippincott, Robin. *Mr. Dalloway*. Sarabande, 1999.
Lloyd, Will. 'Fools, Frauds, and Firebrands'. *New Statesman* 6 October 2023.
Lodge, David. (1965) *The British Museum Is Falling Down*. Penguin, 1981.
Longenbach, James. 'The Women and Men of 1914'. In Helen M. Cooper, Adrienne Auslander Munich and Susan Merrill Squier, eds. *Arms and the Woman: War, Gender, and Literary Representation*. University of North Carolina Press, 1989: 97–123.
Lowe, Alice. *Beyond the Icon: Virginia Woolf in Contemporary Fiction*. Cecil Woolf, 2010.
MacKillop, Ian. *F. R. Leavis: A Life in Criticism*. St. Martin's, 1995.
McLaughlin, Ellen. 'Septimus and Clarissa'. June 2014 (unpublished typescript).
McNichol, Stella, ed. Virginia Woolf. *Mrs Dalloway's Party: A Short Story Sequence* Harvest/HBJ, 1973.
Majumdar, Robin and Allen McLaurin, eds. *Virginia Woolf: The Critical Heritage*. Routledge & Kegan Paul, 1975.

Mansfield, Katherine. *The Dove's Nest and Other Stories*. Alfred A. Knopf, 1923.
——. 'Three Women Novelists'. In *The Gender of Modernism: A Critical Anthology* ed. Bonnie Kime Scott. Indiana University Press, 1990: 309.
Marler, Regina, ed. *Selected Letters of Vanessa Bell*. Pantheon, 1993.
Mendelsohn, Daniel. 'Not Afraid of Virginia Woolf'. *The New York Review of Books* 13 March 2003: 17–20.
Miller, J. Hillis. '*Mrs Dalloway*: Repetition as the Raising of the Dead'. In *Fiction and Repetition: Seven English Novels*. Harvard, 1982: 176–202.
Mitford, Nancy. (1949) *Love in a Cold Climate*. Vintage, 2010.
Moody. A. D. 'The Unmasking of Clarissa Dalloway'. *Review of English Literature* 3.1 (1962): 67–79.
Nicolson, Nigel, ed. *Vita and Harold: The Letters of Vita Sackville-West and Harold Nicolson*. Putnam's, 1992.
Nünning, Angsar and Vera Nünning. 'The German Reception and Criticism of Virginia Woolf: A Survey of Phrases and Trends in the Twentieth Century'. In Caws and Luckhurst: 68–101.
O'Rourke, Meghan. 'To the Madhouse'. *Slate Magazine*. Posted 6 January 2003.
Outka, Elizabeth. *Viral Modernism: The Influenza Pandemic and Interwar Literature*. Columbia University Press, 2019.
Packer, Ann. *Songs Without Words*. Knopf, 2007.
Pająk, Paulina. 'Trans-Dialogues: Exploring Woolf's Feminist Legacy to Contemporary Polish Literature'. In Dubino et al.: 332–353.
Plunket, Robert. Review of *The Hours* by Michael Cunningham. *The Advocate* 8 December 1988.
Prose, Francine, ed. (2003) *The* Mrs. Dalloway *Reader*. 2nd edition. Harcourt, 2004.
Proust, Marcel. (1922) *Swann's Way*. Transl. C. K. Scott Moncrieff. Chatto & Windus, 1976.
Pryor, William, ed. *Virginia Woolf & the Raverats: A Different Sort of Friendship*. Clear Books, 2003.
Rascoe, Burton. Review of *Mrs Dalloway*. *Arts & Decoration*, September 1925.
Reed, Christopher. (1991) 'Bloomsbury Bashing'. In Brenda Helt and Madelyn Detloff, eds. *Queer Bloomsbury*. Edinburgh University Press, 2016: 36–63.
Reynolds, Susan Salter. 'Breakfast with Virginia Woolf'. *LA Times Book Review* 16 March 2003.
Rivers, W. H. R. 'The Repression of War Experience'. In Fernald, ed. *Mrs. Dalloway*. Norton, 2021: 252–270.
Rogat, Ellen Hawkes. 'The Virgin in the Bell Biography'. *Twentieth Century Literature* 20.2 (April 1974): 96–113.
——. 'Visiting the Berg Collection'. *Virginia Woolf Miscellany* 1.1 (Fall 1973): 1–2.
Rose, Jacqueline. 'Smashing the Teapots'. Review of *Virginia Woolf* by Hermione Lee. *London Review of Books* 23 January 1997: 6–7.

Rosenbaum, S. P., ed. *The Bloomsbury Group*. University of Toronto Press, 1977.
Rothstein, Edward. 'Critic's Notebook; A Cozy Familiarity Dissolves into an Unsettling Future'. *New York Times* 11 March 1998: E2.
Sackville-West, Vita. *The Letters of Vita Sackville-West to Virginia Woolf*. Ed. Louise A. DeSalvo and Mitchell A. Leaska. William Morrow, 1985.
Shapiro, Dani. 'Why My Fall Made Me Feel So Ashamed'. *New York Times* 24 October 2023.
Shields, E. F. 'The American Edition of *Mrs. Dalloway*'. *Studies in Bibliography* 27 (1974): 157–175.
'Shopping Power'. *New York Times* 15 December 1993.
Showalter, Elaine. 'Bring out the Cardies and Cocktails: It's Time We Celebrated Dallowday'. *The Guardian* 13 June 2016.
——. Introduction. *Mrs Dalloway* by Virginia Woolf. Penguin, 1992.
——. 'Literary Criticism'. *Signs* 1.2 (Winter 1975): 435–460.
Sigler, Amanda. 'Expanding Woolf's Gift Economy: Consumer Activity Meets Artistic Production in "The Dial"'. *Tulsa Studies in Women's Literature* 30.2 (Fall 2011): 317–342.
Silver, Brenda R. *Virginia Woolf Icon*. Chicago, 1999.
Smyth, Katharine. *All the Lives We Ever Lived: Seeking Solace in Virginia Woolf*. Crown, 2019.
Snaith, Anna. *Virginia Woolf: Public and Private Negotiations*. Macmillan, 2000.
Solomon, Anna. *The Book of V*. Henry Holt, 2021.
Solomon, Asali. *The Days of Afrekete*. Farrar, Straus & Giroux, 2021.
——. '"For there she was": Writing About Now and Then with *Mrs Dalloway* and Virginia Woolf'. Presentation at 'Virginia Woolf and Ecologies' conference, Florida Gulf Coast University, 8–11 June 2023.
Spurling, Hilary. *The Unknown Matisse. A Life of Henri Matisse: The Early Years, 1869–1908*. Knopf, 2000.
Steinem, Gloria. 'Self-Discovery: A Noble Journey'. *LA Times* 12 January 2003.
Tate, Trudi. '*Mrs. Dalloway* and the Armenian Question'. *Textual Practice* 8.3 (Winter 1994): 476–486.
Terentowicz–Fotyga, Urszula. 'From Silence to a Polyphony of Voices: Virginia Woolf's Reception in Poland'. In Caws and Luckhurst: 127–147.
Tomalin, Claire. Introduction. *Mrs Dalloway* by Virginia Woolf. Oxford University Press, 1992.
Trombley, Stephen. *All That Summer She Was Mad: Virginia Woolf, Female Victim of Male Medicine*. Continuum, 1982.
Usui, Masami. 'Who's Afraid of Celebrating Virginia Woolf in Japan?' *Virginia Woolf Miscellany* 54 (Fall 1999): 7.
Varga, Adriana. 'The Translation and Reception of Virginia Woolf in Romania (1926–1989)'. In Dubino et al.: 42–61.
Walbert, Kate. *Our Kind*. Simon & Schuster, 2004.

Waldman, Katy. 'Deborah Levy's Search for a Major Female Character'. *The New Yorker* 18 June 2023.

Walker, Ben. 'At the Design Museum'. *London Review of Books* 30 March 2023.

Wicht, Wolfgang. 'Installing Modernism: The Reception of Virginia Woolf in the German Democratic Republic'. In Caws and Luckhurst: 102–126.

Willis, J. H. *Leonard and Virginia Woolf as Publishers: The Hogarth Press 1917–1941*. University Press of Virginia, 1992.

Wilson, Jean Moorcroft. *Virginia Woolf, Life and London: A Biography of Place*. Cecil Woolf, 1987.

Woolf, Leonard. *An Autobiography, vol. 2: 1911–1969*. Oxford University Press, 1980.

Woolf, Virginia. (1976) 'Am I a Snob?' In *Moments of Being*. 2nd edition. Ed. Jeanne Schulkind. Harcourt, 1985.

———. *The Diary of Virginia Woolf*. 5 volumes. Ed. Anne Olivier Bell and Andrew McNeillie. Hogarth, 1977–1984.

———. *The Essays of Virginia Woolf*. Vols 1–4 ed. Andrew McNeillie; Vols 5–6 ed. Stuart N. Clarke. Hogarth, 1986–2011.

———. 'Introduction'. *Mrs Dalloway*. The Modern Library, 1928.

———. 'Kew Gardens'. In *The Complete Shorter Fiction of Virginia Woolf*. 2nd edition. Ed. Susan Dick. Harcourt, 1989.

———. *The Letters of Virginia Woolf*. 6 volumes. Ed. Nigel Nicolson and Joanne Trautmann. Harcourt, 1975–1980.

———. 'Modern Novels (Joyce)'. In Suzette Henke, 'The Modern Tradition'. *The Gender of Modernism: A Critical Anthology*, ed. Bonnie Kime Scott. Indiana University Press, 1990: 622–645.

———. (1925) *Mrs. Dalloway*. Annotated and with an introduction by Bonnie Kime Scott. Harcourt, 2005.

———. (1925) *Mrs Dalloway*. Edited by Stella McNichol with an introduction and notes by Elaine Showalter. Penguin, 1992.

———. 'Mrs Dalloway in Bond Street'. In *The Complete Shorter Fiction of Virginia Woolf*. 2nd edition. Ed. Susan Dick. Harcourt, 1989.

———. 'Old Bloomsbury'. In *Moments of Being*. 2nd edition. Ed. Jeanne Schulkind. Harcourt, 1985.

———. *A Passionate Apprentice: The Early Journals, 1897–1909*. Ed. Mitchell A. Leaska. Harcourt, 1990.

———. 'The Prime Minister'. In *The Complete Shorter Fiction of Virginia Woolf*. 2nd edition. Ed. Susan Dick. Harcourt, 1989.

———. (1940) *Roger Fry*. Ed. Diane F. Gillespie. Blackwell/Shakespeare Head, 1995.

———. (1929) *A Room of One's Own* and *Three Guineas*. Ed. Michèle Barrett. Penguin, 1993.

———. 'A Sketch of the Past'. In *Moments of Being*. 2nd edition. Ed. Jeanne Schulkind. Harcourt, 1985.

——. '22 Hyde Park Gate'. In *Moments of Being*. 2nd edition. Ed. Jeanne Schulkind. Harcourt, 1985.
——. (1915) *The Voyage Out*. Penguin, 1992.
Wright, G. Patton, ed. (1925) *Mrs. Dalloway* by Virginia Woolf. Hogarth, 1990.
Wussow, Helen, ed. *Virginia Woolf "The Hours": The British Museum Manuscript of* Mrs. Dalloway. Pace University Press, 1996.
Young, John. 'Canonicity and Commercialization in Woolf's Uniform Edition'. In Ann Ardis and Bonnie Kime Scott, eds. *Virginia Woolf Turning the Centuries: Selected Papers from the Ninth Annual Conference on Virginia Woolf*. Pace University Press, 2000: 236–243.
Zhang, C. Pam. *Land of Milk and Honey*. Penguin, 2023.

Illustrations

Endpapers Morris Beja. 'The London of *Mrs. Dalloway*'. *Virginia Woolf Miscellany* 7 (Spring 1977), 4.

Frontispiece Vanessa Bell, *Mrs Dalloway's Party* ('The Party', 1920). Courtesy of Howard Ginsberg. © 2024 Artists Rights Society (ARS), New York / DACS, London.   ii

1. Author's copy of *Mrs Dalloway*, Penguin Modern Classics, 1972.   viii
2. Virginia Woolf in armchair at Monk's House, 1931. MS Thr 560 (Box 1: 5), Houghton Library, Harvard University.   2
3. [Mrs Dalloway. Outline] At Home: or The Party. Holograph outline 1922 Oct. 6 in Virginia Woolf, 'Jacob's Room holograph Part III'. Berg Collection of the New York Public Library. By permission of the Society of Authors on behalf of the Estate of Virginia Woolf.   4
4. Leonard Woolf with pipe at Monk's House. MS Thr 560 (Box 1: 4), Houghton Library, Harvard University.   5
5. T. S. Eliot at Monk's House. MS Thr 562 (Box 1: 108), Houghton Library, Harvard University.   14
6. *The Nation & Athenaeum*, 1 December 1923.   20
7. Area railings, Tavistock Square. MS Thr 564 (Box 4: 152), Houghton Library, Harvard University.   29

ILLUSTRATIONS 209

8	Gerald Brenan.	34
9	Leonard Woolf in armchair at Monk's House, 1931. MS Thr 560 (Box 1: 3), Houghton Library, Harvard University.	42
10	Virginia Woolf on a bench with Lytton Strachey. MS Thr 564 (Box 2: 83), Houghton Library, Harvard University.	48
11	Cenotaph unveiling, 1920. *The Graphic*, 20 November 1920. Photograph by Horace Nicholls.	54
12	Vanessa Bell, sketch for the cover of *Mrs Dalloway*. Victoria University Library. © 2024 Artists Rights Society (ARS), New York / DACS, London.	73
13	Stack of editions of *Mrs Dalloway* (Mark Hussey).	82
14	Vanessa Bell, cover for the first edition of *Mrs Dalloway*, Hogarth Press, 1925. Victoria University Library. © 2024 Artists Rights Society (ARS), New York / DACS, London.	85
15	*Mrs Dalloway*. Introduction by Virginia Woolf. The Modern Library, 1928. Victoria University Library.	90
16	Advertisement for Uniform Edition of Virginia Woolf on back cover of *A Room of One's Own*, Hogarth Press, 1929.	93
17	*Mrs. Dalloway*. Leipzig, Bernhard Tauchnitz, Collection of British and American Authors, 1929. Victoria University Library.	94
18	Advertisement for *Mrs. Dalloway* in *The Dial*.	95
19	*Mrs. Dalloway*. Introduction by Virginia Woolf. The Modern Library, 1928 (alternative dustjacket).	99
20	Vanessa Bell arranging flowers outdoors, Duncan Grant standing nearby. MS Thr 557 (Box 1: 200), Houghton Library, Harvard University.	108
21	*Mrs. Dalloway* Harcourt editions from the mid-1950s.	125
22	*Mrs. Dalloway*, transl. Simone David, with Preface by André Maurois. Paris, Librairie Stock, 1929. Victoria University Library.	129

23 *Mrs. Dalloway*, transl. Herberth E. and Marlys Herlitschka. S. Fischer Verlag, 1955. Victoria University Library. — 130

24 *Mrs. Dalloway* transl. Herberth E. and Marlys Herlitschka. Frankfurt-am-Main, Fischer Bücherei, 1964. Victoria University Library. — 131

25 *Mrs. Dalloway*, transl. C. A. Jordana. Barcelona, Edicions Proa-Badalona, 1930. Victoria University Library. — 131

26 *Misis Dalauej*, transl. Mariana Nedelčeva. Sofia, Narodna Kultura, 1989. Victoria University Library. — 132

27 *Mrs Dalloway*, transl. Simone David, with Preface by André Maurois. Paris, Stock. Livre de Poche, 1982. Victoria University Library. — 134

28 *La Señora Dalloway*, transl. Andrés Bosch. Barcelona, Editorial Lumen, 1975. Victoria University Library. — 138

29 *La Señora Dalloway*, transl. Ernesto Palacio. Buenos Aires, Editorial Sudamericana, Colección Horizonte, [1939] 1944. Victoria University Library. — 167

30 R. E. Parrish, '*Mrs Dalloway*: The Gritty Reboot'. www.reparrishcomics.com. — 175

Legend of Morris Beja map

(1) Clarissa, who lives in Westminster ('how many years now? over twenty'), crosses Victoria Street; later, Peter crosses it after leaving Clarissa's home.
(2) Clarissa passes Buckingham Palace and enters St. James's Park.
(3) Walking north from the Park, Clarissa feels how 'Arlington Street and Piccadilly seemed to chafe the very air in the park'; she then crosses Piccadilly by Green Park.
(4) Clarissa walks 'towards Bond Street', which 'fascinated her', and stops at 'Mulberry's the florists'.
(5) The motor car goes 'down Bond Street', passing Clarissa, who then walks into Brook Street, the street where Richard will later call upon Lady Bruton.
(6) The car crosses Piccadilly and turns 'down St. James's Street' – that is, towards St. James's Palace, where 'the Prince lived'.
(7) Lucrezia and Septimus are 'on a seat in Regent's Park in the Board Walk'. Later Peter will sit in the Park and fall asleep.
(8) Maisie Johnson asks the Smiths 'the way to Regent's Park Tube station'; later, at this spot Peter will hear that song of 'the battered woman', before taking a taxi to Lincoln's

Inn (see No. 19) to see 'the lawyers and solicitors, Messrs. Hooper and Grately'.

(9) Crossing Victoria Street, Peter hears by the bell of St. Margaret's that it is 'precisely half-past eleven'.

(10) Peter goes up Whitehall, noticing the statue of the Duke of Cambridge by the War Office, and then 'all the exalted statues, Nelson, Gordon, Havelock', until he reaches Trafalgar Square.

(11–12) Peter notices a girl in (appropriately) Cockspur Street and follows her as she crosses Piccadilly, goes up Regent Street, across 'Oxford Street and Great Portland Street and... down one of the little streets'.

(13) Rezia and Septimus leave Regent's Park for Sir William Bradshaw's office in Harley Street, walking by way of Portland Place.

(14) After their appointment with Dr. Bradshaw, the Smiths return to their 'lodgings off the Tottenham Court Road'.

(15) Leaving Lady Bruton's on Brook Street (see No. 5), Richard Dalloway and Hugh Whitbread separate 'at the corner of Conduit Street'; Richard continues walking south, crossing Piccadilly and Green Park.

(16) Richard crosses through Dean's Yard on his way home.

(17) Elizabeth and Miss Kilman have tea at the Army and Navy department store on Victoria Street, and then Elizabeth takes a bus on Victoria Street towards the City.

(18) Having ridden on the bus up the Strand, Elizabeth gets off at Chancery Lane and then walks up Fleet Street 'in the direction of St. Paul's', but she then turns 'back down the Strand' and gets on a bus to Westminster.

(19–20) Leaving his solicitor's office in Lincoln's Inn, Peter walks towards his hotel in Bloomsbury, on his way hearing 'the light high bell of the ambulance' and stopping 'by the pillar-box opposite the British Museum'.

(21) Peter leaves his hotel, enters or walks along Bedford Place, and strolls down towards Westminster by way of Whitehall. Finally, 'it was her street, this, Clarissa's; cabs were rushing round the corner, like water round the piers of a bridge, drawn together, it seemed to him, because they bore people going to her party, Clarissa's party'.

Acknowledgements

My thanks to Kim Walker, who came up with the idea of a biography of *Mrs Dalloway*, and to Alun Richards and his colleagues at Manchester University Press. I am grateful to an anonymous reader who made wise suggestions for revision. My thanks to Marielle O'Neill for timely answers to random questions, and to Alice Staveley for sharing her Hogarth Press research. Thanks to Drew Shannon, Matthew Cheney and Laura Cernat for allowing me to quote their reflections on *The Hours*; to Ellen McLaughlin for sharing with me a typescript of her play; to the late Murray Beja for permission to reproduce his map; to R. E. Parrish for letting me reprint his wonderful cartoon; and to Howard Ginsberg for providing an image of *Mrs Dalloway's Party* (sorry it couldn't be in colour!). I am grateful to Edward Mendelson for catching a textual error just in time. Thanks to Kim Jones who, with characteristic generosity, sent me from his collection a scan of the typescript of Woolf's introduction to the Modern Library edition of *Mrs Dalloway*. My thanks, as always, to my heroic interlibrary loan librarian Xiaohong (Sheila) Hu at the Mortola Library, Pace University Pleasantville; to Carolyn Vega, Curator of the Berg Collection at the New York Public Library, and to the NYPL Permissions and Reproductions office; to Mary Haegert and Angela Sun at the Houghton Library, Harvard University, for their assistance with the Monk's House

Photograph Albums; to Roma Kail at the E. J. Pratt Library, Victoria University; to Siobhan Donnelly at ARS; to Zoe Stansell at the British Library Manuscripts Reference Service; and, once again, to Sarah Baxter at the Society of Authors. None of the work I do, and have done, on Virginia Woolf would be possible without the sustaining, vibrant community of Woolf scholars around the world, too numerous to name but you know who you are! And finally, I could not have written this book without the reassuring and thoughtful responses of my two favourite (& voracious) common readers, Alexandra Truitt and Evelyn Leong.

Index

Note: Characters in *Mrs Dalloway* are indicated by (*MD*)

Abel, Elizabeth 136, 143
Adichie, Chimamanda Ngozi 150
Ahmed, Sara 139–140, 164
Albee, Edward 126, 150, 151
Ali, Monica 148–149
Allen, Walter 105, 116
'Am I a Snob?' (Woolf) 8
Antigone 52
Apollinaire, Guillaume 39
Armenian Genocide 61, 121
Asheham House 12
Ashley Adams Trio *see Flowers for Mrs. Dalloway*
ASMR 174
Asquith, Margot 104
Atkins, Eileen 152, 153, 154
    see also Mrs Dalloway (film)
Auerbach, Erich 115–116

Bailey, Paul 140
Baldwin, Stanley 58
Ballets Russes 112
Beach, Joseph Warren 98–99, 100
Beach, Sylvia *see* Shakespeare & Company
Beja, Morris 48

Bell, Clive ix, 9, 10, 31–33, 37, 38, 59, 65, 66, 67–68, 74, 76, 95, 110–112
Bell, Quentin ix, 126, 134, 136, 137, 140, 163
Bell, Vanessa vii, ix, 2, 5, 6, 7–10, 17, 38, 59, 67–68, 72, 73–74, 75, 106, 107, 108, 111, 119, 163, 168
Bennett, Arnold 15, 16, 18–24, 44, 88, 102, 165
    see also 'Mr Bennett and Mrs Brown'
Beresford, J. D. 44
Berg Collection 114, 137, 138
Bergson, Henri 97–98
Between the Acts (Woolf) 156
Birrell, Francis 111, 127
Black, Robin 109
Bletchley, Sarah (*MD*) 56
Bloomsbury Group 9, 10, 59, 75, 84, 96, 102, 117, 127, 134–135, 165
Blunt, Wilfred Scawen 37
Boas, Ralph 100
Bowley, Mr (*MD*) 58–59, 171
Brace, Donald *see* Harcourt Brace
Bradbrook, Muriel 105

INDEX

Bradshaw, David 60, 69, 176
Bradshaw, William (*MD*) 28, 50,
    60–61, 63, 64, 69, 80, 85,
    117–118, 147, 153
Braque, Georges 38
Brenan, Gerald 11, 19, 26, 33, 34, 38,
    83, 92, 112, 113, 169
British Library 24, 137, 138, 177
Brooke, Rupert 13, 33, 75
Bruton, Millicent (*MD*) 56, 57, 60, 62,
    69, 80
Bucknam, David 171
Bullett, Gerald 100

Carey, John 117
Case, Janet 84, 88, 92, 107
Cendrars, Blaise 39
Cenotaph, The 53, 54
Cernat, Laura 167
Cézanne, Paul 87
Chalfant, Kathleen 171–172
'Character in Fiction' (Woolf) 21–24,
    39, 89, 114
Chekhov, Anton 84
Cheney, Matthew 166–167
Colefax, Sibyl 68, 102
Common Reader, The 17, 22, 39, 44, 47,
    72, 83, 84, 88, 92, 96, 129, 172
Common Reader: Second Series, The
    103, 108
Cox, Katherine (Ka) 75
Craig, Maurice 27, 30
Craiglockhart War Hospital *see*
    Rivers, W. H. R.
Criterion, The see Eliot, T. S.
Cunningham, Michael *see Hours, The*
    (novel)
Cusk, Rachel 145, 146
Cyrus, Miley 174

Daiches, David 126
Dalloway, Clarissa (*The Voyage Out*)
    5–6, 8, 9

Dalloway, Clarissa (*MD*) 8–9, 22, 25,
    26, 36, 41, 43, 44, 45, 49–50, 52,
    53–55, 56, 59, 61–65, 66–67,
    68, 69, 71, 76, 80–81, 85–86,
    88, 91, 96, 98, 99, 104, 118–125,
    135, 139, 141, 144, 158, 180
  connection with Septimus Warren
    Smith x, 26, 51, 54, 62, 73, 79,
    81, 91, 97, 99, 109, 118, 178,
    179, 180
Dalloway, Elizabeth (*MD*) 54, 55–56,
    63–64, 65, 67, 68, 117, 120,
    121, 122–123, 124, 145, 152
Dalloway, Richard (*MD*) 41, 49, 50,
    55, 57, 58, 60, 61, 80, 85, 118,
    121, 124
Darling, Miranda 149
Darwin, Gwen *see* Raverat, Gwen
Davies, Margaret Llewelyn 12, 32, 103
Delattre, Floris 97, 128
Dempster, Carrie (*MD*) 43, 51, 171
DeSalvo, Louise 141, 142, 160
Devonshire House 68–69
Dial, The 25, 74, 95
Dickinson, Violet viii, 10, 68–69, 72
Dostoevsky, Fyodor 19, 20, 100
Doyle, Arthur Conan 19, 24, 88
Dreadnought Hoax, The 23
Dreher, Rod 165
Duckworth, George 6, 7–8, 67
Duckworth, Gerald 5, 6
Duckworth, Stella 6, 7, 10, 68

Eliot, T. S. 13–14, 16–17, 18, 22, 25,
    34, 36, 39, 57, 66, 101, 103,
    104, 110, 111, 112, 113, 154
Ellmann, Richard 110
eugenics 60–61

First World War 3, 10, 11, 12–13, 17,
    27–28, 35, 41, 52, 61, 64, 101,
    104, 116, 119, 141, 153, 158,
    178

Fisher, Herbert 31–32
Flowers for Mrs. Dalloway 171
Forster, E. M. 22, 26, 83
Freedman, Ralph 115
Freud, Sigmund 21–22, 98, 126
Freund, Gisèle 107
Friedan, Betty 102
Fry, Roger 23, 27, 37, 38, 40, 69–70, 83, 88, 98

Galsworthy, John 15, 16, 22
Gandhi, Mohandas K. 60
Garnett, David 95, 111
Garsington Manor *see* Morrell, Ottoline
George, Lloyd 31
Gillet, Louis 110, 128
Goldstone, Harmon H. 97
Gorris, Marleen *see* Mrs Dalloway (film)
Gosse, Edmund 110, 128
'Gothic Fiction' (Woolf) 104
Grant, Duncan 59, 102, 107, 108
Graves, Rupert 153
Grice, Bonnie 171
Guy, Derek 150

Hadley, Tessa 140
Hameed, Uzma *see* Woolf Works
Harcourt Brace 73, 74, 76, 81, 95, 125, 159
Hardwick, Elizabeth 118
Hardy, Robert 153
Hare, David 159, 161, 162
Hatchards 49, 54, 104, 177
Head, Henry 27, 31
Heffer, Simon 117
Hemingway, Ernest 127
Henderson, Ellie (*MD*) 66
Henke, Suzette 114
Hensher, Philip 165
Herman, Judith Lewis 141–142
Hirvonen, Elina 152

Hoare, Dorothy M. 99
Hogarth House 1, 11, 12, 13, 33, 46, 113
Hogarth Press 4, 13, 14, 17, 21, 39, 46, 47, 57, 72, 73, 74, 76, 80–81, 83, 88, 89–90, 92, 147
Holms, J. F. 88
Holmes, Dr (*MD*) 28, 30, 31, 64, 79, 117
Holtby, Winifred 97
Hopwood, Francis 28–29
'Hours in a Library' (Woolf) 104
'Hours, The' (Woolf) 20, 24–25, 79
Hours, The (film) 126, 150, 159–163, 164, 165–166
Hours, The (novel) 126, 150–152, 154–169
Hours, The (opera) 173
Howard, Maureen 127
'How Should One Read a Book?' (Woolf) 41, 91–92, 108, 120
Hughes, Richard 87
Humphrey, Robert 115
Hungerford, Edward 105–106
Hutchinson, Mary ix, 65–66, 67–68, 111, 112
Huxley, Aldous 35, 128
Hynes, James 144, 148
Hyslop, Theophilus 27, 37

India 57, 60, 104
Isherwood, Christopher 147–148

Jacob's Room (Woolf) 3–5, 14, 17, 18, 19, 22, 24, 35, 38–40, 74, 92, 95, 111, 127–128
James, Henry 9, 40, 112
James, William 114
Johnson, Maisie (*MD*) 43, 51, 171
Jones, Danell 23
Jones, Gail 146

INDEX

Joyce, James 14–17, 18, 19, 22, 23, 70, 86, 89, 96, 98, 103, 105, 109–114, 115, 116, 127, 128, 129, 134, 160, 166, 175–176

Kennedy, P. C. 87–88, 100
'Kew Gardens' (Woolf) 17, 36, 128
Keynes, Geoffrey 11
Keynes, John Maynard 11, 59–60, 85, 107
Kidman, Nicole 159, 160, 161–162, 166
Kilman, Doris (*MD*) 55, 56, 62–65, 68, 96, 117, 118–125
Korkeakivi, Anna 148

Lamb, Walter 63
Lanchester, John 144, 146–147
Lapaire, Jean-Rémi 172
Larkin, Philip 59
Larreta, Antonio 167–168
Larsen, Libby 171
Larsen, Nella 143
Lawrence, D. H. 18, 22, 35, 113, 128
Leavis, F. R. 103, 104, 127
Leavis, Q. D. 103, 105, 123
Lee, Hermione 10–11, 75, 109, 163
Lessing, Doris 161–162, 164
Levy, Deborah 148
Lewis, Percy Wyndham 102–103, 104, 109, 110, 111–112, 113
Lippincott, Robin 170–171
Little Review 15, 16, 110, 114
Lodge, David 145, 146
Lopokova, Lydia 55, 85
Lubbock, Percy 40, 44
Lushington, Kitty *see* Maxse, Kitty

MacCarthy, Desmond 18, 102
MacDonald, Ramsay 57
McDowall, Arthur 100
McElhone, Natascha 153, 154
McEwan, Ian 146

McGregor, Wayne *see Woolf Works*
McLaughlin, Ellen 171–172
McNichol, Stella 138–139, 168
madness 11, 33, 43, 78, 124, 134, 137, 153, 161
  see also shell shock
Madwoman in the Attic, The 136
Manet and the Post-Impressionists 23, 27, 37–38
Mansfield, Katherine 7, 13, 18, 19–20, 38, 47, 65, 113, 114, 169
'Mark on the Wall, The' (Woolf) 4, 128
Matisse, Henri 23, 37, 38
Matthaei, Louise 62–63, 119
Maurois, André 127–128
Maxse, Kitty 5–6, 7–8, 25–26, 86
Mecklenburgh Square 107
Mendelsohn, Daniel 163
Mercer, Lindsey Augusta 171
Miles, Josephine 126
Miller, J. Hillis 53, 179
Mirrlees, Hope 39
Mirsky, Dmitri 117
Mitchell, Elise (*MD*) 51
Mitford, Nancy 146
'Modern Fiction' (Woolf) 22, 39, 84, 114
  see also 'Modern Novels'
Modern Library vii, 26, 89–92, 98, 99, 100, 118, 168
'Modern Novels' (Woolf) 14–15, 18, 21, 22, 70, 110, 114
Monday or Tuesday (Woolf) 17
Monk's House ix, 1, 2, 5, 12, 14, 41–42, 47, 72, 77, 83, 155
Moody, A. David 118
Moore-Brabazon, John 135
Morrell, Ottoline 10, 11, 12, 34–35, 68, 112
Morrell, Philip 10, 85, 118
'Mr Bennett and Mrs Brown' (Woolf) 20–24, 44, 74, 114, 163

Mr. Dalloway see Lippincott, Robin
Mrs Dalloway (Woolf)
    discussion groups 96, 100, 145, 160
    drafts 8, 15, 24–26, 39, 43, 44, 47, 65, 91
        see also 'Hours, The' (Woolf)
    editions in English vii, 73, 77, 79, 80, 81, 92–93, 118, 127, 129, 143, 160
        see also Modern Library
    letters from readers 77, 89, 96–97
    manuscripts 24–25, 26, 47, 69, 78, 91, 138
    maps 48–49, 55, 147
    narrative modes 16, 26, 35, 96, 98, 105, 110, 115, 116, 128, 157, 172, 179
    party consciousness 8, 66, 139, 171
    sexuality 123, 135–136, 156–158
    translations 93, 127, 129–133, 143, 154, 168
    tunnelling process 36, 43–44, 105–106, 163
    see also entries on specific characters
Mrs Dalloway (film) 152–154, 176
'Mrs Dalloway in Bond Street' (Woolf) 3, 18, 25, 34, 58, 91, 95, 139
Mrs. Dalloway Reader, The 168–169
Mrs. Dalloway's Party 138–139, 140, 168–169
Muir, Edwin 88
Murray, Gilbert 32
Murry, John Middleton 18–20, 24, 47

'New Dress, The' (Woolf) 139
Night and Day (Woolf) 6–7

'On Not Knowing Greek' (Woolf) 31, 44–45
'On Re-Reading Novels' (Woolf) *see* Lubbock, Percy

Orlando (Woolf) 93, 94, 133, 175
Oslo Twins 171
Outka, Elizabeth 178–179
Owen, Wilfred 29–30

Packer, Ann 151
Partridge, Ralph 11, 33
Peterson, Lisa 171
Pfeiffer, Pauline 127
'Phases of Fiction' (Woolf) 71
Picasso, Pablo 23, 38, 175
Pole, Isabel (*MD*) 59, 68, 104
Portrait of the Artist as a Young Man, A see Joyce, James
post-impressionist exhibition
    see Manet and the Post-Impressionists
Pound, Ezra 103, 110, 114
'Prime Minister, The' (Woolf) 3, 25–27, 28
Proust, Marcel 18, 47, 69–71, 75, 96, 98, 103, 109, 112, 116, 128
PTSD *see* shell shock

Rascoe, Burton 100
Raverat, Gwen 33, 47, 74–75, 77–78, 102
Raverat, Jacques 16, 67, 74–78
Redgrave, Vanessa 153, 154, 175
Reed, Christopher 165
Reverdy, Pierre 39
Richards, I. A. 101, 103, 104
Richardson, Dorothy 15, 19, 22, 96, 98, 109, 114, 116
Rivers, W. H. R. 30–31
Rogat, Ellen Hawkes 135–136, 137
Romania 133, 167
Room of One's Own, A (Woolf) 18, 70, 94, 101, 105, 127, 136, 139, 144–145, 153
Rose, Jacqueline 11
Rosnay, Tatiana de 150

INDEX

Sackville-West, Vita 24, 66, 82–84, 92, 153, 170
Sanger, C. P. 84, 92, 179
Sassoon, Siegfried 11, 12–13, 30, 31
Savage, George 27
Schiff, Sydney 112, 113
Scrutiny see Leavis, F. R.
Seldes, Gilbert 16
Seton, Sally (*MD*) 66, 68, 135, 156, 157, 171, 179, 180
Shakespeare & Company 111, 127
Shakespeare, William 54, 59, 104, 153
Shannon, Drew 166
shell shock 13, 27–31, 36, 141–142, 152, 153
Showalter, Elaine 68, 136, 137, 169, 175, 177
Silver, Brenda 140, 165, 175
Sitwell, Edith 22, 68
'Sketch of the Past, A' (Woolf) 66–67, 137
Smith, Lucrezia Warren (*MD*) 29, 30, 41, 43, 50, 51, 53, 55, 67, 79, 80, 85
Smith, Septimus Warren (*MD*) 11, 25–33, 34, 35–36, 41, 43, 44, 47, 51, 56, 59, 68, 77, 78, 79, 83, 86, 91, 99–100, 101, 104, 106, 134, 137–138, 141, 142, 174
   connection with Clarissa Dalloway x, 26, 51, 54, 62, 73, 79, 81, 91, 97, 99, 109, 118, 178, 179, 180
Smith, Zadie 144, 146, 147, 177
Smyth, Ethel 97, 119
Smyth, Katharine 108
Solomon, Anna 151
Solomon, Asali 144, 148
Southborough, 1st Baron *see* Hopwood, Francis
Steinem, Gloria 164
Stephen, Adrian 6, 9, 97
Stephen, Dorothea 119–120
Stephen, Julia Duckworth 6, 7
Stephen, Karin 97–98
Stephen, Laura 6
Stephen, Leslie vii, 6, 9, 119
Stephen, Thoby 6, 9–10, 68
Strachey, Lytton 5, 8, 10, 16, 21, 23, 47, 48, 59, 70, 72, 85–86, 103, 112, 126
Strauss, Richard 53
Sunak, Rishi 58
Swinnerton, Frank 23–24

Tavistock Square 1, 29, 46, 47, 49, 74, 107
Thackeray, Minny 6
Thackeray, William Makepeace 6
Thomas, Jean 120
Three Guineas (Woolf) 141
Todd, Dorothy 47, 66
Tomalin, Claire 118
To the Lighthouse (Woolf) 23, 37, 83, 93, 94, 103, 116, 128, 149, 165
trauma *see* shell shock

Ulysses see Joyce, James

Valéry, Paul 74
van Gogh, Vincent 23, 37, 38
Vogue ix, 47, 66, 96, 107
Voyage Out, The (Woolf) 4, 5, 8, 9, 11, 25, 127, 137, 156, 157

Walbert, Kate 145
Walsh, Peter (*MD*) 25, 39, 41, 43, 45, 49, 50, 51, 53, 55, 56–57, 58, 60, 68, 71, 76, 80, 85, 86, 87, 88, 100, 119, 121, 146, 155, 162, 176, 179
Waves, The (Woolf) viii, 170
Weaver, Harriet Shaw 110, 113
Wells, H. G. 15, 16, 22
West, Rebecca 13
Westminster Abbey 65, 124

Whitbread, Hugh (*MD*) 50, 55, 60, 63, 64, 67, 80, 85, 118, 158
Who's Afraid of Virginia Woolf? see Albee, Edward
Woolf, Cecil 12
Woolf, Leonard vii, 1–6, 10, 11, 12, 13, 14, 16, 21, 24, 27, 30, 33, 41–43, 46, 49, 60, 62, 65, 72–73, 74, 76, 77, 82, 92, 105, 107, 108, 110, 111, 113, 119, 132, 137, 139, 155, 163, 176
Woolf, Philip 12
Woolf Works 173
Writer's Diary, A (Woolf) 105, 110

Years, The (Woolf) 156
Younghusband, Francis 28–29